T0146808

GHOSTS

ALSO BY BILL NOEL

GHOSTS

A FOLLY BEACH MYSTERY

Bill Noel

iUniverse, Inc.
Bloomington

Ghosts
A Folly Beach Mystery

Copyright © 2012 Bill Noel

This is a work of fiction. All of the characters, names, incidents, organizations, and dialogue in this novel are either the products of the author's imagination or are used fictitiously.

iUniverse Star
an iUniverse, Inc. imprint

iUniverse books may be ordered through booksellers or by contacting:

iUniverse
1663 Liberty Drive
Bloomington, IN 47403
www.iuniverse.com
1-800-Authors (1-800-288-4677)

ISBN: 978-1-938908-10-1 (sc)
ISBN: 978-1-938908-11-8 (e)

Library of Congress Control Number: 2012914933

Printed in the United States of America

iUniverse rev. date: 8/16/2012

Cover photo by the author.
Author photo by Susan Noel.

PROLOGUE

At 4:35 p.m. on April 19, 1957, Clint Mussleman, an engineer on the Atlantic Coast Line's passenger train that ran from New York to Miami, returned home from a grueling extended shift. Home to Clint was a small weather-beaten cottage on the barrier island of Folly Beach, South Carolina.

Clint stood in the wooden Folly Pavilion, which overlooked the majestic Atlantic Ocean. The exhausted engineer wanted to get one last look at the ocean, the reason he had moved to the island, before heading home to the mundane chores that had accumulated in his absence. An hour later, he'd had his fix of the ocean breeze, which mixed with the smoke from his Camel cigarette, and he absentmindedly flipped his smoldering cigarette butt to the floor, where it landed on a sheet of discarded tissue paper in a corner of the well-known landmark. Clint took a deep breath, filled his lungs with the briny sea mist, and felt refreshed as he headed home to the dreaded chores. Moments later, the wadded paper provided enough kindling to burst into flames, which rapidly spread to the dried wooden supports of the large structure.

Oblivious to anything but typical teenage thoughts, sixteen-year-old identical twins Charlotte and Cassandra Harmel leaned over the seaward side railing on the pavilion. Their conversation bounced from how they had muddled through another week of school, to their dreaded math class, to the next day's road trip to visit their favorite aunt and uncle in Georgetown. Charlotte thought she smelled smoke and started to look around, but she was distracted when her sister excitedly pointed to a dolphin gracefully heading up the coast.

Three blocks from the beach, Frank Fontana stumbled out of Perk's, his favorite bar and poker-playing hangout. He began his quest to find a friend, or even a stranger, who would "lend" him a few dollars so he could continue his nightly round of barhopping and bumming drink money. Frank, a drunk by hobby and a bum by profession, was known by everyone who had spent more than a week on the small island. Worthless, irresponsible, and stumbling drunk were some of the kinder words bandied about to describe the shell of a man who had served his country with distinction in World War II.

By 5:45 p.m., a stiff wind rushing in from the Atlantic had swept the flames horizontally from the corner where the wayward cigarette had landed. The wind-dried, aging supports and walls of the pavilion ignited as if they'd been soaked in kerosene.

Charlotte and Cassandra were jolted from their animated conversation when the fire, thirty feet behind them, attacked the roof and burned through two support beams. A third of the roof tumbled to the floor. A ball of rolling flames consumed their escape route before they could reach it.

Frank had successfully staggered to Center Street, the literal and figurative center of Folly Beach, and was weaving his way toward Kokomo's Lounge, his second-favorite bar and bumming spot. Part of his addled brain heard raised voices coming from the nearby beach. The sun was on its daily glide to the horizon behind him, and a new ball of light invaded his bloodshot eyes from the direction of the pavilion. He squinted and said to himself, "What in hell?"

He didn't know how accurate he was.

Folly's small and disorganized fire department garnered all its equipment and personnel and descended on the pavilion, which was now consumed in flames that reached more than fifty feet to the sky. The pavilion and Frank's destination, Kokomo's Lounge, were engulfed in the raging inferno in front of clusters of locals who had gathered like bugs around a torch.

Frank's few healthy brain cells clicked in. His mind raced back to Normandy in the rural countryside of France and June 6, 1944, D-day, where he and more than 160,000 American and Allied troops had been thrust onto the beach in a torrent of German firepower. Frank had been luckier that day than thousands of his fellow soldiers. He'd survived—at least physically.

Frank's gait and focus grew stronger as he ran toward the pavilion. For reasons never understood, the drunk heard high-pitched screams coming from the hell on earth—screams no one else heard or admitted to hearing.

He yelled for the firefighters to aim their impotent stream of water at the entrance of the rapidly deteriorating building. He screamed for able-bodied men in the crowd to rush into the structure. He heard someone on the other side of the flames, but those near him only heard blathering—profanity-laced incoherent pleas from the town drunk.

Frank shoved two firefighters to the ground before running toward the fire-engulfed pavilion. Spectators nearest Frank later recalled him cursing them for being "bloody cowards" as he sprinted into the black smoke-filled structure.

By 8:15 p.m., the sun had disappeared behind the marsh side of Folly Beach. The pavilion and nearby buildings were reduced to a pile of smoldering, blackened rubble. Those in the crowd, which had swelled to more than five hundred at its peak, had wandered back to their separate lives, and the exhausted firefighters and police began to comb the charred ruins for the body of Frank Fontana, the drunk who had inexplicably stormed into the deadly flames.

What the firefighters found shocked the tight-knit community. The scorched, lifeless bodies of Charlotte and Cassandra Harmel were trapped under a ceiling beam that had fallen during the early stages of the blaze.

Something else troubled the good citizens of Folly Beach. Dozens of witnesses had seen Frank Fontana run into the burning building, yet the thorough search of the pavilion failed to turn up even the most minute trace of his body. What had happened to him? It was highly unlikely that the flames had turned him completely to ash. Surely some body parts would have been found. So if he'd gotten out, people asked, then why had he disappeared, vanished like a fog under the heat of the morning sun? Gradually, over time, most folks in Folly Beach stopped wondering and got on with their lives. But not everyone did.

CHAPTER 1

"**I've got a job,**" said Charles.

Miracles occur when you least expect them, I thought. "Like with real hours, paycheck, W-2?"

He tilted his head in my direction as if I'd lapsed into Mandarin. "Huh?" he articulately replied.

I suspected the W-2 reference had thrown him. My best friend, Charles, hadn't received a paycheck since Ronald Reagan had dozed through meetings in the White House and gas cost barely over a buck a gallon. Charles was the ripe old age of thirty-four at the time.

"Let me guess," I said. "Off the books ... no taxes?"

"Of course."

Charles had held several "tax-free" part-time jobs during the last twenty-six years of his voluntary retirement—jobs that had included delivering packages for the surf shop; helping restaurateurs clean up after extra-busy days; and even, heaven forbid, manual labor, assisting contractors in building and rebuilding homes on the island. I knew he wanted me to ask what was different about his latest job. I wasn't ready to give him that satisfaction.

Charles and I were sitting at my favorite table in the Lost Dog Café, the best breakfast restaurant on Folly Beach. During the five years that I had lived on the small bohemian island a handful of miles from Charleston, I had eaten hundreds of morning meals at the Dog, many of them with my unlikely friend Charles. Along with hundreds of meals, I had heard Charles ask thousands of questions. He was a fact and rumor collector extraordinaire. My nosy genes paled by comparison, and it irritated him greatly when I failed to ask the obvious questions—but I wasn't nearly as concerned about every who, what, why, where, and when of the world. Besides, I knew he was genetically wired to tell me what his alleged "job" was.

It was approaching seven thirty, and the sun had reared its orange head minutes earlier. Christmas was a week away, and the sun was as late to rise as most of the full-time residents. Folly Beach was in hibernation. Folly was probable one of the best-kept secrets along the South Carolina coast. It didn't get as much attention as its neighboring beaches on Isle of Palms, Sullivan's Island, or Kiawah. However, in the last few years, vacationers who wanted a peaceful beach with a laid-back feel and proximity to Charleston, one of the most historic and beautiful cities in the country, had rediscovered it. The flocks of vacationers who swarmed—some would say overran—the half-mile-wide, six-mile-long island during the summer months were miles away, engulfed in their full-time jobs and school and only dreaming of their next vacation.

Charles and I, occupying one of the three tables of diners, had received the full attention of Amelia, the server. She was one of the few current employees who had been working at the Dog when I moved to Folly after taking an early retirement from a large health-care company in my home state of Kentucky. She arrived with our breakfast burritos and interrupted Charles's sketchy explanation of his new job.

"I know you're foaming at the mouth to hear about it," said Charles a few moments later. "So here goes."

He had surely mistaken the shard of egg white on the corner of my mouth for foam, but he tended to get cranky when someone interrupted one of his stories with reality. "Umm," I merely mumbled.

"Cal's hired me to use my detective skills to find out who's been stealing from him." Charles leaned back in his chair, put his hands behind his head, and smiled.

I couldn't tell if he was waiting for applause or was ecstatic about his burrito. I did what I usually do when I don't have a clue what to say. "Umm," I repeated.

"Chris, come on. It's a real job this time," he continued. "Cal's Country Bar and Burgers has a new bartender, who happens to be yours truly." He pointed at his head and continued to smile.

Cal's was one of Folly's popular watering holes, and up until a year ago, it had previously been called GB's Bar. Its former owner had abandoned the successful business when he was forced to move off-island. The landlord, not wanting the daunting task of finding someone to lease the less-than-pristine building in the down economy, had approached my friend Calvin Ballew, a country music performer who had actually had one hit record, although it had topped the charts nearly fifty years ago, and had been a regular performer at GB's. Cal had never managed anything—including himself—but the deal the landlord offered was too good to pass up.

Charles had as many "detective skills" as Cal had bar-owner talents, which was slightly fewer than a chipmunk had for piloting a 747. Now I was smiling.

I chewed on my burrito and on what Charles had said. "And what do you know about bartending?" I asked.

"I'm glad you asked, my skeptical friend." He nodded, his eyelids narrowed. "Last week I read *Bartending for Dummies*, and now I'm on the second chapter of *Bartending 101: The Basics of Mixology*." He gave another brisk nod. "So there."

After a few years of observing Charles consume adult beverages, I could say with certainty that his mixological vocabulary would consist of five words: Light, Bud, red, white, and pink. The last three were only because wine was my drink of choice, and he occasionally ordered for me.

At five feet eight, Charles was a couple of inches shorter than I, and he was twenty or so pounds lighter. He was sloppy, disheveled, outgoing, a voracious reader, and he viewed employment as the work of the devil. I prided myself on my appearance—neat and well groomed but not necessarily attractive, although I had been described as "relatively handsome" and even "cute" by a couple of biased observers. I had no interest in reading anything other than the headlines in the paper, and I was way on the reserved side of shy. Conversations with strangers didn't come easily. We were about as opposite as two humans can be, but because of the quirky pull of Folly, we became quick friends. On the other hand, both our ages began with the number six, although Charles had only recently arrived at that milestone. I had been there three years. Oh, and we both loved photography.

I inhaled and was rewarded with the soothing smell of coffee from a nearby table. "When do you begin your two new careers—neither of which you have a whit of experience for, I might add?"

"As President G. W. Bush said, 'I think we agree, the past is over.' That experience thing is overrated." Charles carefully placed his fork on the plate, folded his arms in front of his chest, and stared at me.

One trait of Charles's was his tendency to quote US presidents. It was both endearing and irritating, often at the same time. I didn't challenge the authenticity of the quotes, mainly because I didn't care if they were accurate. He was such a consummate collector of all things trivial and often irrelevant, that the citations were most likely factual. But so what? The comforting smell of bacon whiffed through the air, and the muted conversation from the next table barely distracted me from assimilating the former president's deeply profound statement.

I'd heard what President Bush had allegedly said, but I didn't recall Charles answering my question. "And when do you begin your new careers?" I repeated.

"Tomorrow," he said, tapping the table with his left hand. "But don't worry—I'll still be your sales manager."

Sales manager was a bit strong in describing Charles's unpaid involvement in my emotionally rewarding money-pit business, Landrum Gallery. I had opened the photo gallery on Center Street, the home of 90 percent of the retail business on the island, and instead of throwing cash in the Atlantic, I threw it away on utilities, rent, taxes, insurance, and countless other expenses that put me deeper in the hole each month.

After taking early retirement and moving to Folly, I had saved enough money from a couple of lucky real-estate investments and a buyout package from work to purchase a small cottage a couple of blocks from the beach and still make ends meet. I didn't have a cushion of cash to lose thousands each year on the gallery, and I was ready to fold my expensive hobby when the most unlikely event occurred. Charles and I had each inherited five hundred thousand dollars from an aging widow named Margaret Klein. We had saved her life, and since she didn't have any living relatives, she'd left her estate to us.

I had been directing some of my unearned fortune to paying the bills and keeping the gallery open three days a week instead of the seven-day routine I had fallen into, for I'd realized that retirement should mean something more than working every day. Charles, to the untrained observer, was the same Charles that he was before the windfall. I saw how extravagant he had been when he bought his own camera and returned the loaner of five years to me. He had talked about having his 1988 Saab convertible repaired in order to transform it from yard art to a licensed roadworthy vehicle.

"So what's going on at Cal's that he needs a bartending detective?" I asked.

He wiped catsup off his upper lip, wadded his napkin, and dropped it on the plate. "Tell you what," he said. "Let Heather and me buy your chow tonight. I'll tell you all about it."

Heather Lee was Charles's self-anointed "main squeeze," or his "only squeeze," as she was known to everyone else. Charles had never bought me a meal, so I thought tonight's event was going to be historic and the most memorable thing that would happen to me today.

I was wrong.

CHAPTER 2

The thermometer hovered in the midthirties, with a brisk wind out of the northwest. That would be almost balmy in much of the country this close to Christmas, but it was well below average on Folly, and much of the populace claimed to be freezing. I had already wrapped my 185-pound body in a down-filled jacket and covered my rapidly balding head with a Tilley, my tan sailcloth fedora-style hat that I'd fallen in love with years ago. I smiled when I realized that I was overdressed for the short jaunt to the street and my new Infiniti SUV to drive three short blocks to Rita's Restaurant. The SUV had recently replaced a dented ten-year-old Lexus.

I had just opened the door on my way out of the house when the house phone's ring drew me back inside. I almost ignored it but was afraid it was Charles with a change in plans.

I should have followed my first instinct.

"Is this Chris Landrum … the one who lived in Louisville?" asked a female voice. It sounded vaguely familiar, but I couldn't place it.

"Yes," I said after hesitating.

"Thank God," she responded. Then dead air.

"Hello?" I said.

"Chris," she continued after another awkward pause. "This is Joan."

Charles, Heather, supper, and cold weather all cascaded down a snowy slope. My mind raced back decades. My heart rate accelerated; I began to sweat. It wasn't because I was overly bundled.

"Joan Landrum?" I barely got the words out. I didn't remember carrying the cordless phone to the living room and sitting down, but that's where I was, so I must have.

"It's Joan McCandless now, but yes."

The last time I had spoken to her was twenty-four years ago, when her name was Joan Landrum and she had just become my ex-wife.

"Uh, wow … Hi. How are you?" I hoped she didn't think I'd suffered a stroke, but I felt as if I had. Was it really her? Could Charles be playing a sick trick? No, the voice sounded familiar, and it began to come back to me. We had been married twenty years when she came home from work and tearfully told me that she wanted a divorce. She said she was tired of being married.

She giggled. "I guess you're surprised to hear from me."

You guess! I thought. "Uh, yes. I am." I was beginning to get my bearings—sort of. "Where are you? What's up?"

"I'm in Gatlinburg. My husband and I moved here from California a few years ago. He's retired."

"Oh," I said, slipping back to stroke-speak. I hesitated and hoped that a tree would fall on the phone lines and cut the connection. I could probably think of more things to say to a recorded message trying to sell me storm windows than I could to say to my longtime ex-wife. I tried again. "What's up?"

"Nothing really," she said. "We were married a long time, and you were a big part of my life. I googled you and found several Chris Landrums. One of them had saved an elderly lady from a hurricane a couple of years ago, and the story said that the hero was originally from Louisville. I called information and got this number and took a chance." She hesitated. I heard "White Christmas" playing in the background. "Sorry if I startled you."

She had gone to a lot of trouble for "nothing really," but I didn't push it. I also knew that I was late for the rendezvous with Charles and Heather. Tardiness to Charles was somewhat akin to bashing baby seals with a Louisville Slugger.

"That's okay," I said. "I was surprised. How are you doing?"

"Oh, fine. I know you must be busy with Christmas around the corner." Another hesitation. "Chris, I need … Never mind," she said.

"I just wanted to wish you a merry Christmas and see how you're doing and to—"

"To see how I'm doing?" I asked, incredulous. "We haven't spoken in years. What do you want?"

There was silence on the other end of the line. I could hear her breathing. Did I hear a sob?

"You still there?" I asked, a little more gently this time.

The line went dead, and I just stood there for a long moment, staring blankly at the phone as if I expected it to start explaining the mysteries of the world, like ex-wives. I shook my head, vaguely disturbed by the ghost from Christmas past that had just blown in on the cold Atlantic wind.

Chapter 3

It was dark as I parallel parked on East Arctic Avenue in front of the entrance to the Folly Beach Fishing Pier and across the street from Rita's. The restaurant had opened a few years ago and had quickly earned the reputation as one of the best beach restaurants in the Charleston area. It was located on perhaps Folly's most sought-after retail spot, the center of the business district and fewer than a hundred yards from the Atlantic Ocean, the Pier, and a public beach.

A cheerful hostess greeted me at the door and nodded toward a booth on the Center Street side of the restaurant. Charles and Heather were seated on the far side of the booth with a clear view of the entrance. Charles glanced in my direction and then looked at his left wrist, shaking his head. His gesture would have been more meaningful if he owned a watch, but the significance wasn't lost on me. I was late, but even he would have agreed that this time I had a good excuse. Heather, not nearly as time obsessed as Charles, truly seemed glad to see me—tardy or not.

I removed my coat, threw it and my hat on the seat, and slid in the booth opposite the couple.

"Suppose your new ride isn't as quick as your old one," he said. "On time ain't what it used to be."

I ignored his barb, smiled at Heather, and told her she looked especially nice and seasonal. She wore a red-and-green striped blouse and dark green slacks. Most people wouldn't have noticed anything other than the floppy bright red Santa's hat perched on her curly brown hair. Heather was attractive and in her midforties, but she looked younger. Freckles on her nose added to her wholesome appearance.

She was oblivious to Charles's complaints. "Wait till you hear about Chucky's new quote job unquote," she said.

I loved it when she called her bench bud Chucky. He would correct anyone else who dared call him anything other than Charles. He riled at Chuck or any close version, and Heather was the only person who dared to say Chucky in his presence. She was so cute when she said it.

My growling stomach and the smell of frying hamburgers reminded me that I hadn't eaten since breakfast. I asked Charles to hold his story until I ordered. I wasn't certain how much I wanted to divulge about my odd call. Each of us ordered a variation of Rita's world-renowned, or at least island-well-known, burgers, and we requested two orders of fries to share. I asked Charles if he would be ordering an exotic drink since he was now a mixologist. He said sure, a Bud Light; he told Heather that that was what she wanted too. I ordered red wine.

Heather was on the front edge of the seat and beaming. "Okay, okay, Chucky. Tell him."

Clearly not finished berating me for being late, he frowned at Heather, but in a rare moment of wisdom, he chose to change the subject and give in to her. Charles and Heather had gone from being a lukewarm item a year or so ago to sizzling. They were made for each other. Both were quirky, outgoing, and artistic in an offbeat way. Charles's preferred photographic subject matter consisted of discarded candy wrappers, which, in the best of times, would only appeal to the most lopsided art connoisseur. Heather's singing talent would appeal to the deafest listener, but she plied her hobby with reckless enthusiasm and charm.

"Cal's having a rash of thefts," began Charles. "Well, not actually a rash—closer, I guess, to a couple of thefts." He looked out the window toward the Sand Dollar bar across the street, and then back at Heather, and finally at me. "How about I start at the beginning?"

Heather nodded enthusiastically, and I said, "Please do."

"Cal's not quite an experienced bar owner," said Charles.

That was an understatement since Cal had begun his career as a bar owner less than a year ago. His only experience in bars prior to that was as an entertainer and regular consumer of their products.

"Move along, Chucky. Move along," said Heather.

He gave her another frown, but it quickly turned to a smile as he patted her knee. "Cal hasn't mustered the subtleties of inventory control," said Charles.

"Means he can't count how much stuff he's got," interrupted Heather.

I grinned. "Thanks, Heather. I'm sure Charles would have got around to saying that—eventually." I didn't want to dampen her enthusiasm by telling her that Charles had already told me part of the story.

"Okay, okay," said Charles. "Cal thinks that some of his expensive bottles of bourbon are disappearing."

"How much?" I asked.

"Not sure," said Charles. "Have you already forgotten about his inventory control issues?"

"Then how does he know they're missing?" I asked.

"Yeah, Chucky, how?" said Heather as she quickly shifted her gaze back to Charles.

He smiled at Heather and then turned and gave me a frown. "Don't know for sure," said Charles. "He said he keeps buying bourbon and his cash drawer doesn't have enough money to pay for it."

How could an accountant have possibly said that better? I thought. "So he really doesn't know if there's a problem?" I said.

"Yeah, Chucky," chimed in Heather.

"That's why he hired me," said Charles, as though nothing could be more logical. "He wants me to use my investigative skills and cipher out if there's a thievery problem." He raised his right hand and pointed his index finger upward. "And if there's a problem, then solve it."

I nodded. Charles was my best friend, so shouldn't I be supportive of whatever he wanted to do—regardless of how idiotic? Nah! "Charles, must I remind you *again* that you are not a detective? You have no experience at being a detective. In fact, you don't have any experience as a bartender. And Cal, as great a singer and person as he is, knows as much about running a bar as a panda does about needlepoint."

I couldn't tell if Charles heard most of what I had said. He was staring off into space. "Those," he finally said, "are good points, and I appreciate you reminding me. You're right."

Progress, I thought. "Good," I said.

"Those are great reasons why I took the job. It'll give me valuable experience, and who wouldn't want to be a mixologist? And it'll be great teaching Cal more about the bar business. Thanks for being supportive."

Heather looked at the smiling Charles and then turned back to me. "Needlepoint ain't that hard to pick up. I bet a panda could do it."

Logic continued to fly out the window; food flowed into our stomachs; and adult beverages washed the food down and common sense away. By the end of the night, I didn't care if Charles wanted to pretend he was a bartending detective, if Heather wanted to pretend she was the next country megastar, or if she wanted to visit the zoo and teach needlepoint to the entire population, pandas et al.

The night had belonged to Charles, so I didn't mention my strange and disorienting phone call. Besides, I wasn't certain that I wanted to tell anyone. I also realized that my lifelong tendency to close up and not share my innermost feelings and thoughts with those close to me was probably a major cause of my divorce.

CHAPTER 4

The first three days of Christmas week were busy in the gallery. I had opened only on weekends since receiving the inheritance. After Thanksgiving, I opened the doors six days a week. Charles said that I owed it to the photo-buying public, and since he was my unofficial sales manager, he wanted me to open as much as possible. I'd hinted at it at times but had never told him that the onset of winter had always been a depressing time for me; the extra hours gave me something to take my mind off the season.

Charles had finished selling two large framed photos to a condo owner who was in town for the holidays. It was a little after four, but the sky was darkening as sunset approached. We had moved to the small office, break room, storeroom, and occasional party room behind the gallery. Charles was off work at Cal's after putting in two, as he put it, "interesting" nights of bartending and detecting. He convinced me with minimal arm-twisting that it was "almost happy hour" and we should skip the coffee that we had been sipping most of the day and go straight to the beer, wine and cheese bar—the counter and refrigerator—and celebrate a successful day at the gallery. I laughed and reminded him that his proposed activity often occurred regardless of whether any photos had been sold. He succinctly summed it up with, "So?"

He asked if I'd mind if he invited Heather to "our party," and he suggested that I might want to ask Amber. Heather was fine with me, and he grabbed the phone to call her. I quietly said that I didn't think so about asking Amber.

Amber and I had dated for a couple of years. Charles insisted that we would get back together, but I had serious doubts. Amber was the most-tenured server at the Lost Dog Café, and I still saw her there several times a week. We were cordial, and I enjoyed talking to her.

I'd had a few casual dates over the last several months with Karen Lawson, a detective with the Charleston County sheriff's office and daughter of Folly's chief of police, Brian Newman. She and I had met in the most unlikely of situations—over the body of a well-known Charleston developer. I had been on Folly for only a few days when I figuratively, and nearly literally, stumbled onto the murder victim and rapidly became the next target of the killer. I seemed to have bad luck like that at times, being in the wrong place at the wrong time and subsequently getting caught up in crime scenes. I didn't go looking for trouble, that's for sure, but I did somehow have a knack for letting it find me.

I got to know Karen better when her father suffered a near-fatal heart attack two years ago. She and I had shared time with her dad in the hospital room and then time with each other over a couple of meals and drinks at a watering hole near the hospital in Charleston.

It had been three days since I had received Joan's call, and I was finally comfortable sharing the conversation with Charles and Heather. We were sitting around an old kitchen table in the back room. I had left the gallery lights on and the door unlocked in case any last-minute Christmas shoppers were inspired to stop in.

"Who's Joan?" asked Heather before I completed two sentences.

"She's Chris's ex," answered Charles for me.

Heather jerked her head my direction. "Like ex-wife or something?" she said.

I was wondering what "or something" meant and didn't answer quickly enough. Charles came to the rescue. "Yep," he said. "He married his high school sweetheart back when he was in college, sometime around the Civil War." He examined the ceiling as if trying to figure out if I was for the North or the South, and then he took a swig of Bud Light. "Stayed hitched for two decades, and then she wised up and dumped him."

I would have preferred my version of the story. Unfortunately, Charles had the facts correct—except about the Civil War.

"I never would have guessed," said Heather.

Not in the mood to guess what she never would have guessed, I quickly moved the story along. "She called to wish me merry Christmas and ask how I was doing," I said.

"You haven't heard from her in something like three hundred years. She dumped you back in dinosaur times. Now she calls to see how you're doing. Right?" Charles nodded and stared at me.

"Yeah," I whispered.

"And you think that's normal?" he said.

"Not a bird blink of normal there," said Heather.

"So what do you think?" I asked. I wasn't certain that I wanted to know, but I also knew that he was going to tell me regardless.

"You need to start from the beginning," responded Charles. "Tell us everything she said."

"Everything," said Heather.

The odds weren't good that I could avoid the dynamic duo, so I stepped out of my comfort zone and shared as much of the conversation as I could remember. I left out my multiple "umms" and pauses.

Heather tilted her head in my direction. "You know—"

Charles aimed the palm of his right hand at Heather and interrupted. "Hold that thought."

He quickly pushed his chair back and headed to the small refrigerator in the corner, just as quickly returning with two more beers and the half-empty bottle of Cabernet from the counter. He handed Heather one of the beers and put the wine bottle beside my glass. "You were saying, sweetie?"

"Thank you, Chucky," she said with a grin.

After "sweetie" and "Chucky," I was thankful that Charles had brought the wine.

She continued. "You know, Chris, I'm a psychic." She pushed a palm to her forehead. "When you were telling about the call, vibes told me your ex was reaching out to you. She needs help." Her shoulders shook—from psychic vibes, I assumed—and she took a sip of beer.

What I did know was that Heather *thought* that she was a psychic. She also thought she was a good singer. I knew absolutely nothing about what a psychic is, does, or if psychic powers exist, but I did know good singing when I heard it. If she was as wrong about being a psychic as she was about being a singer, her powers were nonexistent.

I glanced at Charles and then turned to Heather. "Maybe she meant what she said. She was thinking about me and wanted to know how I was doing and to wish me merry Christmas," I said. I realized how unlikely that was before I finished saying it.

Charles hadn't spoken for a few minutes—a position that clearly made him uncomfortable. "Heather may be right," he said. "There's more to it. Think of it, Chris. You've been here five years, I'm your closest friend, and you've mentioned your ex once in all that time, and that was years ago. She hasn't had any contact with you for more than two decades, and now you suddenly get a Christmas greeting. Something's up."

Heather nodded enthusiastically.

It had been a long day, and I wasn't anxious to relive more ancient history. Charles and Heather had been making syrupy eyes at each other and leaning closer together. He suggested that it was time for the party to end. I quickly agreed, and we headed our separate ways. Well, I headed my separate way. Charles and Heather appeared to be heading to the same destination.

*   *   *

I had tossed and turned during the night and replayed my brief conversation with Joan. I thought there was more than a thoughtful holiday greeting in her voice, but I might have imagined it. Of course, Charles and Heather's take might have influenced me.

Joan had left me, and I'd tried for years to blame her for the breakup, but I was only trying to fool myself. I was focused—perhaps even obsessed—with my career and getting ahead in the highly competitive corporate environment. She tried time after time to understand what I was going through at work. I closed her out. Was I doing it again?

It was four days before Christmas, and I wanted to open the gallery early. If it wasn't busy now, it never would be. Before beginning the frigid three-block walk to the gallery, I googled "Daniel McCandless, Gatlinburg, Tennessee" and got three hits. According to the sketchy references, Daniel had co-owned Jaguar of Knoxville, a luxury car dealership on the outskirts of Knoxville. Two of the three references were about a diabetics benefit golf tournament that he had chaired. The third showed a photo of Daniel standing in front of a new white Jaguar. The story talked about how he had sold his share of the dealership to his partners, Tag Humboldt and Alil Munson, and how he looked forward to a retirement of golf and travel. Daniel appeared to be in his late sixties, and he was tall and burly, with stylish, longish hair and a mustache. There were no photos of Joan.

A search for Joan came to multiple dead ends. There were no references to anyone by that name connected with Gatlinburg or the surrounding area. There was neither a Joan nor Daniel McCandless listed in the white pages websites. The only Joan McCandless in Tennessee lived in Memphis, several hundred miles from Gatlinburg, which was on the edge of the Smoky Mountains in east Tennessee. I was irritated with myself for not getting her number when she called and the caller ID showed *blocked*. On the other hand, did I want it?

*   *   *

Thursday and Friday flew by, and fortunately I didn't have time to ponder ancient memories or try to figure out why I had received the unusual call. Christmas was two days away, and Charles divided his time between selling photos and selling beer, wine, and spirits. Christmas Eve Eve, he arrived decked out in a red Christmas sweatshirt, with a white face of Santa on the front and surrounded by tiny flashing green LED lights. When he pushed Santa's nose, the shirt played the first few lines of "Here Comes Santa Claus." Well, that's what he said it played; I couldn't tell because it skipped every other note. "What do you expect for seventy-five cents at the church bazaar, the Boston Pops?" he said.

I had seen Charles wearing approximately seven zillion different sweatshirts and T-shirts over the years. He had nearly as many shirts as he had books in his small apartment. His domicile reminded me of a horror movie where alien books attach themselves to everything and take over the world. They had already gobbled up his apartment.

Charles not only collected shirts and books but was also one of Folly's great repositories of rumors and occasionally facts. He would be exposed in his new career as a bartender and self-proclaimed detective to a new source of rumors as rich as earthworms in a compost heap. During the few hours that he devoted to the gallery, he shared how he hadn't realized how much the spirit of the season was inspired by spirits of another kind. He told me that last evening he had waited on one of South Carolina's august members of the state senate, who was one of the greatest proponents of tighter enforcement on drunken driving. The senator asked Charles to put his double shot of bourbon in a plastic Pepsi cup. Another prominent Folly resident told him that if his wife called, Charles was to say that he hadn't ever seen her husband in Cal's.

I ruined Charles's festive mood when I interrupted his stories and asked if he had found the thief. He responded that he hadn't even found where Cal stored the peanuts.

"I've been there a few nights," he said. "I don't know who it is, but I think I could narrow it down." He pointed a handmade wooden cane that was his constant companion in the direction of Cal's. "Think it's either Nick or Kenneth ... Could be Dawn, Tara, or Kristin ... Then again, I wouldn't rule out Dustin or Beatrice."

"Who're they?" I asked.

"They work there," he said.

"So it's an employee?" I asked.

"Yep," he said, continuing to point the cane out the door. "Or maybe someone who isn't."

I tried another tack. "Think the bottles are walking when the bar's open or someone's getting in after closing?"

"Yep," he repeated. "Certain about that."

"And I questioned whether you'd be a good detective," I teased.

He ignored my slight. "Nick usually closes; has since before Cal took over. He told me that every once in a while after everyone's gone, he hears noises from the restrooms."

"He ever find anyone?" I asked.

"Said he hasn't. Checks both restrooms and all around them and never finds anything."

"Animals?" I asked.

"Didn't ask," said Charles. "I'd think if he found a possum or a giraffe in the men's room, he'd mention it."

No argument from me. "Ghosts?" I asked.

I was teasing, but Charles looked at me as if I had solved the crime. "Heather says so. She's a psychic, you know." He nodded in my direction.

I nodded back.

Charles said, "Not sure I'm a believer."

"Better chance it's a giraffe," I speculated.

"Unlikely," said Charles, maintaining a straight face. "Ceiling's too low." He spread his arms out. "Before you ask, the door's too narrow for a hippo."

I sighed and said that I guessed he would need more time to figure it out.

"Likely," he said.

CHAPTER 5

Christmas Eve was a busy night in the bar business, and Charles was scheduled to work until closing. Cal, to Charles's delight, had decided to close at 11:00 p.m. instead of the usual 2:00 a.m.

I had spent the last two Christmas Eves with Amber and her son in their small second-floor apartment on Center Street. They, and Charles, were the closest I had to a family, and I had been delighted to spend Christmas Eve sharing stories and watching the excitement of Amber's son, Jason, as the magical hours of Christmas approached. Now, with the sun beginning to set over the marsh, the loneliness of being by myself on this special night started to get to me. I thought about keeping the gallery open until midevening but knew that "not a creature was stirring," and the only purchases that would be made on Folly Beach would be at Bert's, the island food market that never closed, and in the handful of bars that remained open.

I walked to each room in my cottage and turned on every light. The artificial brightness couldn't overcome my black, dejected mood.

I called Amber and listened to the phone ring thirteen times. Yes, I counted. I knew after the fifth ring that she wasn't there, but I didn't have the heart to hang up.

I finally conceded that I wasn't going to hear her sweet, warm voice on Christmas Eve. I stared out the side window at the dark winter night and then called Karen. She answered her cell on the first ring. We shared a couple of pleasantries before I realized that I didn't know what to say … or exactly why I had called. I finally stumbled through enough words so she knew that I was asking her if she wanted to get a drink. She thanked me but said that she had caught a double homicide and, most likely, would be working all night and Christmas Day. "Murder doesn't take holidays off," she said.

"Merry Christmas," I said. I wished her well with the investigation and said we would talk later.

"You bet we will," she said.

I blushed. But I would still be alone tonight. It sucked.

Television tempted me, but I didn't touch the remote. All I would find would be festive celebrations, mushy old movies celebrating Christmases past, and discussions about peace on earth. I grabbed a three-month-old issue of *American Photo* and mindlessly flipped through the pages before dropping it beside the chair.

I walked to the kitchen, poured a large glass of Cabernet, and sat at the table. Was Charles right? Had Joan called for something other than to ask how I was doing? Why had the call thrown me off? Why couldn't I have asked if she needed anything or wanted to tell me something? Why would she call after not speaking to me all those years? Why?

My thoughts moved closer to home. Where were Amber and Jason? They didn't have relatives within hundreds of miles. Did she have a date? A date on Christmas Eve could be serious. I wasn't an expert, but this was not a casual date night, was it? Was I happy for her if there was someone in her life? Then there was Karen …

Sleep didn't come quickly, but it did come. *What a way to spend Christmas Eve*, I thought as I drifted off.

*   *   *

Christmas Day was expected to only reach the midforties, twenty degrees shy of average for late December. It wouldn't be cold enough for kids to slide around the island on their new red sleds. I was showing my age and my childhood in a more northerly climate by thinking of sleds. I doubted anyone here owned one.

Having those thoughts as I stood in the shower told me that my mood had improved drastically from the night before. I caught myself humming "Jingle Bells" and had to smile. Here I was, not having to ever go to work again, living in my own paid-for cottage a couple of blocks from the ocean, having accumulated more close friends than I had known in Kentucky, and other than being a few pounds over my ideal weight, I was in good health.

Cal had announced two decisions after taking over the reins of GB's Bar earlier this year. First, he renamed it Cal's Country Bar and Burgers and then told everyone who would listen that he was having a "big-ass" Christmas party. He said that he had been on the road more Christmases than most Americans had lived through, and he hadn't had anyone special to share the day with since he could remember. Through his travels, he had seen countless men and women in the same fix. "By golly," he said, "I am going to do something about it."

Cal's Country Christmas Celebration, a mere proclamation in the summer, was now about to come to fruition, and if anyone on the island was not aware of it, he or she had not seen a telephone pole, bulletin board, store window, or read the *Folly Current*. Cal and his staff had plastered notices on nearly every empty wall, pole, window, and car that had not moved for a couple of days.

The party was to begin at noon, and Cal had asked his newest employee, Charles, to get there a couple of hours early to help get ready. Charles, who loved to share, asked me to join him to help with the "prefestivities." I thought that sounded more like grunt work than something good, but I didn't have anything better to do. "Sure," I said.

I arrived and quickly realized that Cal had developed a better sense of the business than I had suspected. Charles was the only employee there, and Cal was giving him a list of what needed to be done. Cal told his regular (higher-paid) staff not to arrive until the party was about to begin. The underpaid under-the-table private detective was earning his keep.

Cal's was larger than several of the bars on Folly Beach. About a dozen tables—a combination of four-tops and barstool-height two-tops—were spread haphazardly around the room on a dark brown beaten-down carpet. Restrooms bookended a small raised wooden stage that anchored the back wall. A twelve-by-twenty-foot laminate dance floor was directly in front the stage. A beat-up wooden bar dominated the right side of the building, and a tiny kitchen and storeroom were behind it.

"Howdy, Kentucky," said Cal as I entered the heavy front door. Cal had the slightly irritating habit of calling people by the name of their state of origin. Charles and I had been trying to break him of the habit, but with limited success. Cal waved his right hand around the room. "What do you think?"

The formerly tired-looking bar sparkled and flashed. Strands, strands, and more strands of flashing green, red, and white lights were strung from the ceiling, the front of the bar, the bandstand, and around the door frames that led into the restrooms.

"Wow!" I said.

Cal beamed. His tall, slim torso stood straighter than I remembered. His full head of long gray hair was topped by his sweat-stained Stetson, a small strand of battery-powered Christmas lights blinking around the crown. "Chris," he said, "this is a dream come true."

Perhaps we were making progress—Chris instead of Kentucky. "Wow," I repeated. "This is almost beyond words."

He interpreted that as a compliment, and his smile grew larger. "Think anybody'll come?"

After all his work, I sincerely hoped so. "No doubt," I said, more confidently than I felt. Folly was nearly deserted over the holiday. There were a few vacation property owners in town for the week, but most of the full-time residents had families and wouldn't venture out. But there were always a few "strays," as Charles called them, around—singles and some couples who would rather be in a bar than alone with their significant others on this special day.

"I would've had more money to decorate," said Cal as he tilted his head toward Charles, "if Mr. Detective there had caught the cat who's stealing me blind."

Charles held five fingers in the air. I got a full view of his blue-and-gold sweatshirt with a large *A* on the front and a polar bear walking across his chest. I absolutely, positively wasn't going to ask about it. He had also traded his Tilley for one of those soft red Santa hats with a white fuzzy ball on top, which fortunately only made appearances this time of year. The hat was similar to the one Heather had worn the other night at supper. I hoped the hats weren't multiplying.

"Five days," said Charles, rolling his eyes. "Five days, I repeat. I've only been on the case five days. And besides, Cal, no one is 'stealing you blind.' You're only missing a few bottles of bourbon."

Cal set down the lights that he was stringing on the third artificial Christmas tree in the room. "Umm, Michigan," he said, rubbing his chin. "I sort of forgot to tell you that some money's missing."

"Hey, boss," said Charles. "Don't you think that's something you should be telling your detective?"

The Hank Williams Sr. look-alike nodded generously. "Yeah. I know I should have, but, Charles, I sort of don't know how much is gone. Seems like I should have more than I do—a lot more."

Charles was clearly ready to give Cal a lecture on no-telling-what, so I jumped in. "Cal, was the cash taken when the bar was open?"

"Don't know," he said. "See, I leave the money in here after I close, and I don't count it or take it to the bank until morning."

"Gee!" said Charles. His gaze was lasered on Cal. "You don't count it after closing?"

"You know I don't," said Cal. "You work here, remember?"

"Five days, remember?" said the increasingly irritated detective as he repeated his five-fingers-in-the-air gesture. "I've only been here one night at closing. I didn't see what you did with the money."

"Oh yeah," said Cal. "Forgot."

"Walk us through the process you follow at closing," I requested.

Cal removed his Stetson, flicked off the switch that controlled the tiny Christmas lights around the crown, and moved to the table closest to the bar. "This time of year," he said, "I close when everyone's gone. Sometimes it's as early as nine."

Charles and I pulled chairs up to the table.

"And?" said Charles.

"And then I lock the front door. Either I or one of the folks working locks the side door."

"That part I knew," said Charles. "I locked it Thursday."

Cal tapped his hand on the table. "You want my story or are you going to interrupt?"

Charles made a zipping motion across his mouth and then waved for Cal to continue.

"Don't see that often," the bar owner said with a laugh. "Anyway, I take the loot out of the register and dump it into a shoebox behind the counter. By that time of night, I'm exhausted." He stood and walked behind the bar, motioning for us to follow. We crowded into the tight space, and Cal pulled out an old Reebok tennis shoe box from under the bar. "And then I stick the box in this cabinet."

Next to the open shelf area were two twelve-by-twelve-inch beat-up wooden doors with rusting silver keyholes. One of the keyholes was plugged with some unknown substance; the other one was in better condition. Cal took a loose key from the pocket of his jeans and used it to open the unplugged lock.

"Credit card stuff too?" asked Charles.

"Yep. And then I lock it in," he said. He then demonstrated the highly complex process of turning the key.

After he locked the box in the cabinet, he told us to return to the table.

"And in the morning?" asked Charles.

"Take the box out and dump the money on the bar. I count it and write down the amount. And then I fill out a deposit slip and mosey to the bank," said Cal.

I pointed at Cal's pocket. "Is that the only key?" I asked.

"No way, Jose," he said with a grin. "Afraid I'd lose it and then be up a creek without a key." He pointed back over his left shoulder. "Got one hidden back there on the top shelf under a bottle of Maker's Mark. Another one's hidden in the water tank behind the toilet in the gals' restroom."

I looked at Charles and then at Cal. "I'm surprised no one's stolen it before," I said.

Cal stared down at the counter. "Well, Kentucky," he said, "it sort of has been taken."

"How many times?" asked Charles.

"Three other times."

Charles tapped his cane on the floor. "Thanks for sharing," he said with a large dose of sarcasm.

Thank goodness Cal had made a career out of singing. Security consultant wouldn't have been one of his top three thousand talents.

CHAPTER 6

Nick and Tara, two of the paid employees, dragged themselves to the bar a few ticks before noon. Cal, Charles, and I had finished decorating, started the grill, and tuned the small Sirius XM Radio receiver to one of the 24-7 Christmas music channels. We had also sighed and shaken our heads at Cal's lax, to put it kindly, control over the bar's revenue. Rather than being shocked by the thefts, I was amazed that Cal had any money when he went to count it in the morning.

Nick was the only "real" bartender who would be working the party. He tended bar at Cal's and had done so for the previous two years while it was under Greg Brile's ownership. Nick was six feet one and thin as a piece of rebar. He had the look of Ichabod Crane from *Sleepy Hollow* and a mouth that comfortably emoted every profanity known to the Western world. He would have made George Carlin blush. Cal overlooked Nick's shortcomings since he was heads above the other two paid bartenders—and heads, torso, legs, feet, and stilts above Charles in the mixology department. Besides, the other two bartenders had declined to work Christmas Day.

To counter Nick's crudeness, Cal had asked Tara to give up her holiday to serve as his gift to the citizens of Folly Beach. She had graciously agreed, arriving with a smile and bubbly enthusiasm. She was the longest-term employee and had been serving customers—good and bad—for seven years. She knew most of their food and drink choices, laughed at their stale and occasional off-color jokes, and made everyone feel important. Her appearance was also drastically different from the dour, gnarly Nick's. She was in her midthirties, and in the words of her husband, she was the "cutest thing that ever skipped across the bridge to Folly Beach." She also had a refreshing sense of humor and pointed out to her husband, a tattoo artist, that she didn't have to be too cute to be better looking than most of his clients. Cal's regular customers, particularly the males, agreed with her husband.

Both hands of the large neon-ringed Miller Beer clock on the wall were pointing straight up, and Cal paced the floor, for the third time wiping the tops of the tables. "What if nobody comes?" he kept mumbling, more to the tables than to anyone nearby.

"They damned well better," snarled Nick. "Sure won't be many tips when everything's free. Fifteen percent of nothing's … hell, it ain't much."

Tara put her arm around Cal's waist. "I think it's a fine thing you're doing," she said, and then she stuck her tongue out at Nick. "Nicest thing that's happened in this old dive since I've worked here."

The front door opened before Nick could grunt at Tara, and in walked Folly's Arlo Guthrie look-alike, Jim "Dude" Sloan.

"Here be the place?" he asked no one in particular.

"Yep," said Cal, who then rushed to the door and put his gangly arm around Dude's shoulder as if to keep him from backing out. Cal's crowd went from nobody to Dude—some would say that was no change, but Cal was happy.

Dude owned the surf shop and had been on Folly Beach for the last twenty-three years. As Amber had once aptly put it, "Dude surfs to the beat of a different wave." Charles had always contended that the short, thin sixty-year-old immigrated to Folly from another planet. Dude owned a tie-dye shirt factory or had a closet full of the colorful glow-in-the-dark holdovers from the 1960s. He took off his two-sizes-too-large corduroy coat, and his Christmas attire looked suspiciously like his other 364-days-a-year garb.

"Merry Christmas, Dude," said Tara. "Something to drink?"

Dude's face morphed into a smile. "Me be thrilled to have you fetch a libation," he said.

Dude normally confined his words to an average of about a half dozen. I would say that many words in a sentence, but Dude's words seldom achieved the common definition of a sentence. He must have been in the holiday spirit.

He perused the room. "Where's Mad Mel and CR?"

"Not here," responded Charles. "Or don't think so. What's a CR?"

Dude looked at Charles for the first time since he walked in. "Caldwell Ramsey." His head bobbed.

Of course, I thought. *Who else could it have been?* "Who's Caldwell Ramsey?" I asked.

"Mad Mel's cohabiter," said Dude.

Mel Evans, better known as Mad Mel, was a retired US Marine who owned a marsh tour boat—*Mad Mel's Magical Marsh Machine*—and ran groups through the marsh between Folly and James Island. He would take anyone, but he specialized in college students who wanted to get away from the police and party on the sandbars that dotted the waterways around the barrier islands. I had never experienced one of his "party cruises," but I suspected that he was a wee bit lax on checking IDs of his imbibing passengers. Dude had introduced Mel to Charles and me back in the summer.

Cal's ears perked up when he heard Dude mention Mad Mel. "Is Mel coming?" he said.

"Said so," said Dude.

"And will he actually bring his significant other?" said Charles.

"Said so," repeated Dude.

The aroma of sizzling burgers on the grill got Cal's attention, and he asked Nick if he would get some sandwiches ready. Nick mumbled a profanity and stomped to the kitchen.

The creaky door opened again, and three of Folly's singles peeked in and asked if the bar was open. It was cold outside, yet two of them didn't have coats and the third man had a dirt-stained army blanket wrapped around his shoulders. Cal, seeing that his crowd had swelled mightily, gave a dramatic wave and said, "Welcome."

I didn't know the newcomers, but Charles whispered that they were good guys, adding, "They're a bit behind in their happy lives and overly dependent upon the good graces of their fellow men."

"Huh?" I whispered back.

"They're bums," explained Charles. "Adjust."

I didn't know about that, but they did look like three gentlemen who needed a nice Christmas party, and that was what Cal was hosting.

Cal walked the three to the bar and made sure they got the first burgers off the grill and paper cups of fruit punch. One of the men glanced around and asked if, by chance, anything stronger was being served. "Later," said Cal.

Red plastic bowls piled high with potato chips and Hershey Kisses were beside the cups of punch on the bar. A stack of red and green paper plates waited to be filled.

Brenda Lee's "Jingle Bell Rock" filled the air.

Cal's Christmas wish and dream was in full swing.

CHAPTER 7

Free food, drink, and human contact proved to be a winning formula. By one o'clock that afternoon, Cal's Country Bar and Burgers looked like an airline terminal the day before Thanksgiving. Cal increased the volume twice on the radio. Nick started handing out bottles of beer in time with the cheerful music. The mood of the celebrants increased in time with the music and the beer.

I was pleasantly surprised to see my friend William Hansel. He was my height, carried less weight, and was five years younger. He was dressed in nice slacks, a white dress shirt minus a tie, and a navy blazer with brown leather arm patches. He looked like a professor getting ready to address an attentive class—not too surprising since that was what he was, a professor of hospitality and tourism at the College of Charleston. He appeared as out of place in Cal's as a walrus in a carrot patch.

"Good afternoon and merry Christmas," said William as I shook his outstretched hand.

William had been my neighbor for a brief period when I first arrived on Folly. He was not only out of place in Cal's—but in most of what he did. He was an African American living on an overwhelmingly white island. He was a Republican; he hated travel and the field in which he taught; and he prided himself on being prim and proper on an island where casual and bohemian ruled.

"And merry Christmas to you as well," I replied. Simply talking to William brought out a more formal tone. I didn't want to be graded down for verbal slovenliness. "It's good to see you."

His eyes took in the room. "I kept observing the flyers posted about town promoting the generous gesture on the part of Mr. Ballew," said William in his distinctive deep voice. "Thus I decided to take advantage of his hospitality."

William's wife had died of cancer a dozen years ago, and he lived in a small, neat cottage a couple of blocks from Cal's. I walked William over so Cal could formally greet him.

Mad Mel arrived with his "cohabiter," Caldwell, and immediately began hurling insults at Dude, his longtime friend. The barbs had been flying between Mel and Dude for nearly two decades, and a Christmas ceasefire evidently wasn't to be. Mel was the opposite of Dude. He was a few years younger, half a foot taller, and had a few zillion fewer hairs on his head. He was bald. Dude's friend had a constant frown on his face and looked as if he could wrestle a gorilla into submission. Mel, with his US Marine background, focused on his tasks at hand, but Dude appeared to have trouble focusing on anything.

This was the first time that I'd met Caldwell. His facial expressions were much friendlier than his partner's were. Mel was more than six feet tall, but Caldwell towered above him. Although Caldwell was African American, his skin wasn't much darker than Mel's. I heard him mention to the master inquisitor, Charles, that he had played basketball at Clemson in the mideighties.

I helped Nick refill the punch bowl but mostly listened to him gripe about having to work for meager tips and tell me that he thought that Charles was the worst bartender he had ever seen. "Between you and me," he said in a conspiratorial tone, "I think the reason Cal hired Charles was because they're friends." He nodded toward the center of the bar. "Look over there. Charles ain't even working; he's talking to … well, talking to damned near everyone. Ain't a bartender supposed to be near the bar?"

I remained silent and nodded. The good news was that Charles's undercover detective career was still a secret—at least from Nick.

"What the hell is that damned bear doing on your shirt?" said Mel.

He was halfway across the room and staring at Charles's sweatshirt. I was certain his booming military voice was heard by all.

"What's the damned *A* stand for? Assho—"

"Whoa!" Charles interrupted. He held both hands in front of him, palms facing Mel. "Alaska, the University of Alaska." He rolled his eyes as if to say, *Who doesn't know that?* "They're the Nanooks. It's Eskimo for polar bear."

"Well, excuse me," said Mel, who then surprised me, and likely everyone nearby, when he smiled. "Merry Christmas, Charles."

My cell phone rang before I imagined everyone breaking out into "Here Comes Santa Claus."

"Is this Chris Landrum?" asked a female voice.

I hesitated and then said, "Yes."

"My name is Charlene, Charlene Goode," she said. "I'm a friend of Joan's. She asked me to call."

My stomach turned sour, and I was having a hard time hearing the person. "Yes," I said. I walked to the rear of the bar, where fewer revelers were loitering.

She hesitated, but I didn't say anything. I realized that she must have called the house and the call was forwarded to my cell phone—a feature that sounded good at the time I had it added. I was now beginning to regret the decision.

"I hate to bother you on Christmas," she finally continued, "but Joan insisted that I call."

"No problem," I said.

"Her husband was killed yesterday ... Joan wanted you to know, uh, and wanted to ask a favor."

The merriment in the room faded. "What happened?" I asked.

"They say it was an accident." She emphasized *say*. "Daniel was on the way over the mountain to the casino in Cherokee. His Mercedes went over the cliff. It burst into flames. He was killed instantly."

I had moved one of the chairs to the corner and slowly lowered my body in the seat. "God, that's terrible," I said. "Is there anything ...? What can I do?"

"Well," she said, "that's why Joan asked me to call." She hesitated. "I hate to ask, but Joan wants you to come over here."

"Why?" I said without thinking. "I mean, what can I do?"

"To be honest, I don't know," said Charlene. "She keeps saying that you were the logical one in the family. She said you could figure most anything out." There was a pause. "But to tell you the truth, I tried to talk her out of having me call. I don't know what you can do … I don't know what she has in mind. I'm sure she'd understand if you said no."

Is this a dream? I wondered.

"Let me have a number," I said. I walked to the bar to get a pen. "I'll call back. It might not be until tomorrow."

She gave me a number where Joan could be reached, adding that she was under a doctor's care and might not be able to talk. I wrote the number on one of the red bar napkins. "I look forward to hearing from you," she said. "I'll tell Joan what you said." She hung up.

I pushed END CALL and stared at the phone.

CHAPTER 8

A dozen "strays" had ventured in and voraciously attacked the peanut butter sandwiches as well as the burgers and grilled cheese sandwiches that Nick and Tara churned out as quickly as the grill would allow. Charles had finally found his spot behind the bar and handed out beer and soft drinks. If someone requested something more complex like bourbon and Coke, Charles shrugged and said that "the boss" wouldn't let him fix it.

I convinced the bartending detective that he could pour me a glass of Cabernet without using too much brainpower, and I took the drink and walked around the room. I met a couple of folks I had occasionally seen around but had never met. I spent some time talking to Mel and Caldwell, and I listened to Dude's sentence-challenged version of why Christmas wasn't a big sales day at the surf shop. Apparently, this was only the second year that he had been closed on December 25. I would have questioned him more on the logic, or illogic, of why he had ever opened on Christmas, but my mind was stuck on the phone call and the extraordinarily strange request that I come to Gatlinburg.

Charles and Nick were behind the bar. Nick shook his head and then pushed Charles away from the beer cooler. Charles started to say something but backed away instead. Cal caught the action and moved behind the bar at three o'clock to give Charles a break. It was most likely motivated by hearing customers bemoan the limited drink selection and the near battle between his two barkeepers. I cornered Charles before he could begin one of his usual lengthy conversations with anyone he could corral.

"Did you see what that troublemaker did?" he asked.

"Yeah," I said. "What happened?"

"Don't know," said Charles. "He just said he thought I was worthless and gave me a shove."

"Sorry," I said.

He shook his head. "Yeah. Merry Christmas!"

"You'll never guess about the phone conversation I had," I said.

"Santa called and said that if you're a good boy next year, he might bring you something," he said. "Did I get it?"

He was back to normal. I shared that he wasn't within a mile of close and then told him about the call.

"The ghost of Chris's past!" said Charles, without an apology to the other Charles, Dickens. He shook his head. "No offense, but why does she want you? What aren't you telling me?"

"I have no idea," I said. "No idea."

Charles examined his wrist, the spot where those who owned watches would be wearing one. Skin, hair, and the sleeve of his blue University of Alaska sweatshirt were all that he could have seen. "So," he said, "when are we leaving?"

I started to laugh but realized he was serious. "I'm not leaving," I blurted. "So there isn't a *we* going anywhere."

Charles cocked his head to the left and said, "Tonight or in the morning? I need time to pack."

"What part of 'I'm not going' slipped by you?" I asked.

More apparently slipped by him. "Morning would be better," he said. "I promised Cal I'd help clean after the party. Eight or nine?"

I took his elbow and nearly shoved him out the side door. It was cold, but I didn't plan to be out long, and there was too much noise in the bar for Charles to hear me clearly.

"Charles, I haven't talked to my ex in a quarter of a century." I cradled my arms close to my body and stood between Charles and the door so he couldn't slip back into the comfort of Cal's. "I didn't know her husband. I didn't even know she was married. Finally, I have no idea why she wants me in Tennessee."

Charles held up his right hand, palm stuck in my face, and

interrupted. "It's cold out here, and I've heard enough excuses. First, it hasn't been a bunch of years since you heard from her. She called a week ago. You said she seemed hesitant and wanted to tell you something. And most important, it'll drive me crazy not knowing what she wanted!" He hesitated and then pointed back at the door to the bar. "Again, are we leaving tonight or in the morning?"

Maybe I felt more responsible for the divorce than I was willing to admit. I guess I did feel guilty about how I'd treated her, closed her out of my professional life. But that was two decades ago, and what was happening now was several hundred miles from here. Besides, I knew Charles enough to know that if *we* didn't make the trek, he would pester—more accurately, torment—me about it until my dying day. And, if he could figure out how, from then until the end of time.

That was the only reason I said, "In the morning. Eight."

The sentimental words of "I'll Be Home for Christmas" greeted us as we reentered Cal's.

CHAPTER 9

Charles was pacing in front of his small apartment on Sandbar Lane as I pulled up. I had called Charlene and told her that a friend and I would come to Gatlinburg, although I didn't know how I could help. She thanked me, gave me directions to Joan's house, and said she'd tell my ex. It was seven forty-five, but I knew that in Charles Standard Time, that equaled eight o'clock. His canvas Tilley hat was cocked crookedly on his balding head. He carried his ever-present handmade wooden cane; didn't have on a jacket, even though it must have been in the low forties; and sported an orange sweatshirt with a ferocious lion on the front, roaring above the words HIWASSEE TIGERS.

Neither his attire nor his pacing surprised me, but I was confused by the two suitcases by his door. I recognized his battered and faded Samsonite case from the trip we'd made to Kentucky a couple of years ago. What was totally out of place was a new brown suitcase next to Charles's well-traveled carryall.

I wasn't nearly as surprised by the pristine suitcase as I was when William Hansel stepped out of Charles's apartment. When he saw me pull up, he walked to the gravel and crushed-shell parking area in front of the building.

Charles looked back at William and then walked to the driver's side of my SUV. "Good news, Chris," he said with a wide grin. "William can go."

"Oh." William closely watched my expression. "That's great," I said, hoping I wasn't giving away my surprise.

"Yeah," said Charles. "After you left Cal's last night, I was talking to William and asked him what he was doing since classes were out for the year."

William stood directly behind Charles. "That is correct," he said in his bass voice. "If I may, Charles, allow me to tell Chris about your benevolent offer."

Charles tipped his Tilley in William's direction. "Please do," he said.

William stepped closer to the car. He wore the same navy blazer that he'd had on at Cal's, but he had the good sense to have a cashmere topcoat over it. "I was sharing with Charles that I had a dearth of activities for the balance of my winter respite, and he graciously and unexpectedly offered me the opportunity to visit the Great Smoky Mountains with the two of you. I've never been there, I might add." He smiled at Charles and turned back toward me. "I trust that my presence is acceptable." He took off a gold, red, and brown plaid motoring cap and held it in front of his chest, offering a slight bow.

"Of course it is," interrupted Charles.

I felt uncomfortable sitting in the car while Charles and William lingered at the door. I got out and walked toward the suitcases. "That's great," I repeated. I was still in the holiday spirit, so I didn't scream at Charles about inviting another person to join in our trip to visit my ex—my ex who just lost her husband and hadn't seen me since before many of William's students had been born.

"I assume Charles told you why we're going," I said. "It's not a vacation." I wanted to give him a chance to back out in case my buddy had failed to tell him about Joan and the death of her husband.

"He clearly communicated the sad and unusual nature of the visit," said William. "He also shared that there certainly would be time to vacate the world of work during the visit."

I paused a second to figure out what he was talking about. Much of his conversation could have leapt off the pages of a nineteenth-century literary novel. It was refreshing to hear proper, although a bit antiquated, grammar coming from someone I knew. But it did take extra concentration, which was something I'd wager his students often lacked. "And," I finally continued, "I don't know how long we'll be there."

"I will be comfortably attired for up to six evenings," said William. He nodded toward his suitcase.

"If they sell sweatshirts," said Charles, "I can only hold out for seven months."

Twenty-four hours ago, my plan was to enjoy a peaceful, quiet day after Christmas holing up in my home—avoiding the gallery, stores, and the mad rush of people returning gifts and spending the gift cards burning holes in their pockets. Twelve hours ago, my plan was to leave my peaceful home and drive to Gatlinburg with Charles while spending the entire trip wondering why I had agreed to go. One hour ago, I had loaded my vehicle with two suitcases, one person I'd known would be in the front passenger seat, and an unexpected surprise occupying half of the rear seat.

Through the magic of my SUV's satellite radio, Willie Nelson shared that he was also "On the Road Again." I helped William adjust the heat from the rear seat control while Charles fiddled with the navigation system and announced that we were 357 miles from my ex.

Perhaps we were only 357 miles away from my learning why I had to dredge up ghosts from the past—and what effect it would have on my life. If recent history was an indicator, I had reason to worry.

*   *   *

We limited our conversation the first third of our trip to topics that people kill time with. Charles, the master of gathering irrelevant information, shared that he had worn the tiger-logoed sweatshirt because Hiwassee College was in Madisonville, Tennessee, near Gatlinburg. Neither William nor I had asked, but that minor detail didn't stop Charles. When he started telling us that the student enrollment was about four hundred, William wisely interrupted and asked if I knew the weather forecast along the route. Clearly, William wasn't ready to listen to the names of Hiwassee's students, or the faculty, or the administration, or the maintenance crew.

The weather was mild for this time of year, and the last thirty miles or so would be on well-maintained interstate highways. There was an increased chance of snow the closer we got to Asheville and the mountains. Before leaving home, I'd checked the Internet and found that forecasters didn't appear worried about any weather delays in Asheville, east Tennessee, or in Gatlinburg. If they weren't worried, neither was I. Besides, if there was snow, it would be a chance to try my all-wheel drive feature, which one had little use for in the mild seldom-below-freezing climate of Folly Beach.

The conversation got more interesting as we skirted around Columbia, South Carolina's capitol. William had napped for a half hour, and he then shook his head awake and looked at Charles. "I couldn't help noticing yesterday that you appeared to be filling food containers and getting malt beverages for the customers at Cal's establishment," he said. "Is it possible that you are in the employment of Mr. Ballew, Cal as you call him?"

William was clearly unaware of Charles's venture into the world of private detecting. I glanced at Charles and waited for his reply.

Charles shrugged in my direction and then turned to the rear seat. "William," whispered Charles, as if he didn't want the trucker barreling past us at eighty miles per hour to hear. "This is highly confidential. Shareth not with others, okay?"

I nearly swerved off the road—*Shareth not?*

"Of course, Charles," said William. He leaned toward the front seat.

Charles then whispered the entire story about how Cal had approached him with the problem; how he and Charles had decided on the plan of action; how Charles had been on the job for a week; and how he had already read two books on bartending and thought that he was getting the hang of mixing drinks. He also told me that unless the thefts stopped, Cal might have to close the bar.

"So," said the professor, "you have found employment where you work a week and earn vacation days?"

William surprised me with that glimmer of humor, something that wasn't his forte. At least I thought he was trying to be funny.

"Cal understood that Chris wanted to make this trip and wanted me to go along for support," said Charles. "He said the thief would wait to get caught."

I threw Charles a look, wondering where that bit of fantasy had come from.

Snowbanks began to appear on both sides of the interstate as we entered the Blue Ridge Mountains near Asheville. The low clouds mated with the higher elevations, and light flurries danced in front of us like fireflies in late summer. December was a problematic time to be traveling in the mountains, and I hoped that we didn't run into any unexpected heavy snow, or worse, ice.

"So Chris," said William, "please forgive me if I'm being too nosy, but how long were you married?"

I glanced in the rearview mirror and saw a sheepish expression on William's face. He was a private person and seldom asked personal questions. "Considering that we've kidnapped you and are taking you to visit my ex-wife, I don't think you could be too nosy," I said with a laugh. I wanted to put him at ease. "We were married for nearly twenty years. She was my high school sweetheart. We were in college together and married our senior year."

Charles couldn't bear to be left out. "Then she dumped him. As President Carter said, 'I have often wanted to drown my troubles, but I can't get my wife to go swimming.'"

William cringed, so I laughed and ignored the presidential remark. "Charles isn't far off, for once," I said. "Joan was incredible. She would do anything for me. I loved her dearly."

"If I may be so bold to ask," said William, "what happened?"

I noticed Charles leaning closer. "You may," I said. "It's a good question. I put work first and wouldn't let her be part of it. And then her paranoia had her concluding that I was having an affair."

Charles's eyes widened; I couldn't see William's.

"I wasn't," I said, answering his unasked question. "Sadly, I did a lot of traveling for work, and she was at home with her imagination running wild." I shook my head. "And then Joan came home one day and said she was tired of being married. She said that I was boring. To be honest, she was right."

William had his arms crossed on Charles's headrest, and he inched closer to the front. "That must have been a different Chris Landrum than the one I've come to know," said William.

I smiled. "I think I'm the same guy—boring or otherwise. It's people like Charles, Larry, Mel, and Dude, and even you, who keep finding trouble for me."

We left the snow flurries thirty minutes past Asheville, and the bright blue sky reflected in the fields of snow covering the bare trees and brown grasses along I-40.

The mechanical female voice from the navigational system eventually told us to take the next exit to the Foothills Parkway, saying that we were thirty miles from our destination. Accumulated snow on the grasslands was nearly a foot deep, and plowed snowdrifts exceeded a couple of feet along the road. Kudos to the road crews. The parkway was clear.

"How often do you talk to your ex-wife?" asked William. He appeared more comfortable with the personal questions.

"Exactly twice," answered Charles for me.

"Twice?" said William. "That's interesting."

I agreed, especially since the two conversations were twenty-four years apart and the second conversation was a week ago and somewhat cryptic.

My cell phone rang. The caller ID read HEATHER, so instead of answering, I handed it to Charles.

"Hello, sweetie," he said.

I nearly gagged.

"No," he said. "We're not there yet … Yes, he's taking good care of me."

I rolled my eyes.

He laughed. "I think your psychic vibes are right," he said into the phone. He then looked over at me and at William in the backseat. "Umm, me too … Yes."

He hit the END CALL button and hooked the phone back on the charger.

"Well?" I said.

"She said she had a strong psychic vibe saying that we were going to have an interesting trip."

I didn't think it took a psychic to tell us that, but I didn't say it. I had been to Gatlinburg a couple of times when I lived in Kentucky, but I had never entered the resort town from the east. A sign for the Gatlinburg Community Center was the first indication that we were close. Charles commented that we would get to Gatlinburg before we got stranded. I willed myself to remain more optimistic. My main concern was to get out of Gatlinburg before getting stranded.

There was no doubt we were in Gatlinburg when we passed under a huge GATLINBURG WELCOMES YOU lighted display that spanned the road. Red, blue, and white lights were shaped like mountain peaks.

We drove down a steep hill and hit the intersection of Parkway, the main road though town. I finally recognized where I was. Christmas lights were everywhere, and the city looked like a cross between a Swiss village and a Disney version of the most festive Christmas ever. Oversized electrified candles, Christmas trees, stars, caroling snowmen, candy canes, and American flags with fireworks bursting in the background appeared to be placed at every empty spot in the city. Even William, the most proper person I knew, said, "Wow!"

The sidewalks had been cleared, as had been the main street. Several hearty tourists walked arm in arm along the sidewalks, puffs of frozen breath preceding them.

"Now what?" asked Charles. And he was the one person who always had a plan—good or bad.

"See my ex," I said, although I would rather have purchased a pound of Gatlinburg's famous fudge and scampered back to the beach.

CHAPTER 10

A large church youth group was in town for a conference during the week between Christmas and New Year's, so we were lucky to get the last two rooms at the Hampton Inn, the hotel that I had stayed in on previous visits. It was located close to the entrance to the Great Smoky Mountains National Park and in walking distance to the main retail area of Gatlinburg. I would be footing the bill, so I took a room by myself and let William and Charles share.

After throwing our luggage in the rooms, we piled back in the car to head to Joan's house. The friendly navigation voice told us to turn right on Ski Mountain Road and then we would be a half mile from our destination. I'd paid more for the SUV than I had ever paid for a vehicle, so I felt obligated to obey.

Charlene had given me an address and told me that Joan lived in a log cabin near Ober Gatlinburg, a ski resort tailored to everyone from the youngster who had never slipped on a ski boot to the experienced skier. It overlooked the city like a medieval castle.

"Think her cabin is larger than the one Abe Lincoln lived in?" asked Charles. We had passed log homes in varying sizes on the way up the hill.

My guess would have been yes, but when the pleasant Infiniti voice told us that we had reached our destination, I was shocked. I asked Charles to double-check the address before I pulled into a circular drive in front of the massive log structure that looked more like a mountain lodge than a "log house."

"Yep," he said. "Abe's cabin could fit in the guest bath."

The log mansion was perched on the side of the mountain. The gravel circular drive was on the only level spot on the property. I could see three stories of windows from our vantage point, but there could have been more. Each level had a large porch across the back of the house, which overlooked the snow-covered mountains and the ski slopes of Ober Gatlinburg. I guessed that the house was more than five thousand square feet, not counting the large decks.

I stopped behind a new metallic blue Jaguar XK convertible. It was spotless. It looked as if it had been airlifted to the place where it rested. Its chrome wheels were so pristine that they looked as if they had just arrived in the driveway via UPS. My car was covered with salt and road muck, and clumps of snow were in the wheel wells. I wondered how the Jaguar could have remained so clean; surely self-cleaning wasn't an optional feature. Before I could spend more time pondering the mystery, the nine-foot-high front door opened and I came face-to-face with the person I'd once loved and shared a life with.

I almost gasped, but not quite, when I saw Joan. There was a deep sadness in her eyes, and something else too. Her face gave me the distinct impression that she was in torment beyond the immediate grief of losing her husband. I wondered for the first time whether she might have been right, that there was more to Daniel's death than a tragic car wreck during what was supposed to be one of the happiest times of the entire year.

Joan stepped on the oversized porch and squinted toward the SUV. It was in the low thirties, and she wrapped her arms around her chest. We were backlit so she wouldn't be able to tell much about her visitors. At five feet eight, she was a couple of inches shorter than I was. She wore an oversized gray sweatshirt, leg-hugging black slacks, and dark brown work boots. Naturally blond hair had cascaded around her shoulders the last time I saw her. It was now mostly gray and short, and it barely covered her ears. We were the same age, but she looked younger than I imagined I did. She was trim when we were married, and I doubted that she had gained half a dozen pounds since then. The thought struck me that she may have had some help keeping her face as youthful as it appeared. I probably wanted to think that since time hadn't been that kind to me.

I hesitated and then walked to the porch to speed up the introductions so we could get out of the cold. Charles and William had stepped out of the car, but I knew they were intentionally lagging behind me.

"Chris, God, it is you?" she said. Her voice was more gravelly than I remembered. "Thank God you've come." She put her trembling arms around me and squeezed. The smell of alcohol was on her breath. After what seemed like an eternity, she let go and stepped back. Her eyes were red from crying.

"How are you?" was all I could think to say.

Then she noticed my friends who awkwardly stood at the bottom of the steps, clearly not knowing what to do. She waved her arm toward the door. "Please come in. How rude of me. Let's get inside."

That was all it took for Charles to bound up the six steps to the porch, his cane tapping each step. William took more time. Joan backed into the entry and stood aside so the three of us could squeeze past her. I introduced Charles and William. She gave each a tentative hug and welcomed them to her house. The heat from the powerful furnace felt good.

Joan turned away from us and waved for someone to come forward. "Charlene ... Char ... let me introduce you to Chris and his friends," said Joan.

I stepped forward and extended my hand to the attractive, angular-featured five-three brunette. The overly sweet aroma of her perfume arrived before her hand. Char introduced herself before Joan could say my name. "Thank you for coming," she said in the high-pitched voice I recognized from the phone.

I noticed that Joan had glanced toward William and then back to me, shrugging however slightly. She probably couldn't remember his name, so I did the honors and introduced William and Charles.

"I hope you don't mind my being here," said Charlene. "I stopped to see if Joan needed anything, and she wanted me to be here when you arrived."

The three of us nodded. Besides, how could I complain? I had dragged Charles and William along.

I looked around the room. From the entry, I could see a massive great room with floor-to-ceiling windows on two sides and a deep wooden deck stretching across the entire back of the house, providing a panoramic view of the snow-covered Smoky Mountains. The celebrated mountains filled most of the background. Joan waved us toward an L-shaped beige leather sofa that faced a ski lodge–sized fireplace and a large flat-screen television above it.

Charles, William, and I sat side by side on one side of the oversized sofa, and Joan and Charlene faced us from the other side. My ex-wife sniffled, wiped back a tear from her cheek, and sat erect and quite regal.

"Charlene told me you were coming," said Joan, breaking the ice. "But I didn't believe it … I hoped you would but knew it was a lot to ask since … well, since it's been so long."

William looked around and said, "You have a lovely domicile, Mrs. … uh …"

"McCandless," helped my ex. "Please call me Joan."

"How long have you lived here?" asked Charles.

I knew he and William were trying to make conversation, but all I wanted to do was scream, "What do you think I can do to help? Why call? *Why?*"

Joan smiled at Charles. "Daniel …" She looked at the floor and then back at Charles. "Daniel and I moved here three years ago. We fell in love with this house and made an offer the first time we saw it."

"William's right," said Charles. "It is lovely."

"Here I am being rude again," she said. "Can I get you something to drink … something to eat?" She motioned toward the ultramodern kitchen that opened to the great room. On the granite countertops were three platters covered with aluminum foil and two or three smaller clear Tupperware bowls—the kind neighbors bring after a death in a family. Her hands were trembling as she gestured, and I was afraid she'd fall if she tried to stand. She and Charlene had nearly empty glasses in front of them.

I declined for the three of us.

Joan started to stand but fell back on the couch. Charlene grabbed her before she fell sideways. She put her elbows on her knees, lowered her head, and placed her hands on the side of her head. "I should have been with him," she mumbled. "I wish I were."

She didn't move for the longest time. When she slowly raised her head, her cheeks were tear covered and her eyes redder than when we'd arrived.

I leaned toward her. "What happened?"

She blinked at me. "There's a casino across the mountain in Cherokee. It's a little over an hour from here." She pointed in the direction of the Great Smoky Mountains National Park. "We go over once a week. Daniel says ... said ... it was his way of giving money back to the Indians to pay for white people stealing their land umpteen years ago."

"Indians?" said Charles.

She turned facing him. "Cherokee is an Indian reservation. They own the casino. It was sort of his joke."

Charles and William nodded.

The lamp on the table beside the couch flickered as if it were laughing at the joke.

"It agrees," said Charles, his head twisting toward the lamp.

Joan forced a smile. "That happens a lot lately. The electric here is erratic at best," she explained. "Daniel's going ... was going to call an electrician ... Never mind."

"I see," said William, as formal as ever.

"Anyway," Joan continued, "we would go, usually on Saturdays, have supper, and then gamble for a couple of hours. Two thousand dollars was our limit, so it wasn't a big deal."

Charles gulped and then covered it with a deep cough. Two thousand dollars wasn't a big deal to him either; it was a humongous deal. Up until the inheritance this year, his net worth had never approached two thousand dollars. And when I considered the casino's odds of winning, I realized that Mr. and Mrs. McCandless could easily drop a hundred thousand dollars a year on their weekly jaunts.

"Did you always go with him?" I asked.

"Most of the time. I missed twice this year—I wasn't feeling well the other night, and he didn't want to go without me." Tears began to flow again. "I almost pushed him out the door. If he stayed home ... if I had gone with him ... if ..."

Her head was back down between her hands. William sat stoically on the front of the supple leather couch. Charles nervously wiggled, and I had no idea what to say.

Charlene put her arm around Joan. "This has been a terrible time for us," she said, nodding toward Joan.

Joan reached for her near-empty glass and asked Charlene if she could get her a refill. I noticed that Charlene hesitated and knew that Joan had had enough. Thinking food might help, I said, "Come to think of it, we could use a snack if it's no trouble."

Joan twisted her head toward the kitchen. "There's no shortage of food. Help yourself."

"That's so kind," said Charles. He got up and indicated to William that he should follow him.

"What would you like to dring ... drink," she slurred.

"A soft drink or water would be fine," I said.

She managed to get to her feet, and she reached for my arm. "Let me show you something," she said, leading me to the far side of the kitchen. Charles and William stood at the counter and watched me go.

She led me to a room off the kitchen and turned on the light. Because we were on the first floor, it wouldn't qualify as a wine cellar, but it would have fooled even the most astute wine connoisseur. Three of the walls were covered, floor to ceiling, with dark wooden wine racks and must have held six or seven hundred bottles. The racks were the same color as the floors in the great room, and, most likely, throughout the rest of the house.

"Daniel fandies ... fancies himself a collector of fine wines," she said. "The shelves are Indonesian mahogany. He said that was good for several reasons, none of which I understood. I favor bourbon." She smiled. "Red wine, right? Have a favorite?"

I didn't argue. She was in enough turmoil without my insisting on a soft drink. "Anything already open," I said. I didn't think she needed to hear that I favored anything with a screw top over wine from a box, but I was surprised that she had remembered my color of wine.

She poured a glass of Cabernet from a nearly full bottle on the three-by-three-foot butcher-block table in the center of the room. The long-stemmed Riedel glass was a vast upgrade from the plastic containers I usually drank from. She treated herself to a generous helping of Blanton's single barrel bourbon and took a sip. I started back to the great room, but she held her arm out to stop me.

"I should have been with him," she said—the same message and tone she had used earlier.

Clearly, she wanted to talk to me alone, so I leaned against the wine racks. "What happened?" I asked.

She took another sip. "Newfound Gap Road is the way to Cherokee. It twists and turns and goes over the mountain like a giant anaconda." She cringed as if the analogy frightened her. "In the winter, it's often closed because of snow. They're usually quick to clear it since it's a major road from here to North Carolina. It can still be dangerous."

I remembered making the trip one summer and told her I understood.

"They said he was going too fast—*much too fast*, they said—and must have not seen the curve." She looked down at her trembling hands. I waited patiently. "Not see the curve! They said he didn't hit the brakes. They said he went over the cliff without slowing down. They said his car burst into flames when it hit the bottom of the gulley."

Her cadence was frightening. She said it from rote. "They said" was like a kettledrum pounded on by a sledgehammer.

She then whispered, "They said he was burned beyond recognition. They said it was a terrible accident—terrible accident."

She took another sip of bourbon. Voices from the couch were the only sounds I could hear.

"What?" I said.

She slammed her glass down on the table. Bourbon sloshed out and ran down the side of the table.

"He was murdered!"

She picked up her glass and a bottle of wine and abruptly turned, leading me back to the butter-soft couch in the family room. The log fireplace gave the room a warm glow. Lights from cabins twinkled in the distance from the nearby mountains. William was telling Char something about his classes, and Charles glanced over at me. I could almost see the question marks in his eyes. They all had paper plates on their laps, filled with food from the kitchen.

I had lost my appetite.

CHAPTER 11

When we were in college, Joan had thought that a friend had stolen her term paper and used it in another class. Nothing came of it, and she never had more than a suspicion. She had a flat and was convinced that a guy who kept asking her out had sabotaged the tire. A tech at the tire store found a roofing nail in the tread, but Joan remained certain it was no accident. She also believed that her father was cheating on her mother. She couldn't present a shred of evidence, but it didn't stop her from believing it. Her older sister, who tragically died in her midthirties of a brain hemorrhage, had constantly teased that Joan was paranoid and was the first to believe anything bad said about anyone. I was never certain how much of her sister's comments were actually teasing.

Those memories stormed back to me when she said "murdered."

She plopped down beside Char, eyeing each of us seriously. "My husband was murdered," she repeated.

"Is that what the police said?" asked Charles.

"A terrible accident," she repeated. "The police called it a terrible accident."

What have I gotten into? "Why do you think he was murdered?"

"I don't think—I know," she said. She set her goblet on the coffee table, gazed down at it, and then picked it up and downed what little was left in the glass. She stood, walked to the wall of windows, and peered out.

"Okay," I tried again. "How do you know he was murdered?"

She went back to the kitchen and poured another glass of Blanton's, holding the Cabernet bottle in the air and motioning to me. By now, I needed a refill, but I declined. She called over to William and Charles and asked if they wanted something stronger to drink. They declined. Char had served them beer while Joan and I were in the wine room.

She took a seat on the couch. "Before we moved here," she said, "Daniel and a partner owned a group of luxury auto dealerships across California. They sold Rolls-Royces, Bentleys, Lamborghinis, and a few Aston Martins. They had showrooms in San Francisco, Beverly Hills, Santa Barbara, and Carmel, where we lived." She paused and turned to smile faintly at us. "We met three years after I left Kentucky. I was at a fund-raiser to help save some small fish with a name I couldn't pronounce. He was tall, had a mustache and stylishly long hair, and was dressed in an expensive three-piece suit." Her eyes were far away, almost as if she were reliving their meeting in her head. "Dashing was how I described him. He was a little older than I. That night he talked about ballet, opera, and fine wines. To use an old-fashioned term, I was smitten."

She had met Daniel three years after I had had any contact with her, but the description of that night still bothered me a little. I also wondered what her story had to do with the accusation that his death wasn't an accident. I chose the safest way to continue and remained silent. Wisely, so did Charles and William.

She continued. "He told me he was a car salesman. That wasn't exactly what I wanted to hear from the charming gentleman who was in the process of sweeping me off my feet. He could tell I wasn't thrilled to hear his occupation, and he explained that he wasn't exactly what one would call a car salesman—saying that he owned the dealerships and in reality was more of a broker of ultra-luxury vehicles."

"Ultra-luxury?" I asked.

"Selling for more than a hundred thousand dollars each," she explained.

"Oh," said Charles.

I thought it but didn't say anything. The *combined* cost of my last four vehicles may have reached that number.

"He did quite well," she said. "He often teased that he would be happy brokering deals until he died at the ripe young age of one hundred and seven. I was stunned when he came home two days before Memorial

Day three years ago and said he had sold the dealerships and thought we ought to buy a home in the mountains of east Tennessee."

"Did he say why he'd changed his mind?" I asked.

"No, never." She shook her head. "Never."

"Why move here?" asked Charles.

"I'm not certain. We had vacationed in the area three or four years earlier, and he said he loved the mountains and being relatively close to the ocean and the cities on the East Coast. To be honest, that didn't make sense—we were on the Pacific; we had San Francisco and LA close by and the mountains a short hop away."

"Do you think selling the dealerships and moving had something to do with his death?" I was reaching.

She continued to sip bourbon. "Not long after we moved, Daniel was contacted by two men he'd met at a car dealers' convention in Las Vegas. They had recently bought Jaguar of Knoxville. The men owned two other dealerships—sold Nissans and Kias. They were great with volume sales of new and used cars but didn't have experience selling higher-end vehicles. Somehow, they learned that Daniel was here and asked if he wanted to become a partner. They said they desperately needed his expertise."

"What did you think of that?" I asked.

Her eyes became slits. "It bothered me. The reason we were here was for him to retire. I guess it bothered me so much … so much that I ignored anything to do with the Jaguar dealership."

Her eyes were half-closed, and her head nodded a couple of times. She asked if we wanted anything else. I said no, and Charles and William shook their heads. Then she appeared ready to return to her story—I began to wonder if it would ever get around to why she thought he was murdered … and why I was here.

"Chris, we had all the money we needed. He made a mint when he sold the California dealerships, so I was dumbfounded when he accepted their offer. Anyway, he jumped in with both feet and elevated it to one of the top Jaguar dealerships in North America." She paused and then shook her head. "Six months ago, he abruptly walked away from it."

"Why was that, Ms. McCandless?" asked William.

"My degree's in math," she said with a small laugh. "Chris knew that, of course. I was a cost analyst for years. I've dealt with figures and business models all my adult life, yet Daniel never let me in his business world. He took great care of me, buying me anything I wanted; we traveled around the world. But I had to take it on faith that our finances were in order." She shook her head, her eyes continuing to narrow. "I have no idea why he sold."

"Did he get along with his partners?" I asked.

"Guess so … not certain," she said. "I only met one of them a couple of times. I never met the other one. I was so mad that he joined the dealership that I ignored anything about it. Petty, I guess. Well, they—"

Joan jumped and nearly fell off the couch. A large icicle had fallen from the roof overhanging the deck and crashed into a snow-covered rocking chair.

I had little confidence that we would get any useful information, but I gave it another try. "So why do you think he was murdered?"

"Know he was murdered. I don't think it." She had raised her voice and was staring at me with her angry gaze that was beginning to come back to me from decades long gone by. Charlene put her arm around her. Joan took a deep breath and then continued.

"Two months ago, he started getting calls. If I was with him, he would hang up and tell me that it was a wrong number. At first, I thought he was having an affair, but then I heard the other person's voice once—it was a man." She laughed without enthusiasm. "And don't think Daniel was gay. I can assure you that he definitely was not."

I hadn't said anything. Truth be told, I could almost believe that it was the wrong number. "Anything else?" I said.

"I started seeing a man, and sometimes two, watching me when I went to the grocery store. They looked vaguely familiar, but I couldn't place them."

"Could it have been a coincidence?" I said.

"I'm talking about a half dozen times," she said. "Statistical … statistically, that's way more than coincidence."

She abruptly turned to Char. "I hate to ask, but will you pick up the urn in the morning? I don't think I can handle driving yet."

Char agreed "I'll drop it off on our way out of town." She then turned to me. "My husband and I have a business obligation in Memphis tomorrow afternoon or I'd stay with Joan."

"I'm fine. I'm fine," said Joan.

I questioned that but chose not to say anything.

Joan waved her hand in the air and said, "Daniel had two wishes for when he … when he was gone. He didn't want a funeral—he wouldn't tell me why, and I stopped asking long ago. And he wanted to be cremated. I had no problem with that. I want the same …" She began tearing up. "Now who'll be there to cherry … to carry out my wish? Who?"

It was rhetorical, and all of us sat silently.

She took the final sip and stood. "I think I need to go to bed," she said. "In the morning, I'm taking Daniel … Daniel's remains … and spreading them where he said he would like to be."

I simply nodded. What else could I say?

She wasn't done. "Would the three of you come back around ten? I'd like you to go with me."

"Sure, if that's what you want. Don't you have other friends who you would rather be with—friends of Daniel … friends of yours?"

She shook her head. "There's nobody else."

So sad, I thought. "We'll be here," I said. "Is there anything else you need?"

"Yes," she replied, her eyes filling with tears. "Find out who killed my husband."

CHAPTER 12

It was snowing harder as we left Joan's house. I was tense from the long ride and hyper after our strange meeting with Joan. When we reached the hotel, I suggested that the three of us take a walk. Charles thought it was a "decent" idea, and William said he'd go, but he didn't show any enthusiasm. A couple of inches of the white stuff had fallen since we'd arrived, and Charles, and to a lesser degree William, complained every step of the walk from the hotel past some of the shops lining the main street of Gatlinburg. I reminded Charles that if he had brought anything heavier than sweatshirts, he wouldn't be freezing. He said that his red Tennessee Temple Crusaders sweatshirt was "just fine, thank you." He then added a snarl and shook the accumulation of snow off his hat at me. William seemed to enjoy the give-and-take—although I took far more than I gave.

Charles turned to me as we passed the Pancake Pantry, one of the city's culinary landmarks. "Chris," he said as he rubbed his hands together, "did I pester you on the ride back from Joan's house?" He shook his head as he asked. "On this hundred-mile walk through a raging blizzard, did I ask you about what you and Joan talked about in that monster wine room?" He continued shaking his head. "William, you know the answer is no and no, don't you?"

"My friend," said William, "allow me to refrain from participating. I am simply along for the ride." He smiled.

"Hmm," said Charles. He turned back to me. "Whatever. The point is that you have a passel of information that William needs to know, and all you want to do is walk and tell me that I don't know how to dress."

William needs to know? "Okay, William," I said, "let me tell you what I learned."

I shared what Joan had said about his death and where the accident had taken place. More than anything, I shared my observations about her mental state. I was interrupted approximately seventy-five times by Charles, who wanted to know every detail of the conversation. William's questions were kinder and gentler. He was concerned about how Joan was and whether I was okay. I told him that Joan was obviously devastated, but that I was fine. A half-truth was better than no truth at all—sort of.

I badgered Charles to stop in a gift shop on our way back to the hotel and buy something more weather appropriate than his sweatshirt. His shivering body didn't argue, but he was disappointed when the store didn't sell college logo wear. He settled for a heavy orange fleece jacket with the image of a black bear on the breast pocket. I had several things bouncing around in my mind, but worrying about Charles freezing to death on my watch was no longer one of them.

*   *   *

Joan had been watching for us through the side glass at her front door, and she stepped out onto the porch before the car came to a stop. She stood erect and wore black slacks and a heavy black cloth coat with fur lining. Her black leather boots were immaculate, and her smile was almost as shiny as her boots. A black leather purse strap draped over her shoulder, and under her right arm, she carried a foot-long rectangular cardboard box with a gold ribbon around the center. It looked nice enough to be a birthday present, but its contents weren't nearly as festive.

"I knew you'd be on time," she said as she opened the passenger door. Charles had moved to the backseat when we stopped. "You always were."

"That's one of his irritating habits," chimed in Charles.

Spoken from someone who considers himself late if he's less than fifteen minutes early, I thought.

Charles and I once again on our way to a funeral—something that had become too common in the last five years. My gut told me that this was going to be one of the strangest.

Joan directed us to the park's entrance and said we were going to Cades Cove, Daniel's favorite spot. The sun was breaking through puffy white clouds and reflecting off the newly fallen snow. The snow clung to the branches of the countless trees and produced scene after scene for a photographer. I resisted the urge to pull over and grab my camera. Despite the recent snow, the roads had been cleared, and we made good time on the curvy twenty-five-mile drive to the Cades Cove Visitor Center.

Charles "entertained" us with trivia about the national park. He shared that there were ninety historic structures, more than 130 species of trees, and (the one that got my attention) two bears per square mile. The lesson that I should have learned by now was never to let my friend loose in a hotel that had a well-stocked brochure rack. He needed more trivia like I needed shingles.

Joan barely spoke. William remained his respectful self and simply uttered "interesting" after each of Charles's revelations.

The snow wasn't as deep as we entered Cades Cove's eleven-mile-long loop road. Joan asked me to turn left on a small dirt road. The light coating of snow had been undisturbed. We were the first vehicle on the road today.

About a quarter of a mile down the rutted path, Joan pointed to a postcard-perfect small white church. "That's the Primitive Baptist Church," she said. "It was built in the late eighteen hundreds."

William said, "I like it. It's simple and spiritual."

Joan shared one of her few smiles of the day. "Yes, it is …" She opened the door as soon as we came to a stop. "There's a small cemetery in back. Will you join me?"

Charles murmured the names he saw on the tomb markers—"Gregory, Oliver, Shields …"

"This is the oldest church in Cades Cove," Joan interrupted. "Many of these people were the first white people to settle the area. Like everywhere around here, the Cherokee were here first." She turned and walked to the back of the small burial ground.

We gathered outside the rear marker of the graveyard. Joan motioned for us to come closer together. "Daniel and I used to come to Cades

Cove four times a year. We tried to make it each season," she said slowly. "We stopped here often." She waved toward the church. "He found it so peaceful; the last two trips he said that this is where he wanted to spend eternity." She sniffled. "I didn't think it would be … so soon."

We were silent a couple of minutes, and then she continued. "He actually called the park service to see if it was okay to have his ashes spread here. She grinned and nodded. "The ranger said he didn't know if it was legal, but that he had more to worry about than ashes in a cemetery."

Her smile faded. She gazed at the ground and then at us. "Could we have a moment of silent prayer?" she asked, barely audible. We stood in a semicircle, and she put her arm around my waist. Charles and William moved closer until we touched shoulders.

My head was bowed. Not a sound was heard. Until …

"Amazing grace, how sweet the sound, that saved a wretch like me …" William's wonderful soothing bass voice began singing the poignant hymn.

I was stunned. Tears filled my eyes. I had never heard William sing—never knew that he could. The idyllic snow-covered cove and the three of us were being treated to a voice that was usually reserved for the finer opera stages of the world. All living creatures within a couple of hundred yards surely stopped to listen to a melody, lyrics, and a voice inspired by the angels.

"… was blind, but now I see."

Then silence. I was torn between applauding, hugging William, and crying like a baby. But then Joan caught my eye. She had untied the ribbon on the box earlier and held the urn close to her heart during William's awe-inspiring rendition, and now she was carefully shaking the gray gristly and powdery contents in front of her.

She watched as each particle settled on the light covering of snow. Studying her side-lit face, I realized that at that moment, she appeared exactly as I remembered her from the first time I saw her in Mr. Crosby's tenth-grade math class. Tears rolled down my cheeks, and I brushed them away before they froze.

Joan then slowly walked toward the woods behind the cemetery. Charles started to follow, but William held out his arm and stopped him. The three of us remained beside Daniel's ashes. Clouds began to cover the sunny sky, and the temperature seemed to drop.

Joan returned from her slow-paced solace, carefully stepping in the footprints she had created when she walked away.

"Could we continue around the rest of the Cove loop?" she asked as we piled back in the car.

I said of course, and we fell in behind three vehicles for the slow drive through the beautiful, open countryside. She pointed out several historic sites along the way and shared that Cades Cove was once known as Kate's Cove, named after an Indian chief's wife. Charles listened intently to her every utterance, and I knew that at some point, he would be spouting this information back to someone.

Two white-tailed deer bounded in front of the car and stopped in the meadow fewer than thirty feet from the road. They turned and looked at us. I thought I actually saw one of them smile, but I'm sure I imagined it.

We left Cades Cove and headed toward Gatlinburg. "Chris," said Joan, "could I ask another big favor?"

I nodded and then realized that she was staring out the side window, so I said, "Sure."

"I'd like to see where he was murdered."

We had spread the ashes of her husband moments earlier and now this. I glanced at her. "Are you sure?"

"I think so," she said. "We could stop at the visitor center and get something to eat and head to the mountain."

She and I sat in silence for the next half hour while Charles quizzed William about where he had learned to sing and why he wasn't rich and famous. Apparently, William had spent several of his younger years in a church choir. I was surprised when he said he had five major roles in college musicals but didn't pursue it because he was uncomfortable performing in front of an audience.

The parking lot at the single-story stone and glass Sugarlands Visitor Center was nearly empty when we pulled in. We raided the vending machines—the only food available. We three guys would be satisfied with chips and cookies, but I was worried that Joan would be above such a mundane meal. But she got excited when she saw Cheetos in the machine. Money hadn't totally spoiled her.

"Kevin and a park ranger knocked on the door three hours after Daniel left for the casino," said Joan. She had been silently eating

Cheetos after telling me which way to turn after we left the visitor center.

"Kevin?" asked Charles from the backseat.

She turned in his direction. "Officer Norton," she said, "Kevin Norton. He's with the Gatlinburg Police Department and is a friend from church." She turned back toward the window. "It was kind of him to come with the ranger—Kevin's nice like that. He said he was relieved when I answered the door. He was afraid I'd been in the car with Daniel. Everyone knew we went to the casino each week."

A thick layer of ominous gray clouds began to fill the sky, and the snow was deeper along the side as we climbed Newfound Gap Road. The beauty of the scenery was muted by the sadness in Joan's voice.

"Kevin's expression went from relief to stoic when he saw me. The park ranger told me what happened—he put as much emotion in it as he would reading the phone book. He told me right on the front porch. My legs gave out, and Kevin caught me. They kept saying that it was a terrible accident—a terrible accident."

I had no idea how much farther we had to go. The Little Pigeon River was to our left, and the distance from the two-lane road to the nearly vertical drop narrowed to only a few feet in spots. Snow was piled a foot deep on the sides, but the highway crews had done a good job of keeping the driving surface clear. I didn't want to interrupt her grief but had to ask.

She shook her head and focused out the front window. "We should be close. They said it was just before the side road to Clingmans Dome. That's up ahead."

The road took a sharp left, and then we entered a long, straight stretch. Yellow caution signs with an arrow indicating a sharp right turn were generously spaced ahead of the next bend. I slowed and carefully rounded the curve. There were deep ruts in the packed snow along the berm directly where the road twisted right. Two young pine trees were sheared off about a foot from the ground, and tire tracks disappeared over the side. It didn't take a reconstruction specialist to know that this was where Daniel's life had ended.

A motor home closed quickly on my rear bumper, so I couldn't stop at the tragic spot. I continued for a half mile to where the road widened enough to make a U-turn. I slowly drove past the broken pines and edged into a scenic pullover. I stopped fewer than fifty feet from where the car had gone over the edge. My two right tires cut into the snow, but I was able to park safely off to the side. The snow was deep against the passenger side of the car, and we had to exit from my side. Joan gracefully navigated over the center console as if it were an everyday occurrence.

"They told me he must not have seen the curve and drove over the side of the mountain," said Joan.

We were about six feet off the road and looking down the hill where the Mercedes had vaulted to a fiery end. It had snowed since the wreck, but we could see the path the heavy luxury car had taken. There were several blackened trees and burnt shrubs at the bottom of the hill.

"That's possible, isn't it?" asked William.

She glared at my friend. "Daniel has driven this road more than two hundred times." She pointed in the direction of Gatlinburg. "There are five big yellow signs warning about the curve." She turned back toward the spot where the car left the road. "That is where my husband was murdered," she said clearly, emphatically enunciating each word.

I thought the same thing that William had made the mistake of verbalizing but knew it wasn't the time to say anything. Besides, what good would it do?

Several cars passed us while we were checking out the scene. Two of them were traveling too fast for the curve. We moved farther off the roadway and precariously close to the drop-off. I finally suggested that we head back to the safety of the car. Joan nodded, and the rest of us cautiously inched our way back.

We hardly spoke a word on the drive to town.

We pulled into her circular drive. "Chris, do you think you could take me to supper tonight?" she asked.

As was his habit, Charles blurted out an answer before I could say anything. "Sure he could. What time do you want him here? I'll make sure he's not late."

She laughed—the first real laugh since we had arrived. Either Charles had stumbled onto the right thing to say, or he was a well-trained psychologist hidden inside a rough, quirky shell.

We agreed on a time and waved as she entered her log mansion.

Chapter 13

Joan and I sat at a table on the heated side of a large picture window that overlooked a narrow river. A bottle of Kendall Jackson Merlot was on the table between us. We shared the native log and stone dining room with three couples and a table of four in the far corner. Joan had recommended the Peddler Steak House. I told her that if it didn't have golden arches, I was in. She tried to smile and fell short. I hurt for her.

She had exchanged her black mourning clothes for a light gray cashmere turtleneck sweater and dark gray wool slacks. Her short black leather jacket was draped on a nearby chair.

We were on our second glass of wine and had traveled to the large stone and granite salad bar and talked about a storm that was expected to deliver a foot of snow tomorrow evening—all before she mentioned Daniel and his tragic death. I was far from qualified to answer what she asked. "Who would have wanted him dead?" she said.

I filled her glass. "I have no idea. Who do you think?"

"I was awake most of the night trying to answer that," she said. She pushed the lettuce around on her salad plate and then took a small bite. "He wasn't a big gambler—I don't think he owed anyone money. I don't know all the details, but it looks like our bank and brokerage accounts are quite healthy." She took another bite and watched the slowly moving river with ice islands near the center. It was illuminated by spotlights in nearby trees. "He had a large insurance policy: something like two million dollars and double for accidental death." She turned toward me. "If the police didn't think it was an accident, I'd be their top suspect."

She was right. So where did I fit in? She hadn't invited me to Gatlinburg and to dinner without Charles and William simply to introduce me to the Peddler's filet mignon. "What can I do?" I asked.

A waiter crossed the room to deliver two plates of sizzling steaks to one of the other tables. The smell of the still-broiling filets trailed behind.

"I can't turn back the clock," she said. "No one can. But I've looked back many times over the years. I thought back to Louisville and my decision to bail on you. I was convinced it was the right thing to do; I really was."

"I know," I said. "It tore me up, but you may have been right. I was getting tired of me too, but I couldn't figure how to leave myself." I grinned and hoped she saw the humor.

She smiled. "Regardless, that's water under the bridge. I was wrong. I realized that what I thought was boring or uneventful was your careful, analytical, understated approach."

"Sounds like boring to me," I said. Humor had always been my first line of defense against fear and situations in which I felt uncomfortable.

She asked if I'd remarried, and I said no. She said, "Oh," and she then took a sip of wine. Finally, she turned toward me. "I loved Daniel. I guess I still cared about you and wanted to know if you were okay. If …"

The waiter magically appeared tableside and interrupted Joan's thoughts. He said our food would arrive shortly and asked if we wanted another bottle of wine. I said, "Not yet," but I wanted to shout, "Yes!"

"I actually called directory assistance twice and asked for your number," she said. "Either it wasn't listed or you weren't in Louisville anymore. I … I knew you had your own life and I wasn't a part of it, so I didn't try to find you."

I explained that I had an unlisted number. I'd had to deal enough with employees at the office and didn't want to take my job home.

"Oh," she said again. "Well, when the strange calls started coming and the scary men appeared around town, I thought about calling my friend Kevin but didn't have anything to tell him—thought he'd think I was crazy." She looked down at her barely touched salad and whispered, "Maybe I am."

Our steaks arrived, and I didn't have to respond—thank God.

We commented on how great the steaks looked, and I took the opportunity to order another bottle of Kendall Jackson.

"That's when I googled you. I was surprised but not shocked to learn from a newspaper article how you had helped the police. You were always so analytical and logical. You never met a puzzle you didn't like; I knew you could help. I wanted to tell you more when I called before Christmas, but I didn't know what to say … I really didn't."

She had kept up a strong front all evening, but tears had begun to gather in the corners of her eyes. "And then … and then … he was gone."

I didn't know what I could do to help find the person she insisted had killed her husband. I had serious doubts that it was murder. Nothing she had said had led me to think anything was suspicious. When we were married, I had entertained thoughts that she may have been clinically depressed and paranoid. Had anything changed? And I had never met her husband. Her only friend that I'd met was Charlene.

I felt sorry for Joan. I knew she was hurting and was convinced Daniel's death wasn't an accident. I got all that, but how could I help? Wasn't it police business? Even if I stayed longer, I didn't see what I could do.

Like all good self-respecting cowards, I used an excuse to avoid an awkward situation. For me, it was the pending snowstorm. I told her we were leaving in the morning so we wouldn't get stuck in the storm. I said that William needed to get to work. I didn't mention that he didn't have to be in class for another week. I didn't want to leave her without hope, and I said that I would think about what she'd said and would talk to some police friends at home and get their take. I saw disappointment in her eyes and felt bad about deserting her. I tried to rationalize it by telling myself that she had deserted me.

After taking her home, I walked her to her front door and said that I'd call in a few days to talk about what I could do. She hugged me and then stepped toward the door. I started to turn, and she stepped back and hugged me again—this time so tightly my ribs hurt.

She finally let go and said that she would look forward to hearing from me. I figured I'd wait a week or so and then call to say that I couldn't think of anything to do. I figured that would be the end of a very strange chapter in my adult life.

I figured wrong—way wrong.

CHAPTER 14

The heaviest snow was to blanket eastern Tennessee around noon, and I wanted to be over the mountains and on the down side of Asheville before the bad weather hit. Charles grumbled, and William showed dignified displeasure when I told them that we didn't have time to stop at Pancake Pantry.

"Let's see if I have this right," said Charles as we pulled out of the hotel parking lot. "You had a delicious steak dinner with a beautiful lady at a nice restaurant overlooking a babbling brook after you dumped William and me at a hotel without a restaurant, and we had to trudge through snow and freezing cold to get a sub sandwich and a watered-down soft drink and then trudge back to the hotel and watch reruns of *Cold Case*." He took a deep breath, his first since starting the monologue. "And," he continued, "now you're depriving us of a decent breakfast." He turned to his trudging partner in the backseat. "Is that what he's doing?"

William smiled and showed no evidence of contempt. "I could not have said it better. More succinctly … but not better," he added.

I started to laugh but held it. After all, there was a kernel of truth in Charles's rant. Rather than listen to him gripe each mile of the trip, I promised that I'd stop for breakfast once we got near Asheville.

"Second best is better than no best," he said.

Whatever, I thought.

He wasn't done. "Since we were shut out of the fun last night, it's time you tell us what you learned. And why are we leaving? Shouldn't we stay and help?"

William, who was born with a fraction of the nosy genes that Charles had inherited, leaned forward to hear my answer.

I shared as much as I could, considering that Joan and I had killed two bottles of Merlot. I told them that she undoubtedly believed that her husband was murdered—but when I pressed about why she was sure, she didn't offer anything that sounded remotely plausible.

"Okay," said Charles. "Even if she doesn't know more than what she said, think about the wreck." He pointed straight ahead at the interstate. "There was a long straight stretch before the curve. There were several warning signs. And didn't she say that he'd driven the road a couple hundred times? Surely he saw the curve."

I turned to Charles. "I don't—"

"I think he was killed," interrupted Charles. "You should have stayed."

"And done what?" I asked.

"I don't know," conceded Charles.

William had been following the conversation, and he tapped Charles on the shoulder. "I have driven Folly Road several days a week for many years," said a deep voice from the rear seat. "I know that road like, pardon the cliché, the back of my hand."

"That's my point," interrupted Charles.

"Hmm," said William. "My friend, that is not my point. May I finish?"

"Okay, okay," said Charles.

"My point," said William as he nodded toward Charles. "As a result of knowing the route so well, I occasionally catch myself daydreaming, thinking of what I need to do when I get to the classroom or what I need to purchase at the grocery store on the way home. I am not paying the appropriate amount of attention to driving and my environs. I dislike admitting it, but it seems appropriate. I have come perilously close to hitting another car or missing a turn. Not because I am not familiar with the roadway, but because I'm too familiar with it."

"Good point—I guess," said Charles. "But did either of you notice any effort he made to stop as he approached the curve? I didn't see any skid marks, did you?"

We shook our heads.

"Then," continued Charles, "that's a good reason to think his car was sabotaged—or even that he committed suicide."

"Did Joan happen to mention if Daniel had consumed alcoholic beverages before he left home?" asked William. "Or did he have health concerns? He could have had a heart attack and possibly been incapacitated or died prior to heading over the cliff. Was he depressed?"

"Yeah, Chris," interrupted Charles. "He was several years older than your ex, and she's your age, so he was an old geezer."

I told them that she hadn't mentioned either his drinking or health, physical or mental, but that I agreed. It could have been exactly what the police had concluded—an accident, a tragic accident. My thoughts were clouded by my history with Joan.

We were on the outskirts of Asheville when Charles suggested that we stop talking about the "murder" so the driver could concentrate on finding somewhere to stop.

Flurries had morphed to snow showers and then turned heavy by the time we hit the Asheville exits. I said that all we had time to do was grab a bag of doughnuts and some coffee at a convenience store. Charles grumbled but agreed that he didn't want to be stuck with William and me in a dinky motel along the road. I let Charles run in the store and get whatever he wanted. That appeased him some, enough so he wouldn't complain the entire way down I-26 toward Columbia, Charleston, and best of all, Folly Beach.

We talked and talked about Joan's situation until there was nothing left to say. William frowned as he chewed and swallowed a bite of stale doughnut. "Exactly what does it require to become a private investigator?" he asked. "I would think that there are rules governing the profession."

I was equally interested in his response since, to my knowledge, he had avoided my suggestions over the last six months that he check with the state about regulations. I waited for his answer.

Charles glared at me. "Did Chris tell you to ask that?"

"No," said William. "It simply stimulated my interest."

"Good question," said Charles. He then put an entire minidoughnut in his mouth and chewed as if nothing had been said.

"Thank you," said William. "Perhaps you have an equally good answer?"

I smiled inwardly and nodded toward Charles.

"There are laws," responded Charles, "but they don't apply to me."

Charles had an inherent belief that most laws didn't apply to him. I was curious as to why he felt he was outside the jurisdiction of the private investigator laws. "Why is that?"

He looked over at me and then turned back to William. "Gee," he said, "you two never give up. To be a private investigator in South Carolina, one must accept employment for his or her services. If one does, he or she must have three years of experience working under a licensed investigator and apply to—get this—SLED. Isn't that the dumbest name you've ever heard? I think it means South Carolina Law Enforcement Division. Dumb, dumb, and dumb."

When I heard Charles use "his or her" and "he or she" in two consecutive sentences, I knew he was quoting something. If William had said it, I wouldn't have given it a second thought.

William tilted his head in Charles's direction. "But isn't Mr. Ballew paying you to find out who's stealing from him?"

"Of course not," said Charles. "He hired me to tend bar. If I happen to discover who is absconding with his stuff, it will be merely a coincidence."

"More like a miracle," I mumbled.

"What?" said Charles.

"Nothing," I said.

Charles had deflected the questions about his private investigative efforts. William grinned throughout the discussion; Charles failed to see the humor. He did what I would have done—he changed the subject.

"Chris, what's the latest on your love life?"

I enjoyed Charles's explanations of why he wasn't a detective more than his new line of questioning. William unwittingly jumped from my side to Charles's when he asked, "Oh, is there something incongruous with your relationship with Amber? She's a lovely young lady, and I thought you two were, as my students say, hooking up."

"I believe a more accurate term would be *unhooked*," said Charles.

I wouldn't have put it quite so harsh, but the bottom line was that Charles was right.

"Sorry," said William. "Consequently, are you presently dating anyone?"

"I've been out a few times with Chief Newman's daughter, Karen—"

"Seven," interrupted Charles. He held five fingers from his left hand and two from his right hand in the air. "Seven dates. They went to Charleston for supper three times; once to a brainless chick flick; she took him kayaking, if you can believe that; and twice I haven't found out what they did. But don't worry, Professor—I'm working on it."

"Pray tell, we must be exact," I said, shaking my head. I hadn't been counting, so I didn't know if he was accurate. "She and I've been friends for a few years but only started dating this summer."

"I warned him," said Charles. "Karen and her dad carry guns. Seems like nothing good could come from making either of them mad."

"I've had limited contact with Karen," said William. "But I have great admiration for her father; she seems nice as well."

The chief and William had been acquaintances for years but became closer four years ago, when a friend of William's was murdered. Struggling with the death, William had suffered a nervous breakdown that required hospitalization for several days. Both the chief and I had regularly checked on him.

We were a few miles from Columbia and out of the higher elevations. The snow had stopped. Temperatures were supposed to be in the sixties at home, and I would be glad to stick my coat in the closet—hopefully its final resting place.

I thought William's comment about Karen and her father, Brian, was a good note on which to end the dating discussion. I asked William about his teaching schedule, if he looked forward to getting back into his garden in the spring, and if he had plans for New Year's Eve. Charles couldn't have cared less about those questions, and his chin came to rest on his chest. I had successfully bored him to sleep.

CHAPTER 15

"Gatlinburg got its foot of snow," said Charles as he entered the gallery, where I had been peacefully drinking a cup of coffee. He wore a College of Charleston long-sleeved sweatshirt and his Tilley. He tapped his cane three times on the well-worn wooden floor to officially announce his arrival. He was too cheery for my mood after the last few days.

"Glad we're not there," I said with little enthusiasm. I had spent several sleepless hours the night before, feeling guilty about leaving Joan. She had almost begged me for my assistance. It reminded me of how she had asked me time after time about work back when we were married. I had never given her the time she deserved.

He pulled a chair from the table in the back room and sat. "What's your problem?" he asked. "You know, 'Things are more like they are now than they have ever been.'"

"So what?"

"Don't know," he said. "President Gerald Ford said it, and it seemed appropriate. You'd be in a better mood if you had breakfast yesterday at the Pancake Pantry."

That brought a smile to my face, albeit a faint one.

"Last night Heather and I were ciphering about your ex," he said.

Oh, great, I thought, *a sucky-singing scatterbrained psychic and the world's newest, and probably least qualified, private detective bartender ciphering, whatever that means.*

"Tell me about it," I said.

Charles watched the door to make sure no customers were arriving. "We pondered the death of Joan's non-Chris husband for an hour, and then we … Never mind. I'm not a math whiz like your ex, and neither is Heather, but according to our calculations, one of four things happened. Number one—and the leading candidate according to the police—an accident, a terrible accident. Number two, he was offed by someone. Three, suicide." He stopped and took a drink of coffee before looking my way again.

"Four?" I reminded him, holding up four fingers—after all, he'd said he wasn't a math whiz.

"That was a dramatic pause," he said. "I'm waiting for your full attention. It deserves a drumroll, but I can't have everything."

"Four?" I repeated before he called for a drum and bugle corps.

"Four was Heather's idea. I'm amazed that we didn't think of it." He pointed at me and at his face. "Suppose it needed a fresh pair of adorable eyes to see what was staring at our faces."

"And what was it?" I barked, sharper than I should have.

"Daniel's not dead," said Charles. He had a smug look as he leaned back in his chair.

I searched for upturned lips from across the table. A smile wasn't forthcoming. "Not dead," I said.

"Not dead."

"And that was Heather's idea?" I asked.

"Yep. Hear me out before you hurl the theory to the floor and stomp on it."

"Go ahead," I said. "I'm anxious to hear this one; I really am."

"Look at what we're sure of," said Charles. "Daniel's car went over the cliff. The car made no effort to slow down—we all saw that?"

I nodded.

"Somebody was turned into charcoal at the bottom of that ravine. The body was so burned that Joan should have gotten a discount from the funeral home for the crema—"

"Charles!"

"Okay, I could have said that better," he said. "Anyway, they still don't know if it was Daniel. Joan thinks that he had a boatload of money, but she never knew how much. Remember, she said that he wouldn't let her in on his business."

I nodded again.

"Here's the clincher," said Charles. "Heather said that she got a powerful psychic vibe that Daniel absconded with a ton of money and went back to California ... or Capri."

He was serious, so I didn't laugh—out loud. "Doesn't Heather get her psychic vibes from dead people—spirits or ghosts? If Daniel's alive, who shot her the vibe?"

"I'm fuzzy about that psychic stuff," he confessed. "But it does make sense that Daniel may still be among us."

"If he's alive, who was in the car?" I asked.

"I only started my detecting career last week. I've got to figure out who's stealing from Cal. Joan's your ex; you figure it out."

There was so much to argue with and so little time to do it. I decided that we should wait for customers in silence. I got my wish when Charles said he had to meet with Cal to plan his schedule for the next few days. He also said he would be gathering clues to help catch "the person or persons unknown" who had been stealing from Cal's. Charles had been watching too much television.

I couldn't remember the week between Christmas and New Year's Eve for each of my sixty-plus years, but I did remember some, and I had a vague feeling about the rest. That was usually the worst week of the year for me. The sun began setting at what seemed like noon, and it was dark by five o'clock. It was typically cold—most years either snowy or rainy—and the majority of people I came in contact with were either depressed, angry, or sick. I hated the week, and here I was in the middle of it—this year was not an exception.

On the off chance that I could turn my luck around, I punched Karen's number on my speed dial and hoped that the good citizens under the jurisdiction of the Charleston County sheriff's office weren't in a bad enough mood to kill their fellow citizens. I needed to see Karen more than I hoped she needed to see a corpse.

My luck had changed. She said that she would be delighted to have supper with me. She said she didn't care where and added that I could pick her up at seven.

CHAPTER 16

Karen lived two blocks off Savannah Highway and about nine miles from the bridge separating Folly Beach from the rest of South Carolina. Her two-bedroom white house was slightly larger than my cottage, but it was perfect for her and her nine-year-old cat, Joe Friday, named for the main character in the old television show *Dragnet*.

Joe announced my arrival with a loud purr before I knocked. Karen must have heard her guard cat, for she opened the door as I stepped on her postage stamp–sized concrete porch. She was in her early forties but looked younger. Underestimating her had been the fatal flaw of many criminals. She had a keen, analytical mind, a near-photographic memory, and was able to wade through the manure that bad guys tried to spread when being interrogated.

Tonight Karen looked like anything but a successful detective. Her blue silk blouse complemented her athletic figure. Her chestnut-brown hair was shoulder length and not constrained as she usually wore it on the job. She greeted me with a peck on the cheek, welcomed me back, and quickly added, "Where are we going? I'm starved."

I suggested the Athens Restaurant and Grill a couple of miles off Maybank Highway. I had never been there but had heard good things about it. She agreed, so she was probably thinking that it was a good idea or was too hungry to argue.

The restaurant was light and airy and had a spacious bar and nice outdoor seating area, which, for obvious reasons, was empty the last week of December. The decor was neutral, with dark wood chairs and booths. Traditional Greek music played softly in the background. The dining room was nearly deserted, but the waiter assured us that it would be packed tomorrow and New Year's Eve.

I ordered their private label Cabernet, a marketer's phrase for house wine, and Karen surprised me by ordering an Alexander the Great, something with Greek brandy and a hint of chocolate. She said that she felt like living on the edge. I smiled as I wondered what Charles's reaction would have been if someone had asked him for that drink. I ordered a plate of hummus and pita bread to split.

"How was the trip?" she asked. She knew the basics of why we had gone.

I gave her a rather lengthy version of the three strange days in Gatlinburg. Karen knew I would eventually fill in the blanks. She listened without interrupting—a skill foreign to Charles—and sipped her brandy without losing focus on my ramblings. I finished by sharing Heather's theory and was surprised when Karen failed to disavow it.

The hummus and pita bread disappeared in short order, and Karen said she was still starving. Being a top detective burns a large number of calories. There was only one other couple in the dining room, so the waiter was extra vigilant. Karen ordered the Athens pie, and I pointed to the pastitsio on the menu since I didn't know how to pronounce it.

"You have a good track record at figuring these things out," said Karen. "What's your gut say?"

"I thought you'd ask," I said, rubbing my chin. "To be honest, I can't get a good read. On the surface, I think the police are right about his death being an accident. That may be clouded by my years with Joan. I do think she was paranoid—at least when we were married. I saw some of the same behavior this week. On the other hand, it doesn't make sense that her husband would just drive off a cliff. It was well marked, he was familiar with the road, and the weather wasn't bad." I hesitated. "Couldn't the police tell?"

"Normally, yes," she said. "Most of the time an autopsy would show unusual trauma to the body—trauma not caused by the crash. It should show if the driver had been dead before the crash—heart problems, seizures, bullet to the head … The techs probably would have been able to tell if the car had been tampered with."

"The fire screwed that up, didn't it?" I asked.

She nodded.

"Let's assume he was murdered," I said. "Didn't the murderer take a big chance? If the car hadn't burst into flames and incinerated much of the evidence—car and driver—there would have been a good chance that the police would have found enough to pursue it, right?"

"Yes, but he would have been dead either way."

I thought a second and then continued. "Then, to be sure the accident took place at the right spot, the murderer would have had to be in the car with a gun to Daniel's head and then get out before it went over the cliff?"

"Yes," said Karen. "The killer would have almost certainly been in the car when it reached the cliff. There are ways that he could have increased his odds of it burning—damaged gas line or screwed-up fuel injection system come to mind. Daniel could have been killed elsewhere, driven to the scene, and sent over the cliff with a burning rag in the open gas tank. That'd have pretty much guaranteed a fire when the car hit the rocks."

"True. I guess we'll never know," I said.

"It's not that uncommon. It really isn't. Television makes us think that all crimes are solved. That's the difference between fact and fiction." She glanced at the amber pendant lights over the bar and then back at me. "You said she mentioned a local cop. Do you remember his name? I could give him a cop-to-cop call and see if he found anything unusual."

I did remember, and I gave her his name.

"Chris, there are two other things to remember …"

"What?" I said as our food arrived.

The waiter left the plates on the table and stepped away. The appetizing smell of the attractively presented dishes drew Karen's attention. She hesitated before taking the first bite and looked up at me. "First, if it wasn't an accident or suicide, was Daniel the target? Didn't you say that Joan always went with him, and that no one knew she was staying home?"

"Yes," I said.

"Then she could have been the intended victim?"

I paused and then said, "Yeah … yes."

"And second," she said, "if Daniel was the target, the most likely suspect is Joan. You said that she inherits millions. Double insurance for accidental death, remember? She said she didn't go with him that night. Did anyone see her at home, or did she leave with him and rig some way for the car to go over the cliff? If she was in the car, then she had to get back home. That means an accomplice. Other than the obvious money, did she have reason to want him dead?"

She picked up her fork, attacked the entrée, and then pointed the fork at me. "These are only questions, Chris—only questions."

I hesitated briefly. "I know."

I'd already thought that it could be Joan, but I hadn't wanted to verbalize it for fear that it would come true.

CHAPTER 17

The best thing about the week between Christmas and New Year's Day is that it eventually ends. I'd never been a fan of New Year's Eve parties. I didn't have a burning desire to see the New Year begin any more than I did to stay up until 2:00 a.m. to change my clocks twice a year. I'd make an exception this year—exception to staying up until midnight, not the time change.

The weather reflected my dreary frame of mind. Joan's abrupt reentry into my life only darkened my mood. I'd finally blocked years of guilt about the divorce out of my mind, and now the guilt was slapping me in the face. I hadn't opened the gallery, but I did check on it the day after my date with Karen. No one had stolen all the photos, but two of the fluorescent bulbs in the office had lost their enthusiasm for life.

"Hey, Chris, happy almost New Year," said Larry as I opened the squeaky door of Pewter Hardware. I barely saw Larry's full head of hair as he gazed over the chest-high counter. Larry had owned Folly's sole hardware store for the last decade. The store was tiny, the perfect scale for its five-one, one-hundred-pound owner. I had met Larry my first year on Folly, and we had become friends—and on one occasion, he'd been my partner in crime. Six months ago, in a quirk of karma that I doubted even Heather could explain, Larry, a reformed cat burglar, had married Cindy Ash, a Folly Beach cop.

Larry quickly gave up trying to sell me seventy-three boxes of Christmas lights he was stuck with, but he did sell me a couple of fluorescent bulbs. "Better than nothing—but not by much," he said.

I shared my New Year's Eve plans, and he said he and Cindy might join me. "If she says it's okay," he mumbled.

This would be Cal's first New Year's Eve at Cal's Country Bar and Burgers. More accurately, it would be his first as owner. He had been the featured entertainer the last two New Year's Eves. He said that there was a good crowd each year and expected his first big night as proprietor. This would also be Charles's first New Year's Eve as a bartender. To celebrate that milestone, Cal had drafted the other three bartenders to work. My guess was that two of them would tend bar and the third would bail Charles out if anyone ordered anything more complicated than beer.

I would be there to support Cal and to watch Charles bartend. Could there be a more entertaining way to spend the night? I had mentioned my plan to William on our way home from Gatlinburg and was pleased when he said he'd join me "if I found it acceptable." I did.

I walked to the party. It had already been dark for more than three hours, and it wasn't even nine o'clock. I thought about calling Cal on my way to suggest that he turn his clocks ahead a couple of hours so we could celebrate midnight at ten o'clock, but I decided that would deprive him of hundreds of dollars of liquor sales. Surely I could stay up that late one night a year—surely.

The flaw in my change-the-clocks-and-celebrate-early plan became apparent when I walked in. The place was nearly empty. Three tables were occupied, and the largest gathering was at the corner of the bar nearest the bandstand, where four servers and two of the three bartenders were carrying on an animated conversation. Cal's predominant customer base had been alive to see the first moon launch, so many of them were probably at home napping before their big night out. Charles was on the bandstand helping Cal untangle a clump of wires that snaked to two large speakers and a beat-up black Fender amplifier.

I headed to two unoccupied tables in the far left corner and put my Tilley on one of the tables, rearranging the other so the two touched. Hopefully, my hat would mark my turf for the night. I thought Cal would prefer that to my urinating on the floor.

Tara, the server from Cal's Christmas party, broke away from the gaggle of employees to see what I wanted to drink. Actually, all she said was, "Red?" I nodded. The color of my wine preceded me.

She quickly returned with an extra large pour of wine and acknowledged the table setup. She smiled. "Expecting a large group?" she asked.

"Hope so," I said, returning her smile.

"Good. We need all the tips we can get." She tilted her head toward the group of employees still enjoying the light workload in the corner.

I took my glass and joined Cal and Charles on the bandstand. "You singing tonight?" I asked Cal.

"Couple of sets—popular demand, you know," he said.

"Someone took two cases of Woodford Reserve," said Charles.

"I would have sworn they were here when I left," said Cal as he waved his right arm toward the bar. "But who knows? I'm still learning what's here—who can tell the difference between Woodford Reserve and Knob Creek?"

And he owns the bar, I thought.

"Any doors open this morning? Any sign of forced entry?" I asked.

"Been there, asked that," said Charles the detective. "Locked up tight as a new plastic CD holder."

"I don't get it," said Cal. "A dozen bottles of whiskey gone—poof!"

"Don't worry," said Charles. "I'll get 'em. Ain't that right, Chris?"

I hesitated, watching Cal fiddling with the wires. Then Charles turned to me with a hopeful look in his eyes. "You bet," I said.

Before Charles made more promises than I knew he might not keep, I saw Larry and Cindy walk in and look around. Cindy was a couple of inches taller than her new husband, outweighed him by thirty pounds, had dark curly hair, and was in her late forties, seven years younger than Larry. She wore a baggy sweatshirt and tight jeans; she was off-duty. Larry was attired, as usual, in an orange sweatshirt with the Pewter logo on the breast pocket. They made a cute couple.

I pointed toward the tables in the corner, and they pulled out two chairs. Tara quickly took their order.

Cindy had no more than settled in her chair before she said, "So tell us about your ex."

Larry tapped her arm. "We weren't going there, remember?" he whispered in her ear—more of a stage whisper.

"Oh, Brahman manure," she said. "Charles'll tell us, so let's hear it from the horse's mouth—no offense, Chris," she added as she turned to me.

Cindy had moved to Folly from Knoxville three years ago to join the police force. She was funny, iconoclastic, and had a quick smile and an equally quick temper. Little was off limits to the Tennessee fireball. If she was in uniform and asked you a question, you'd best answer quickly with "ma'am" at the end. She was the perfect yin for Larry's yang.

I gave them the thirty-second version of Joan's situation and our trip to the mountains.

"That's it?" said Cindy as she held her arms out in exasperation.

"Told you," said Larry as he turned to Cindy.

"Night's young." She winked at me. "He's still sober."

William saved me. He arrived at the opportune moment and I hopped up to meet him. He was far from a regular at Cal's, and I didn't want him to change his mind. Cindy had never met the professor, and Larry knew him slightly from the hardware store, so I made the introductions and offered him a chair. Once again, Tara appeared like a fly on watermelon and took William's request for a whiskey sour. I was glad Charles was with Cal and not behind the bar. It was no telling what William would have had to drink otherwise.

"So, William," said Cindy, after the basic social icebreakers were covered, "tell us about your trip to the mountains and Chris's ex."

William looked at me. He didn't say it, but I could feel his scream for help—of course, he wouldn't scream but would use a dozen multisyllable words to express his desire to be bailed out.

I put my arm around his shoulder. "William, let's go say hi to Charles. He asked if you were coming."

William moved more quickly than I'd seen before. He jumped from the chair and scampered toward the front of the room. "I'm sorry," he said to me when we were away from the table. "I didn't know what you wanted Mrs. LaMond to know."

I told him it was no problem, and we talked to Charles and Cal.

Considering the cast of characters who had already arrived, I suspected that the night could get interesting.

CHAPTER 18

Cal's first New Year's Eve party was in full swing. The tables were full, nine patrons crowded around the bar, and three couples waited at the door in hopes that someone would leave. I recognized most everyone. It was low season, and locals took pride in complaining about vacationers and bragging about "retaking Folly" over the winter. Of course, many of the same locals depended on those same evil interlopers for their livelihood.

Cal had completed his first set and was behind the bar playing owner instead of his guitar. I was used to seeing the lanky, stooped, aging singer onstage in his yellowing white rhinestone-studded coat and sweat-stained Stetson, so watching him in his stage garb fiddling with the lid on the beer cooler brought a grin to my face. Charles closely watched whatever Cal did. *The blind leading the blind.*

"Where's my Chucky?"

I recognized the voice without turning toward the door. Heather had strolled in as if she owned Cal's. She was dressed in a bright yellow sequined blouse, a floor-length Kelly green skirt, and a wide-brimmed straw hat. She wore this outfit when she was allowed to perform two songs every Tuesday during open mike night. *Oh no,* I thought. *Please, someone, tell me that she isn't going to screech out the old year.* The only good thing the previous owner had done was limit Heather to one song per week; of course, to the discerning taste of most patrons, that was one ditty too many.

I glanced at the bar, where Charles had been seconds earlier. He wasn't there. Heather looked around. Having failed to see you-know-who, she spotted me and headed my way. My worst fears were realized when I saw her swinging a guitar case in her left hand.

She gave me her best aw-shucks smile and a peck on my left cheek. "Hear you had fun in Gatlinburg," she said, her eyes searching the room. "Enough about that. Where's Chucky?"

I pointed to the bar and said that's where he had been earlier. She carefully placed her guitar case on one of the two vacant chairs and skipped toward the bar. Yes, she skipped.

Cindy looked at the case. "Want me to steal it?" she said. Cindy knew Heather's vocal abilities.

"No," I said. "She'd call the cops, and then you'd have to work."

"Good point." Cindy continued to stare at the case as if it held a nuclear warhead. "Want me to stomp on it?"

Heather returned before we could decide how to eliminate the threat. "Chucky said he'll be taking a break soon." She nodded at the empty chair. "I'll save it for him."

Dustin, the only waiter at Cal's, leaned over Heather and asked what she wanted to drink. He explained that Tara was slammed and had asked him to check on us—Tara told him that we were the VIP group. Dustin was in his early twenties and handsome in a cute sort of way. He had told me on an earlier visit that his goal was to become an airline steward. He said that waiting tables would be good training for serving two hundred people flying six miles above the earth in an aluminum tube. He seemed like a nice guy but was rumored to have a drinking problem. Besides, to the guys at the table, he wasn't as attractive as Tara.

The New Year's Eve party officially began when two middle-aged men on the other side of the room pushed their chairs back and began shoving each other. The shorter of the two overcelebrating gentlemen yelled something about a friend of the other guy stealing his bicycle. I had trouble understanding because his words began slurring and rapidly deteriorating from there.

Cindy started to stand, her cop instincts kicking in, but Larry reached out and lovingly took her arm. "It's New Year's Eve," he said. "Chill."

Before she could argue, Cal had moved his tall frame between the warring celebrants. He wrapped his long arm around the neck of the loudmouth and said something to the other man. Cal had spent more of his life singing for drunken audiences in smoky country music bars than fifty other entertainers combined. I had confidence that he could diffuse the situation.

He didn't disappoint. The two potential troublemakers shook hands, and Cal waved for Tara to come to the table and take a free drink order. New Year's Eve!

Charles arrived as the minor ruckus subsided. The bartending detective wore a fire engine–red long-sleeved T-shirt with MAY YOUR TROUBLES LAST AS LONG AS YOUR NEW YEAR'S RESOLUTIONS—JOEY ADAMS spread across three lines on the front. He dropped his rear into the empty chair so hard that I was afraid the seat would collapse.

I closed my eyes and waited for someone to ask. They weren't closed for more than a blink.

"Cute shirt, Chucky," said Heather. "Who's Joey Adams?"

"Probably the nickname of one of the presidents named Adams," said Larry.

"No clue," said Charles. He looked back to the bar. "This bartending stuff is almost like work."

Charles lowered his head and swiveled it left and right. He motioned for me to come closer and then nodded in the direction of Larry and Cindy. "You tell them why I'm really here?" he asked.

"Didn't think you wanted anyone to know," I said.

"Larry's part of my detective team. He's one of us," said Charles.

One of us! I shrugged.

Charles then motioned for his team member, Larry, and Larry's new spouse to lean closer. Heather wasn't asked, but she joined the rest of us in a variation of a team huddle, and Charles outlined why he "was really here."

Larry started to laugh, but Cindy elbowed him. She then rolled her eyes but didn't say anything. Charles finished his CliffsNotes version of his mission and slowly and solemnly sat back in the chair. Heather broke the awkward silence. "Ain't that something?" she said. "My Chucky's going to break this crime wave wide-open."

Cindy got a mischievous twinkle in her eyes. "Sounds more like a crime ripple," she said. "Charles, I'm a cop, so I'd be interested in what detecting techniques you're using to break this case open."

Charles looked around again, ostensibly to see if anyone was listening. "The Race Is On" blared over the sound system, a handful of couples danced a South Carolina version of the Texas two-step on the laminate dance floor, and a few customers yawned, but most seemed to be getting excited about the arrival of the New Year. Only an hour to go. No one, except those of us at the VIP table, cared one iota about what Charles was saying. Technically, that was wrong, as the thief would have cared, but I knew that he or she wasn't at our tables, and those seated nearby weren't likely suspects.

"I'm glad you asked," said Charles. "I knew you and Larry would want to help. Thanks for offering."

I must have dozed during the offer.

Charles moved his head to within six inches of Larry's face, "Could you use your *expertise* as a hardware store owner to examine the locks? Give me your *professional* opinion on how easy it would be for someone to break in?" He winked at Larry. "I think the booze was stolen overnight; Cal's almost sure it was here last night when he locked up."

Charles's emphasis on Larry's expertise and professional opinion wouldn't have fooled the dimmest of lightbulbs. The wink would have tipped that group off. He sought Larry's talents as a reformed cat burglar, not as a hardware store maven.

"I'll look," said Larry.

"What else are you doing?" said Cindy, who wouldn't let Charles off the hook.

"Well," he said, "I started by throwing off the employees." He paused again and glanced toward the bar. "Only Cal knows my mission, you know. Before we opened tonight, all the 'spects—that's what I'm calling the other employees; they're all suspects—were shooting the bull, jabbering on about how they spent Christmas, guessing about tonight's tips, talking about how they were going to get drunk once they got out of this stinky dive—"

I interrupted before Charles shared more useless information about the "'spects." "Throwing them off how?"

He frowned in my direction but answered. "I innocently said, loud enough for them to hear, 'Hey, what happened to those two cases of

Woodford Reserve that were here last night?' I wanted to see who acted guilty."

"Isn't that brilliant?" said Heather.

Brilliant must have a different meaning to a psychic, I thought.

Larry ignored Heather and said, "Did anyone jump up and holler, 'You caught me; I stole them'?"

"Not yet," said Charles. "Dawn had a puzzled look on her face; Nick looked at Kenneth; Kenneth picked up a bar towel and twisted it." He paused. "Oh yeah, Tara looked toward the storage room, and Kristin said, 'What cases?' I couldn't see what Dustin and Beatrice did."

From the jukebox, Eddie Arnold pleaded for the world to go away.

"Brilliant," repeated Heather.

"Who are those people?" asked Larry.

A legitimate question, I thought, since Larry wasn't a Cal's regular.

"Tara and Dustin have been waiting on you," said Charles. "The other 'spects are the employees working tonight, except Cal and me. We're not 'spects—yet."

"What did you learn from your team meeting?" I asked, partially in jest, partially in the unlikely event that he actually did learn something helpful.

A loud noise that sounded like a tiger with a hairball came from the men's restroom. We all turned in time to see one of the lovable—most of the time—town drunks stumble out of the room, bend over, and deposit a puddle of pureed fries, foam, and about a gallon of beer on the floor. Cindy's loud "Yuck!" spoke for all of us at the table. Dustin had already grabbed a handful of bar towels and the mop from the back room and headed toward the mess.

Charles turned back toward the rest of us as if nothing unusual had happened. "I learned that asking about the missing hooch was a stupid question. I need to reevaluate my strategy."

"Charles," said Cindy, "are you sure none of the employees—excuse me, '*spects*—know what you're up to?"

"Why?" asked Charles.

"It seems Cal has plenty of bartenders," said Cindy. She looked toward the bar, where there were already three mixologists buzzing around, nearly stumbling over each other. "Using my highly trained professional power of observation as a law enforcement officer, it appears that you know as much about bartending as I do about being ambassador to Sri Lanka."

"I don't think any of them know," said Charles.

The waiter reappeared at the table. "Charles, Cal said to tell you that your *extended* break is over, two of our employees are on *urp* duty, and that the bar is calling your name."

"Hah," said Charles as he turned to Cindy. "See, my talents are needed." He stood and took one step toward the bar, and then turned back to Cindy. "How's your Sinhala?"

She said, "Huh?" I was sure the rest of us were thinking it.

Charles tapped his cane on the floor and then half turned to the bar, and then he turned his head back toward Cindy and said, "Official language of Sri Lanka, the world's largest producer of cinnamon." He finally retreated.

I noticed that Cindy wasn't taking notes about Sri Lanka, so I asked, "Why did you ask if anyone knew?"

She watched Charles take his place behind the bar. "People tend to underestimate bartenders and the waitstaff. They think that because they have fairly mundane jobs, they're not bright. It's usually the opposite. They are untrained but astute observers of human nature. They're not easily fooled."

Knowing what I did about Amber and the other servers at the Dog, I knew Cindy was right. "True," I said.

"A couple of other things," said Cindy. "Charles couldn't mix water and more water, much less some of the exotic drinks some of these folks want—and he's the bartender." She paused and looked back at Charles. "Finally, he's a great person and would do anything for anyone. He's funny and liked by most people who know him—"

"But," I interrupted.

"But he knows slightly less than nothing about being a private detective." She shook her head. "He may be after a bourbon and bar cash thief, but to the thief, freedom is a pretty big thing. Charles is a threat."

Charles should have been here instead of behind the bar to hear Cindy's next words—her prophetic words.

"He needs to be careful."

*   *   *

Other than being sleepy, the first few minutes of the New Year didn't feel different from the minutes that had just entered the history books. Cal had begun his final set of country classics at eleven-thirty and started a countdown thirty seconds before the magical hour. He had used his 1960s' Timex watch for the count, so we may have missed the exact stroke of midnight by a few minutes.

The final verse of "Auld Lang Syne" wound down, as did the energy level of everyone at our table—everyone except Heather. We spread hugs around and headed home. Heather said she had cheer to burn and remained seated. "Besides," she said, "Cal may let me sing a song or two later."

I wouldn't put money on it, but I wished her well. I said good-bye to Charles, who was doing on-the-job-training as a bartender. He asked if I could come in later in the morning and help him straighten up. He said that Cal trusted him, and only him, to do the chores. My thought was that Cal didn't want to pay his other help—the 'spects—their higher wages to be there.

CHAPTER 19

I couldn't get "Auld Lang Syne" out of my mind. I started humming it in the shower even though my head hurt from staying out too late last night and—okay, I'll admit it—too much wine. The song also brought back memories of my life with Joan—memories of how I'd put work above our relationship, how I'd not let her know about my fears, aspirations, and conflicts. I hated myself for it, but I couldn't stop being who I was. Maybe I could make up for some of that now, maybe. And then I remembered that I'd agreed to help Charles this morning.

I walked through Cal's side door at ten o'clock.

"About time you got here," said Charles. He said he had been on the job for an hour. From the mess I saw, I couldn't imagine what it had looked like earlier. Crepe-paper streamers were everywhere; empty beer bottles were on the tables, and several were on the floor near the bandstand; bar napkins dotted most other surfaces. The strong smell of beer hung in the air, as did the faint smell of the traditional New Year's Eve regurgitation.

He thanked me for coming and said that Cal was coming in around three. He said that the night had gone smoothly after the VIP table was vacated. He laughed and said that none of the other employees were sad that Cal hadn't asked them to work this morning.

"Grab a broom and start there," said Charles. He waved his arm in the direction of the front door. "I'll start in back." He headed off toward the small storage room.

Seconds later, there was a crash. "Shit!" screamed Charles. Then silence.

I dropped the broom, rushed behind the bar, and hurried into the storeroom. Charles was sprawled out on the floor. He was on his left side. His head rested against the wooden storage shelves just inside the door. His left foot was twisted at an unnatural angle. A Jekel Vineyards wine box leaned on his leg. Red wine poured out of the box and onto the cuff of his frayed jeans.

He gritted his teeth and murmured, "Shit … shit …it hurts. Oh, shit."

I carefully lifted the case and checked his foot. I was afraid to move him. I said to hang on; I was going to call for help. He moaned and didn't try to stop me, so I knew it was serious.

I grabbed the phone behind the bar and punched 911. I told the dispatcher the address and explained what had happened. The calm, professional dispatcher said help was on the way.

I knelt by my friend's head. The room was small, and I was half in and half out the door to the back bar. "What happened?" I asked.

He pounded the floor with his right fist but held the rest of his body motionless. "Don't know," he said. "I opened the door and caught a glimpse of that damned box falling from the top shelf."

Looking up, I couldn't see how the large crate could have simply fallen. The shelves were deep enough to hold the box comfortably, and the other shelves were neatly arranged with nothing sticking out beyond the front lip. Strange.

I wiggled my legs to keep from cramping. I was careful not to jar Charles. He was in enough pain without my adding more. From the angle of his foot, I had no doubt the ankle was broken. It was swollen above the top of his tennis shoe. He was in pain but thought to ask me to call Cal and tell him what had happened. He said the number was near the phone.

Cal answered with a groggy, "Huh?"

I told him who I was and explained what had happened.

Cal slowly regained consciousness, followed by alertness, followed by, "Shee … I'm on my way."

Cal lived in a dilapidated boardinghouse six blocks away. I told him that if he didn't get here before we were gone, to mop the wine off the floor but to try not to disturb anything else. I wanted to have a closer look at the shelf. How could a thirty-five-pound box have fallen? It didn't compute.

I heard a siren and told Charles not to move while I opened the front door for the EMTs. Charles gave a half grin, half grimace and said he wasn't going anywhere.

An orange-and-white Charleston County Emergency Medical Services ambulance was in front of Cal's by the time I figured out how to unlock the door. Two EMTs were out and walking toward me as I gave them a twenty-second summary of the situation. I pointed toward the storeroom, and they hurried to Charles. They couldn't both fit in the room, so the middle-aged female knelt beside Charles's ankle and carefully moved the leg slightly to get a better look. She asked her younger partner to get the stretcher. He slipped past me on his way out. I knew Charles was trying to appear calm and act as if nothing unusual had happened. He wasn't successful. He moaned, and I was afraid that if he clamped his jaws tighter he would need a trip to the dentist after leaving the hospital. The EMT kept repeating in a soothing voice that everything would be okay and that they would have him at the hospital soon.

The second responder rolled a yellow stretcher into Cal's. He couldn't maneuver it behind the bar and into the storeroom, but he lowered it so he and I could lift it over the bar and near the storeroom entry.

Cal barged in the door like a tornado looking for a mobile home park. We were still trying to figure out how to get Charles out without causing further harm. Cal appeared drastically different from how he'd been the night before. He wore threadbare robin's-egg blue sweats, and his mane of gray hair flowed in unintended directions. He could easily have spent the night in a Dumpster. There wasn't room for him behind the bar, but it didn't stop him from jumping on a bar stool and yelling, "Yo, Michigan, you okay?"

Charles laughed and said, "No!"

The female EMT worked to keep Charles calm while her partner, Cal, and I concentrated on how to get him out of the bar once they got him on the stretcher.

Amazingly, our plan worked, and the two EMTs carefully lifted Charles onto the stretcher. The four of us grunted, turned, and wiggled until we were able to lift the stretcher over the bar so they could extend its legs and roll it to the ambulance. We were across the street from the fire and police stations, and a couple of officers I didn't know walked over to see what had happened. They knew Charles and wished him well as he was loaded into the ambulance. He gave them a thumbs-up.

I followed the ambulance to Roper Hospital in Charleston. I realized how much quicker the ride was when I stayed close to the ambulance and didn't stop for red lights. Additionally, because it was New Year's Day, traffic was unusually light. I parked behind the ambulance at the emergency entrance and followed the gurney into an attractive emergency area. The EMTs took Charles directly to an exam room, and a triage nurse was at his side in seconds. It took her five minutes to assess his problem and administer a painkiller through an IV. She said that she was sure the ankle was broken, adding that they would send him to radiology for X-rays and then figure out what to do.

For the next three hours, I sat in the waiting room and watched a steady stream of suffering humanity. *Happy New Year*, I thought.

Between listening to moaning patients, an occasional scream, and the sound of sirens arriving at the emergency room, I kept thinking about the wine box. How could it have fallen? Could Charles have pulled it? He said that when he opened the door, it tumbled down. Could the door have been booby-trapped? If someone placed it to fall, was Charles the intended recipient? If he was, who knew that he would be the first person in the storage room? Didn't Charles say all the employees were around when Cal asked him to come in early? Did the thief know that Cal had hired Charles to find him or her?

Cindy had hinted that others who worked at Cal's probably knew the real reason he was there. If the box was supposed to fall when Charles opened the door, why? Was he getting too close to solving the crime? Were Charles's stumbling, bumbling, crude, unorthodox efforts at detecting actually working? And why would someone go to so much trouble to hurt Charles over the theft of some whiskey and some cash? Was there more to it than met the eye?

That was too many "ifs" for one New Year's Day morning in the emergency room. Fortunately, a nurse came to take me to the exam room where Charles was holding court.

"Good news, bad news," said the doctor. He stood over Charles's bed in the exam room. The doctor's shoulders sagged, and his salt-and-pepper hair was nearly as mussed as Cal's. I guessed that his shift had begun before many of the parties started the night before. I was a couple of feet behind Charles.

"The bad news is that your ankle's broken," he said.

No surprise there. He didn't have to spend years in medical school to figure that out.

"Bring on the good news," said Charles.

The pain meds had done their job; my friend was in excellent spirits.

"There are three bones that come together at the ankle—the tibia, fibula, and the talus." He nodded as if he knew that we understood. "The tibia and the fibula wrap around the talus and form the ankle joint. Those bony prominences at the ankle are the medial malleolus and the lateral malleolus."

Now he's showing off, I thought.

"Have we gotten to the good news yet?" said Charles.

The doc almost smiled before continuing. "The tibia is the larger weight-bearing bone in the lower leg—it carries nearly ninety percent of the weight. The fibula supports the remaining ten percent. You very wisely chose to fracture the fibula."

"So when will I be able to run a marathon?" asked my drugged friend.

"Ever run one?" asked the perceptive doctor.

"Nope."

"That's what I thought," said the doctor. "Let me tell you what's going to happen. Here's more good news. I won't have to operate. We'll splint the ankle. You'll need to keep it on for a few days until the swelling goes down."

"And then the marathon?" asked Charles. He and his meds were enjoying this way too much.

The doctor rolled his bloodshot eyes and shook his head at the same time—multitasking. "And then you'll get a cast. It looks like the fracture is fairly stable, so we should be able to use a fiberglass cast rather than a heavy, awkward plaster one."

"Will my fans be able to sign a fiberglass cast?" asked Charles.

The doctor finally smiled, but I had a hunch that he was ready to kick Charles in his other leg. "I'm sure they will," he said diplomatically. Before Charles could interrupt again, the doc continued. "I know it didn't feel like it, but the fracture is relatively minor. I doubt you'll need the cast for more than a week or so. Oh, and you'll need crutches the entire time. If your job requires a lot of standing, you'll have to be off for a while. Sorry. We'll get you taken care of." He then pirouetted and quickly left the room.

I spent the rest of the day playing nurse and chauffeur. We were at the hospital for three more hours, waiting for the splinting process and the paperwork maze that Charles had to wade through. No, he didn't have health insurance; yes, it was work-related and workers' comp would take care of it; yes, if anything was not covered by workers' comp, Charles would be responsible; no, he did not have any credit cards; yes, he would be paying with cash; and on and on.

After we escaped from the hospital, Charles announced that he was starved, so we had to go to McDonald's. And then we had to practice with his new set of crutches for an hour. And then the drugs wore off, and bed was the only place he wanted to go. I then turned his care and feeding over to Heather, who gave it her best shot, but her best shot did not include grocery shopping and other errands he wanted run. There went two more hours.

We went to Cal's before it opened the next day and tried to figure out how the box could have fallen on its own. No matter how we looked at it, we couldn't see how it was possible. What was possible was that the box had been propped against the top of the door and the door carefully closed. When Charles opened it, the precarious balance was upset and the case fell. Other than the logical conclusion that whoever set it to fall worked at Cal's, all we ran into—or hobbled into—were dead ends.

The next morning, I walked two blocks to the Tides hotel for a hearty breakfast. I had done a lot the last two days, but other than the trip to McDonald's, eating wasn't one of the activities. The hotel's restaurant was empty except for an elderly couple sitting near the window, looking out on the ocean and the Folly Pier. I was exhausted and looked forward to a silent, peaceful breakfast.

My cell phone vibrated and royally screwed up that plan.

CHAPTER 20

"**Thank God I got** you," came a tinny voice over the phone.

This time I recognized my ex-wife. I hadn't talked to her since we'd left Gatlinburg five days earlier.

"They tried to kill me!" she said. The words caught in her throat; the volume increased. "Chris, my God, they tried to kill me."

"Slow down. Who tried to kill you? What happened?"

"My house … my house. They blew it up."

"You okay? Are you hurt?"

"I'm fine. But it was luck." She cleared her throat. I heard her inhale. "I spent the night at Charlene's … It was late … didn't want to drive … Didn't know about the explosion until I went home this morning. Fire engines were everywhere; ice was all over the place; and … half the house is gone … no roof … two walls standing. My God, Chris, they tried to kill me." She started sobbing.

I paused a few seconds and then asked, "Where are you?"

The server set a plate of bacon and eggs in front of me. The bacon smelled good, but I knew I wouldn't enjoy it.

"Charlene's," she said after another sob. She said something else, but it wasn't to me. I heard a second voice in the background, and there was another pause.

"Chris?" said a different and calmer voice.

"Yes," I said.

"This is Charlene. Joan handed me the phone and went in the bathroom."

"What happened?"

"All I know," said Charlene, "is there was an explosion—sometime overnight. She was at my house last night, and we'd … been drinking. She was in no condition to drive, and I insisted that she stay."

I knew this was a delicate subject but asked while I could. "She said someone tried to kill her. Who? Why? How does she know?"

"She called a half hour after she left," Charlene whispered. "She screamed that they destroyed her house and were trying to kill her. I rushed over. It was terrible. Two of the firefighters had wrapped a blanket around her and helped get her back in her car. The heater was blowing full blast, but she was shivering. I thought I'd have to take her to the hospital. I told them I'd take care of her, and they went back to loading their trucks. The fire was out."

"Any idea what happened? Who she thinks is trying to kill her?" I repeated.

"Daniel's killer, she says."

"Was it intentional?" I asked.

"The guys I talked to didn't think so," said Charlene. "They thought there was a gas leak and a spark set it off. Apparently, it happened around three in the morning."

"Does Joan have reason to think it wasn't accidental?"

"To be honest, I don't know why she thinks it was an attempt on her life." She was now whispering, and I pressed the phone to my ear to hear. "She's being paranoid about all this, if you ask me. I hate to say that, but we've been friends ever since she moved here. She's generous to a fault. A great lady. But I think sometimes she wants to believe the worst."

I heard a hand scraping the mouthpiece, muffled voices, and then Joan. "I'm back," she said. "Could you please come? Please?"

I could think of a hundred reasons to say no, but "Auld Lang Syne" reverberated in my head.

I closed my eyes and said yes.

Karen and I had planned to go to supper, so after I kicked myself a few times for telling Joan that I'd return to Gatlinburg, I called Karen to postpone. I never knew where she would be when I called. Several times she was at horrific murder scenes. I got lucky this time. She was in her office catching up on paperwork, and I told her about the call.

"Want me to go with you?" she said.

Of her possible responses, I never would have anticipated that one.

"Uh, sure," I said. "Can you get away?"

"You don't seem thrilled." I could tell she was smiling.

"Sorry," I said. "I was surprised."

"I have vacation time, and to everyone's delight, the year has started off slow on the murder front."

I told her that I planned to leave early in the afternoon so I could get to Gatlinburg early evening. She would check with her boss but didn't think that was a problem. I could pick her up at her house around one o'clock.

How had my peaceful breakfast gone so wrong so quickly? Was someone really out to kill Joan? Or was the paranoia that I had suspected many years ago real and living in the mind of my ex-wife? And did Karen really want to go to Gatlinburg?

And most importantly, how was I going to tell Charles that I was going on a road trip, and that Karen was replacing him?

CHAPTER 21

I got up the nerve to call Charles when we were three hours from Folly Beach—I waited until I was too far along to be chided enough to return for him. I had hoped he would answer and tell me that he was in terrible pain and ready to take more pain meds. He had no business making the long ride with his broken ankle, regardless of how he would argue.

Charles answered on the second ring and said that the ankle hurt every time he stood, and that he felt best when he was in bed. The wisest thing he could do, I suggested, would be to stay there for a few days. He reluctantly agreed.

He said that it sounded like I was in the car and asked where I was. The road was level, but the conversation went downhill quickly. I told him where I was going, and why, and who was with me. His silence was much louder than if he had blown a referee's whistle in my ear. He then proceeded to tell me how comfortable the backseat of my new vehicle would have been, and how he would have been quite content, and how he could have helped me reassure Joan. He sighed and asked if Karen was really with me.

I limited most of my responses to "Uh-huh."

My friend rambled on for ten miles and finally mumbled, "You're right, I suppose. I don't need to be bumping around in your car. Got to take a pill. Have fun."

He didn't really mean to have fun.

"Tell me about Joan," said Karen.

I suspected that she was asking to find out more about my ex and to get my mind off leaving Charles behind. I shared how we had met in high school and had gone to college together. I felt awkward talking about it, but I elaborated some on our lengthy courtship; her family, which only consisted of her parents and a sister; our first few years of marriage, when we were both starting careers and made the decision not to have children right away—right away drifted to never. I shared details about how she'd come home from work one day and told me that she was tired of life with me. She wanted a divorce and planned to move to California. A handful of others knew the bare bones facts of what happened, but I told Karen more details about how I felt, how Joan had reacted the day she left, and other things that I had never shared with anyone. I didn't share that I felt responsible for the divorce; perhaps I'd tell her someday—not now.

Karen was an exceptional listener. Her years as a detective and her ability to put together seemingly random bits of information into a coherent story allowed her to listen without interrupting and then ask questions that glued the random parts together. I had talked for almost two straight hours and didn't realize it until she asked if we needed gas. We were following the curve of the mountains on I-40, and we were almost to the Gatlinburg exit. Drifts of post-Christmas snow were plowed to two and three feet high on the sides of the interstate. Grass in the fields was blanketed with the white stuff. The temperature loomed below freezing, but the pavement was dry.

A large hotel billboard loomed on the right as we exited the interstate. We were more than thirty miles from our destination, but the sign yanked me away from an ancient history lesson to a dilemma. I wanted to stay at the familiar Hampton Inn—but how many rooms to get? Should I assume we wanted two? Should I ask Karen?

The amazing array of festive holiday lights illuminated the sky, sidewalks, vacant lots, and every structure in the city as we entered the Gatlinburg city limits. I was almost used to the abundance of holiday lights, but Karen kept saying "amazing," and "spectacular" every few hundred yards. Her enthusiasm was contagious.

How to address the room problem was foremost on my mind as I pulled into the Hampton Inn's parking lot. Either Karen had read my mind, or she was thinking the same thing.

"One room," she said.

I looked at her. "Sure?"

She nodded. Neither of us said anything as I parked. She stayed in the car, and I went to the office.

There weren't any large groups in the resort community, so the hotel had several vacancies. Ours was on the first floor and only a few doors from the office. Each of us grabbed a suitcase and quietly entered the room. It was chilly, so I adjusted the thermostat.

"Where's Joan?" asked Karen.

"She should be at Charlene's," I said. "I'm supposed to call and get directions."

It was past seven, and we were hungry. We decided that I would call and tell Charlene we could be there in a couple of hours. Karen and I could eat first—we had no idea what the night would bring. We also decided not to tell Joan that Karen was a detective, playing that card only if it seemed appropriate. I didn't want to feed Joan's paranoia.

Charlene gave me directions and said Joan was with her. Karen and I then walked the short distance to Maxwell's Steak and Seafood, one of the area's many nice restaurants, and had a peaceful prime rib supper. I joked that we would need full stomachs before seeing Joan. I joked but was certain that it wouldn't be a joking matter.

The walk back to the hotel was filled with the soothing aroma of smoke from the many wood-burning fireplaces in the resort community and the anxiety of what was to come next.

CHAPTER 22

Charlene's house was on a narrow lane in a hilly, wooded area off the scenic road that connected Gatlinburg to its neighboring community, Pigeon Forge. The house appeared smaller than Joan's and as different as possible. It was a sprawling native stone ranch with a wide drive that ended at a four-car garage. Her husband was an attorney with a well-respected Knoxville firm, and Charlene was active in numerous civic groups. The house reflected their status.

Joan's Jaguar was parked in the back of the drive. I was pleased, in a perverse way, to see that the car had a light gray covering of slushy snow, ice, and salt—a complete contrast to the last time I had seen it. It wasn't immune to the elements. We parked, got out of the car, and rang the doorbell.

A tall, distinguished-looking gentleman greeted us with a strong handshake for me and a practiced smile for Karen. I introduced Karen and myself, and then Charlene's husband, Roland, waved us into the richly appointed entry and said that the ladies were in back and we should follow him. The interior looked like we were in the middle of a blizzard. The walls were snow white, and the floor was white marble. The few pieces of furniture were contemporary, leather trimmed, expensive, and white. Fortunately, Roland wore a black turtleneck so we were able to follow him through the maze of whiteness. Classical music from a high-end sound system seemed to follow us as we trailed behind Charlene's husband.

A family room about the size of a small village shared the color of the rest of the interior. Charlene and Joan were seated on a, you guessed it, white oversized sofa. Each held a glass of what appeared to be bourbon. Joan saw me; she set her drink on the coffee table and rushed across the room. She wrapped her arms around my waist.

"Thank you for coming," she said, her voice barely audible. She had on a burgundy sweater, cream-colored slacks, and a double string of pearls. She looked all dressed up with nowhere to go. Charlene, by contrast, appeared comfortable in pink sweats.

Roland said, "I shall leave you to your conversation."

He and William could carry on a grammatically correct, and extraordinarily boring, conversation.

Joan stepped back and thanked me again. I noticed the bright blue eyes that I was attracted to so many years ago. Her head abruptly turned toward Karen, who had remained in the doorway. Joan had just noticed her.

"Oh," said Joan.

I took the slightly awkward moment to introduce Karen to Joan and Charlene. I simply said that Karen was a friend who had some time off and offered to make the trip. I also explained what had happened to Charles and said that William was back at work and couldn't come.

Charlene played the good hostess and got us each a glass of Cabernet as Karen and I sat in two leather chairs that faced Joan. A massive wood-burning stone fireplace was to our backs, and the heat and crackling of the fiery logs made the house feel like a mountain lodge.

"Chris," said Joan after a lengthy, awkward pause, "you should see it. It's ruined. They tried to kill me. Why … why?" Her hands tightly gripped the sturdy glass that held her amber-colored drink. Her fingernails were chewed to the quick, a habit that she apparently had maintained since we were in college.

I glanced at Charlene, who gave me a barely noticeable shrug.

"Are you sure?" I asked.

"It was sheer luck that I wasn't there," she said. "I spent the night here. This would be my funeral if I'd been home."

That hadn't answered my question, but I didn't pursue it.

"Mrs. McCandless," said Karen, "who would have wanted to kill you?"

Joan turned to Karen and acted surprised that she had spoken.

The surprised expression turned to a quick smile. "Please call me Joan, dearie." Her smile hardened. "I have no idea. It had to be the people who murdered my husband." She shook her head. "I don't know who … or why."

She turned to me as if she had dismissed Karen. "They've been following me, you know," she said.

"Did you see them?"

Joan peered into her glass. "Umm, yes. I think so," she said. "I could feel them staring."

"What did they look like?" asked Karen.

Joan abruptly turned to Charlene. Her drink sloshed around; a small amount splashed on her wrist. "Char, you saw them. You saw the guys watching us. Tell them."

Charlene studied Joan, Karen, and finally me. "I thought I saw two men watching us yesterday when we were at the grocery store, but … I'm not certain."

"Can you describe them?" asked Karen. Her training wasn't going to waste.

Charlene sheepishly said, "I really couldn't tell for sure. They were bundled up in heavy coats, and I think they wore hats." She turned toward Karen and tilted her head. "They could have been shopping. I just don't know."

"Oh," said Joan. Her shoulders slumped as she listened to Charlene's recant.

"I just don't know," repeated Charlene.

Joan turned away from Charlene and stared at the hearth. "Tell me about Folly Beach," she said. "I'd never heard of it before I learned you were there."

Where did that come from? Charlene nodded at me ever so slightly. I wasn't nearly the detective Karen was—or, for that matter, Charles— but I knew it was a hint to change topics. I wasn't sure why Joan wanted me here, but I figured she would get around to telling me when she was ready.

I told her that I hadn't heard of it either until I went there on vacation a few years ago. I gave the short version of how I had discovered the quirky island, why it was such a great location being directly on the ocean yet only a few minutes from one of the most beautiful and historic cities in the country, how I had made so many friends in such a short time, and why I didn't want to be anywhere else.

"How about you, Karen?" said Charlene.

"My dad lives near Folly and works on the island," she began. "I don't live on Folly but nearby." She paused and then added, "I work in Charleston."

"What do you do?" asked Joan.

"I work for the government and so does Dad," she said. Then she held out her empty wineglass. "May I have a little more?"

Charlene started to get up, but Karen waved her off. "I'll get it," said Karen.

Karen walked toward the kitchen, stopping about ten feet from the couches. "I love your decor," she said. "The white seems so appropriate for the mountains and the snow; it seems so bright and cheerful."

"Thank you," said Charlene.

Karen had done an admirable job of deflecting the question about her occupation and then changing the subject. I was impressed.

I made another run at Joan. "Tell me again why you're so sure someone is trying to kill you."

"Damn, Chris," she said, "aren't you paying any attention? They killed my husband. They blew my house to hell. And you wonder if someone is trying to kill me." She sighed heavily.

"And the police said both the wreck and the explosion were accidents. Right?"

She put her arms down to her side and glared at me. "They're trying to kill me. Period."

We'd reached an impasse. I looked over at Karen, and she gave a slight nod. Nothing good would come from pursuing it further. So we spent the next half hour talking about everything imaginable, except the explosion, the alleged threats to Joan's life, Folly Beach, Karen's occupation, and why Joan wanted me to make the long trip.

"I know you must be tired and want to get a good night's sleep," said Joan. She looked at me when she said it, but she glanced at Karen as well. "Could we get together tomorrow for lunch?"

I told her that was fine. She named a restaurant in town, and we agreed to meet at noon. She grinned, and I noticed that her face appeared to have more wrinkles than it had a few days earlier. Her eyes were shadowed with dark rings underneath.

She hugged me at the door and whispered, "Chris, I'm scared."

Does she have reason to be? I wondered.

CHAPTER 23

My nerves had been on end when I'd pulled into Charlene's drive, but nothing compared to how I felt when we stopped in front of the room at the hotel. Big flakes of snow were falling when we'd left Charlene's, and Karen thought I had been driving slowly to avoid slick roads. I was actually in no hurry to get to the hotel and share one room, one bed, with Karen.

Nervous, scared, and anxious would all describe how I felt. What did she expect? What did she want? What did I want? I hadn't been with anyone since Amber and I had parted ways. I still had feelings for Amber and held out some hope that she would eventually want to see me again. Was that realistic? Probably not. I needed to move on.

Karen had said one room. It couldn't have been to save money. Or was it? Then I did something that I would never tell Charles about. I did what Charles would have told me to do. He would have either hurled some obscure quote from a US president at me or simply said, "Get your butt in the room and find out!"

So I did; and we did. Karen headed to the far corner of the room before the door was closed. She turned on the gas fireplace and opened the door that led to the small balcony, looking toward the brook that meandered behind the hotel. I had started to unpack, and she pulled the earth-toned drapes closed. The fire was beginning to heat the room.

I asked what she thought of Joan's story.

She said, "Tomorrow." She then turned toward the knotty pine headboard on the king-size bed, pulling her sweater over her head.

I could wait until tomorrow.

*   *   *

The clock's green LED numerals revealed that it was three thirty—the middle of the night. I turned to my right and saw Karen hugging the far edge of the bed. I grinned, thinking about all the movies that had a bedroom scene after a couple had sex. They'd fall asleep in each other's arms, body parts intertwined, wrapped together, sheets and blankets thrown asunder, and with a full orchestra playing in the background.

In the real world, four hours ago, I was too hot, and Karen was cold. I threw the covers off, and she pulled the sheet and blanket around her neck. I accidentally kicked her when she was almost asleep. And then I tripped on the corner of the bed as I tried to find my way to the bathroom in the dark, unfamiliar room. Reality would make a slightly humorous but unromantic movie.

My eyes popped open at six fifteen, but there was nothing to see. It was still dark. The glimmer of the parking lot lights seeped under the tightly closed drapery. Last night's visit with Joan and Charlene replayed in my head. How could I help? Sure, I knew she was scared, but did she have reason to be? Charlene hadn't supported Joan's story about being watched.

"What're you thinking about?"

I jumped. I had tried to be quiet, and it was still well before seven o'clock.

"Sorry," I said. "Did I wake you?"

She laughed. "No, this is late for me. I've been awake for an hour. I tried not to bother you."

Someone after my early morning heart, I thought.

"I've been awake and didn't want to move and wake you."

"Good," she said. "I'm starved. What's for breakfast?"

"I was thinking the Pancake Pantry, about a quarter mile back down the main street."

She threw the blankets and sheets off and was out of bed before I could ask if that was okay. "So what're we waiting for?" she said.

We were in front of the Pancake Pantry when they unlocked the door at seven. Karen had decided that we needed to walk instead of drive and wasn't deterred by my arguments that it was cold, and a long walk, and the sidewalks could be slick, and that we could get attacked by a hungry bear along the way. So far this morning, I had learned that Karen was an early riser and enjoyed a brisk walk in subfreezing temperatures. By now, I was starving.

We were the first customers, so we had our choice of tables. Karen selected one by the front window.

Karen scanned the menu and quickly ordered a chocolate chip waffle—another plus for the lovely young woman—and I stuck with the traditional Belgian waffle.

"So what's your take on Joan and her idea that someone's trying to kill her?" I asked while we waited for our food.

Karen stared out at the small shopping area and the candy store beside the restaurant. She took a sip of coffee and then turned back to me. "She's scared. I thought she was going to squeeze her glass into shards, and her hands trembled the whole time we were there."

I nodded.

Karen continued. "Other than the trauma of losing her husband and her house exploding, I don't know if there is a threat. Her description of someone spying on her was vague. And her friend was less certain about seeing someone. I've gotten better descriptions out of a dachshund."

Our food arrived, and Karen stuffed the first bite in her mouth before I could pour syrup on mine.

I shared more about how I had suspected that Joan was paranoid. To my knowledge, though, she had never been treated for emotional problems. "She thought I was having an affair for more than a year," I said.

"Oh," replied Karen.

I shook my head. "Work was my mistress. I felt bad about it but never could convince her."

"Because she may be paranoid," said Karen between bites, "doesn't mean that someone's not out to get her. Let's go to the house. I'm no expert, but maybe I can tell something from what's left."

We ate in silence for a short time, with me basking in the warmth of the restaurant, the wonderful odors of breakfast, and the savory taste of the coffee. We finished eating, and I paid the check. The walk back to the Hampton Inn was fast. It was if we were both suddenly on more of a mission than before, though that was nonsense. Nothing much had changed, except that we wanted to get on with finding out about any possible threats to Joan. I put the heat on as soon as the engine warmed up, and we headed over to Joan's place. Snow was still piled a couple of feet deep along the side of the road, but the main routes were mostly clear. Tourism was critical to the economy of the area, and the powers that be did whatever it took to keep the streets passable.

Slowly navigating the winding road toward Ober Gatlinburg and Joan's residence, I got my first glimpse of the shell of what had been a beautiful mountain home. The left half of the structure was standing, but the right side had collapsed on itself. The green metal roof had completely fallen, and icicles clung to every exposed horizontal surface. Yellow police tape was stretched tight around the exterior, and water that had ponded from the firefighters' efforts had frozen. It was heartbreaking.

I was barely able to pull into the circular drive enough to get out of the path of traffic. The supple and very expensive leather sectional that Joan had lounged on during our visit had been dragged out the front door and blocked most of the drive. The firefighters had made an effort to save it, but it had gone for naught. One corner was smoke-blackened from the blast and the resulting fire. There was an inch of ice on the cushions. The smell of water-soaked furniture and charred wood hung over the property. And parts of the roof and insulation were strewn on both sides of the road.

"Crap," said Karen as she saw the couch and then the front—or what was left of the front—of the house. "That couch probably cost more than my house."

An exaggeration, but not by much, I thought.

Karen ducked under the warning tape and proclaimed, "It's okay. I'm a cop."

"Be careful," I said. "You're a cop but not Superwoman. It's slick."

I followed. The massive entry door had been ripped off its hinges and was propped against the door frame. Karen held my arm and tried to move the door, but the ice held it tight. She then grabbed the door frame and gingerly stepped on a piece of the log wall that had fallen across the foundation and was supported by a blackened floor joist.

The wood groaned under her weight but held, and she stepped on the floor joist and leaned left to move toward what used to be the family room.

"Come on," she said, turning back toward the center of the house. She held her arm back for me to grab. The explosion had torn up some of the floorboards, and a couple more had burned through. I could see through to a finished lower level some twelve feet below.

"Hold on to me," I said, reaching for her hand. Her foot slipped on ice, and the floor gave way.

"Oh, shit!" she yelled.

Her left leg disappeared with it. I gripped the door frame and stretched as far as I could toward her. Her left leg was through the floor. I grabbed her wrist and pulled. Her hand slipped a couple of inches, and I squeezed as hard as I could. I thought I was going to pull my shoulder out of its socket, but I wasn't about to let go.

She was inches from safety when I heard a loud crack. Three boards that I was standing on gave way. I still held her wrist, but I was losing footing. I wrapped my right arm around the door frame, but my left leg was dangling between the two floors. If I let go, Karen would plummet a dozen feet to the lower level. If I didn't let go, both of us would take the disastrous fall.

I pulled on the door frame with all my strength, but it didn't help. I swung my right leg up and managed to get it over a floor joist. I took a deep breath and got enough leverage to pull my body back to floor level. Karen swung her free hand up and was able to reach my left leg. My torso was on the stable joist, and I was able to pull myself over to the solid floorboards. Karen remained calm, something I didn't think I could do if I were dangling in midair.

Once I reached the solid flooring, I was able to pull her back to floor level. She flopped down beside me and let out a low moan. I was looking up to where the roof had been a day earlier. It was a beautiful sunny day in the mountains. For a second, I thought it was the most beautiful day ever.

She wrapped her left arm around my waist. Her arm shook, and she gasped for air. "Thanks," she muttered.

We inched our way out of the house and back to the solid porch. She leaned against the frozen door frame and caught her breath. I pulled her close. Neither of our coats was made for subfreezing temperatures, and I slowly and carefully walked her to the car.

The heater roared full tilt, and we both rubbed our hands together to get circulation back. My shoulder ached, and my knee had a sharp pain in it. Karen's eyes were closed, and she rubbed her leg. Neither of us spoke. I knew that she was just as happy as I was to be safe in the car, not to mention walking.

It was at least ten minutes before she said, "Are you okay? Need to go to the hospital?"

"I don't think anything's broken," I said. "I'm okay for now. How about you?"

She smiled. "Just fine … just fine."

We sat for another few minutes. She finally said, "That's where the gas line went in." She gestured to the right side of the house.

I admired her focus. "From the damage, I'd say it was near the site of the explosion."

"You're right," she said. "Look how the metal roof has melted and twisted." She again pointed to the rear corner. "The other side of the house looks pretty good. Water and smoke ruined it."

She unzipped her jacket and continued to stare at the ruins. "From where the power entered the house, the electric panel was probably near there too," she said, casually rubbing her left leg. She grimaced, but she didn't complain. I wanted to comfort her but resisted. I told her about the lights flickering when we visited, and how Joan had said that she was going to call an electrician. Wouldn't the detonator be a logical explanation for the spark?

"It could still have been set," I said.

"If it was, there's a chance that the techs from Knoxville, I assume, could determine what set it off."

"I wonder if the police will even check," I said.

"Let's ask Joan if she told the firefighters or the police about her suspicions. If she did, most likely they'll investigate."

She cringed again as she touched her leg. She still didn't mention the injury.

"How would you proceed if you were investigating this?" I asked.

She took another glance at the house and turned in the seat to face me. "I'd consider four scenarios. First, that it was an accident—a malfunctioning gas furnace, a short in the electric system setting it off, or some other igniter. Second, Joan was the target of both the auto crash and the explosion." She hesitated as if she had thought of something else, and then she continued. "Third, her husband was the original target, and the killer is trying to eliminate Joan because he thinks she knows something. Fourth, her husband faked his death and set the explosion. And fifth," she paused again. "You're not going to like this."

"Go ahead," I said.

"Joan killed her husband and set the explosion to throw the cops off."

She was right. I didn't like it.

CHAPTER 24

We met Joan at Calhoun's, a restaurant across from the entrance to the aerial tram to Ober Gatlinburg and a block from the hotel. The restaurant was nearly empty when we arrived about fifteen minutes early. Karen had offered to stay in the room, but I asked her to come. I wanted her to get a better feel of Joan's mental state and information she might have about the explosion or Daniel's death.

Joan walked in at noon, spotting us near the front window. She stood erect, held her head back—she was in much better shape than she had been in last night. My ex smiled and walked to our booth. She gave me a tentative hug and nodded to Karen, who had remained seated.

Joan ordered a light lager beer; Karen and I ordered Merlot. Joan asked how our evening had been. I simply said we slept well. Neither of us mentioned the ill-fated visit to her house that morning. Joan told us that Calhoun's had some of the best burgers on the strip. That was good enough for me. I wasn't hungry. My stomach was queasy, and my body was beginning to ache all over. And my gut told me that there were too many coincidences. Joan was right about the events not being accidents. But that didn't explain if she was in danger or the cause of the danger.

Joan looked around, and I assumed it was to see if anyone was close enough to hear. No one was. "Chris," she said, "I don't know what to do. My house is gone, and someone here is after me."

"Have you thought about going back to California?" I asked. "Don't you have friends there you could stay with?"

"Not really," she said.

"You could stay with Charlene, couldn't you?"

Her eyes again darted nervously around the room. "She offered, but I wouldn't be comfortable staying here." She paused and then said, "I'm moving to Folly."

Now my stomach had reason to gyrate. "W-why?" I stammered. "When?"

She put her hands on her cheeks, lowered her head, and glanced at me with uplifted eyes. "They killed Daniel … they tried to kill me," she said. I leaned close to hear her soft voice. "They're here." She looked left and then right, as if they were standing in Calhoun's. "I have to get away—go where they won't find me." She hesitated, but neither Karen nor I spoke. "I thought about Folly before you got here. After I heard you talking about it last night, I knew that's where I could go and … hide." She gave a weak smile. "I don't know how long I'll be there, but I don't have a house, and most of my stuff's gone."

"When?" I asked—again.

"Tomorrow," she said.

The burgers may have been great, but after Joan's announcement, mine tasted like catsup-covered sawdust. Joan told us that she had started packing what little was left of her belongings. One of Charlene's husband's clients owned a construction company and had agreed to start repairing her house even if they had to completely demolish it first. Charlene's husband was also handling Daniel's estate. She didn't have to be in Gatlinburg for that.

She's been planning this since the house exploded, I realized.

Karen asked if Joan had learned anything more about the explosion, but Joan waved her off with a slight flick of the wrist. "No." I was no detective, but it was obvious that there was no warmth flowing in Karen's direction.

The rest of lunch was a blur. In addition to my queasy stomach, my head throbbed. Joan asked where she could stay on Folly Beach. I told her about the Tides, the oceanfront hotel that had been completely renovated in the last few years. She said that a hotel wouldn't meet her needs. I didn't ask why. I then suggested that she rent a house. She said that she might, but not now. I thought about offering to let her stay with me, but fortunately I realized how terrible an idea it was before I opened my mouth.

"What about Water's Edge Inn?" offered Karen, the first thing she had said since Joan dismissed her question about the explosion.

The Water's Edge Inn was a relatively new upscale bed-and-breakfast on the marsh side of Folly Beach, within easy walking distance to all the retail the island had to offer.

"Not a bad idea," I said. "It's a bed-and-breakfast, and they also have a couple of larger villas."

Joan nodded in my direction and then toward Karen. "That might work," she said.

I knew the owner and said I'd call to see if anything was available. She would think about it and let me know if she wanted me to call.

Pauses grew longer among the three of us. We had run out of conversation before thinking about ordering dessert. Joan had errands to run and said that she would like to follow us to Folly in the morning. We agreed on a time, and she gave me an extended hug and a cool nod to Karen. She left Calhoun's ahead of us.

The temperature felt twenty degrees colder on the walk back to the hotel. It also could have been Joan's announcement that made me shiver.

"Do you know where the police department is?" asked Karen as we approached the parking lot.

"No," I said. "Why?"

"I'd like to stop by and see what, if anything, they can tell me about the explosion—maybe meet her friend Officer Norton."

We got directions from the office, and she asked to borrow the car. She said it would be better if she went alone. She changed into the most detective-like attire she had with her.

I was stranded in the room with warm, pleasant thoughts about my time there with Karen, thoughts that competed with total confusion about Joan and her announcement that she was moving to Folly Beach—for a week, a month, forever. Who knew how long?

*   *   *

"The sergeant I talked to didn't know much about the explosion," said Karen. She had returned from her fact-finding visit to the Gatlinburg

Police Department. "Officer Norton was most familiar with the situation, but yesterday he and his family headed to Florida on vacation. He won't be back for a week."

"Anything else?" I asked.

"They didn't think it was suspicious. Said it looked like there was a gas leak and it built up in the lower level. A spark from something set off the explosion." She shook her head. "He said it wasn't common but does happen occasionally this time of year."

"Were they investigating?"

"Some, but it would be hard to tell if it was deliberate."

She started to change to her more comfortable jeans and sweatshirt. She wasn't shy about changing in front of me. I didn't complain. A large bruise on her left calf was all the apparent damage from the near-disastrous fall. She was fortunate.

She opened the door to the small balcony and stuck her head out. The low roar of the creek provided a soothing ambiance to the room. She shut the door and said, "So, what are you going to do with your ex-wife?"

Perhaps my imagination was working overtime, but I thought she placed an emphasis on *ex*. Could there be a tinge of jealousy?

"Let's discuss it tomorrow," I said with a smile.

CHAPTER 25

Joan was maneuvering an oversized Bankers Box into the rear seat of her Jaguar as Karen and I pulled into Charlene's drive. Her small backseat was stuffed, and Joan had to turn the box on end before it would fit through the door. She wore a fur-lined dark gray dress coat that would have looked more appropriate at the entrance to the ballet rather than loading boxes. Considering what was left of her house, she was lucky to have saved a winter coat.

She waved and said she was almost ready. I asked if I could help, and she said that there was only one more thing to load and then she'd be finished. Charlene stood in the doorway and gave Joan a hug before handing her a brown leather carry-on suitcase. Joan rolled the suitcase to the car and lifted it onto the front passenger seat. We agreed to stay in contact during the trip. She programmed Folly Beach into her navigation system and promised to call if she got lost.

I followed her out of town, and she waved for me to take the lead when we got on the interstate. The fifty-plus miles of interstate to Asheville were exceptionally curvy. Snow-covered remnants of the recent rockslides that had closed the road for weeks were visible along the way.

I was comfortable driving five miles per hour over the posted limits, but for most of the drive to Asheville, I was distracted by Joan's Jaguar tailgating me. Clearly, her comfort level was significantly different. We stopped for lunch at the Biltmore Estate exit on the other side of Asheville. Joan hinted that since her car had a navigation system, she would be okay if I let her take the lead. I thought that was a great idea since I had no interest in participating in an interstate accident where a new Jaguar convertible rear-ended a new Infiniti SUV. I told her that the easiest spot to meet on Folly would be in the parking lot of the Tides. I said that she couldn't miss it, that she'd understand that when she got there.

Letting Joan lead was one of the smartest decisions of the trip—in hindsight, possibly the only smart decision.

Five hours later, Karen and I pulled into the parking lot of the nine-story hotel, the tallest structure on the island. Joan's car was parked in the unloading area under the entry canopy as if she owned the hotel. Karen and I went inside, where we were greeted by name and with a beaming smile by Jay, one of the hotel's bellhops, who multitasked as concierge, greeter, security officer, and all-around good guy. I asked if he knew where the Jaguar's driver was, and he nodded toward the bar.

Joan was the only person at the bar. The fur-lined coat was draped over the back of her chair, and a glass of an amber-colored liquid was in front of her.

"It's about time," she said as we approached.

"How long have you been here?" I asked.

"About an hour." Her speech was slightly slurred. An hour would have been about three drinks in consumption time. I was never a math whiz, but if she had actually had been there that long, she must have been driving a fraction under the speed of sound.

"I think I'd like to see that breakfast and bread ... I mean bed ... place you talked about," she slurred.

"Okay," I said. "Let me see if there's a vacancy." I nodded to Karen and then to the empty seat on the other side of Joan.

Karen gave me a dirty look but offered to wait with Joan until I got back.

I smiled. "Thanks."

She frowned and said feebly, "You're welcome."

I went to the lobby and called Paul, the owner of Water's Edge Inn. He answered on the second ring and said both villas were rented but one would be available tomorrow. He said he would be glad to show it to my friend. I didn't think *friend* quite described my relationship with Joan, but I let it go.

Jay pulled me aside on my way back to the bar. "That's your friend's fourth drink," he said, gesturing toward the bar. "It's none of my business, but I thought you should know. She doesn't need to be behind the wheel of that Jag." He looked toward the entry.

There was that word *friend* again. I thanked him, and he said there were plenty of rooms in the hotel if she needed one. I thanked him again.

I returned to the bar to Karen rolling her eyes at me and Joan with a crooked grin affixed on her face. A fresh drink was in front of her. I told them about the vacancy tomorrow at Water's Edge and suggested that Joan get a room in the hotel for the night.

Joan glanced up from staring at her glass. "If they get me, please have me cream … cremated … and sprinkle my ashes with Daniel's." Her head nodded back down toward the bar. "Please."

"Come on, Joan," I said. "Nothing's going to happen."

Her mouth opened, but nothing came out. She shook her head and opened her mouth again. My phone rang before she could manage a response.

"You're back," said Charles. "Brought that chick detective back with you. Did y'all get hitched in one of those wedding chapels in Gatlinburg? Did Elvis sing at the wedding?"

I waited for him to take his first breath and said, "Who told you we were here?" I ignored the questions.

"Heather was walking home from work and saw your car. She rushed home and called me." He hesitated. "Dang shame I have to hear from someone else when my best friend gets home. Why didn't you call?"

I huffed for his benefit. "We just pulled in—I had to meet someone at the hotel." I then grinned, knowing that would not only rankle him but lead to a herd of questions from my uber-nosy friend.

"I'm late for work—got to keep Cal's afloat, you know. Come in later and tell me all about your wedding, and I'll tell you about the thief striking again."

"Didn't the doctor tell you not to work for a couple of weeks?" I asked.

"Yeah. So?"

I sighed. "Never mind." I then hung up—a fairly common practice for Charles, but usually he hung up on me. It felt good being on the other side of the dead line.

Chapter 26

Charles was behind the bar in animated conversation with Nick when I walked in. I couldn't tell what they were debating, but Charles's arms were flailing wildly, and he was having a difficult time balancing his crutches under his armpits. He finally put his hands on the crutches and pushed away from the bar, coming over to greet me. It was nine o'clock, and Cal's was one table shy of packed. The long, dark winter nights brought out more and more locals—boredom was a team sport in January.

A small table was available near the dance floor, so I headed there, Charles following. On the way, I heard someone at the next table complaining about how cold it was. I couldn't help but smile. Folly was a balmy forty-five degrees compared to the frigid, frozen, and snow-covered place I had left this morning.

"That dumb-as-a-rotten-pear Nick's driving me crazy," said Charles as he arrived at the table.

I was impressed how well he had skirted around the tables on his crutches and told him so. I didn't want to know why Nick was so dumb. Of course, what I wanted meant little to my friend.

"Yeah, yeah—practice," he said. "Why in Pluto's name would Nick think I could learn how to fix all those strange drinks people want? I think they make some of them up."

"Could be because you're a bartender," I said.

"Hmm," he replied, as if he hadn't thought of that. "So far I'm about as good a bartender as I am a detective." He shook his head.

"Another case of whiskey and the night's moola were stolen while you were gallivanting all over creation with your new squeeze toy."

I slapped my forehead with my right hand. "Charles!"

"Okay, okay," he said. "Your friend Karen. How's that?"

"Better," I said. "What happened?"

"I came in yesterday morning. Cal had asked me to check the place out. He was exhausted from the holidays. He's not used to actually working for a living, you know." He looked back toward the bar. "Anyway, I didn't notice the case missing at first, but I sure knew the shoebox was empty—thirteen hundred bucks gone," said Charles. "At least I got Cal counting it at night now."

"Doors locked?" I asked.

"Exactly," he said, and then he lowered his voice. "But get this. See those four tables over there?" He pointed one of his crutches to the side of the room. I nodded. "The night before the heist, they were where they are now. I straightened the room myself. It only took me a zillion times longer than usual." He pointed one crutch at the ceiling. "Yesterday morning two of the tables were in the center of the room. One of the other two had a deck of playing cards on the corner and four hands of cards, facedown, around the table—like someone had dealt them. There were two empty beer bottles on the table. Two chairs were on their sides on the floor, and another beer bottle was broken on the floor." He raised his right hand. "I swear to God that's what I found. If I didn't have these—" he indicated his crutches "—I would have gone home for my camera and I'd be showing you pictures." He exhaled deeply.

"So," I said, "four people came in through locked doors, played cards, drank beer, and then walked out with a case of whiskey and the money?"

"Yeah. See why you can't leave town?"

"Did you call the police?" I asked.

"Sure," he said. "I called Chief Newman myself; didn't want one of his officers to think I was nuts."

He didn't mind if the chief thought he was off his rocker, I thought.

"Did he find anything?" I asked.

Charles sighed heavily. "No, nary a thing. Said it was a mystery to him—doors were locked and no evidence of a break-in. Said there was no reason to print the furniture since everyone in town except small children and Baptists would have their prints on them. The bottles had smudged prints, and the cards didn't have any."

"What about the keys hidden around here?"

"Cal had Larry change the locks New Year's Day. Now there are only two sets—Cal has one, and I have the other." He tapped his pants pocket. "I thought that would solve the problem; now this."

"Sounds like a mystery," I said.

"Half the solution is admitting there's a problem," said Charles.

"Did a president say that?"

"Maybe," said Charles, "but I heard it from Larry—don't think he's been president of anything except his cell block."

"What are you thinking?" I asked, as seriously as I could.

"You know old Mr. Carr? Used to work at Bert's."

I remembered him from the island's grocery store but more recently from the story he had told me back on Halloween about the pavilion fire in the fifties. He'd said that the ghost of Frank Fontana still haunts the bars where he spent most of his years on Folly Beach, not to mention the Tides hotel, which sits on the site of the long-forgotten Folly Pavilion. According to Mr. Carr, Frank was furious with the good citizens who ignored his pleas to help the two girls on that tragic night many years ago.

I nodded and wondered what that had to do with Charles's theory of what happened.

"He was in last night. The old feller shouldn't have quit Bert's. He's eighty-seven and bored stiff. He hangs out here; we ought to get him a job—"

"Charles."

"Okay. He was telling me that there's been a bar on this site since before Adam and Eve fooled around in the garden—"

"Charles!" I tried again.

"Maybe he said since the early nineteen thirties. Anyway, Mr. Carr was a young pup a decade or so after that and remembered his granddad talking about how there had been two illegal gambling parlors on the island. One of the hot spots was over near my apartment, and the other one was right smack-dab here." He tapped the floor twice with his left crutch.

"So," I said, "your theory is that the other night, four centenarians snuck in through a crack in the wall and played poker for old times' sake—and then took a case of whiskey and a bag of modern currency on their way out."

"Don't be silly. Of course not. That's absurd." Charles shook his head. "It was their ghosts."

Chapter 27

A balmy fifty-five-degree day at the beach sounded good after a few days in the snow. I was looking forward to it until I had my first cup of coffee and remembered that Charles was chasing ghosts who had allegedly had a poker game and then robbed Cal's of whiskey and loot, and that a ghost from my past was moving to my island and waiting for me at the Tides to take her to a villa. It also struck me that after all those years of feeling guilty about the divorce, I could do something to make up for part of it. *But what?* I wondered. I'm certain the New Year could have begun worse than it had, but after only one cup of coffee, I couldn't imagine how.

"Is there somewhere on this dinky island where I can get shoes?"

That was a question that had never been posed to me, but I wasn't surprised when the phone rang, and after an obligatory greeting, Joan got to the meat of the call. It seemed that she had saved "only" five pairs of shoes and "desperately" needed a new pair of flats for the trip to the Water's Edge. I told her that I didn't think she could find anything here dressier than flip-flops or tennis shoes with glitter hearts. That wouldn't do, so I agreed to go with her to Charleston before our trip to the bed-and-breakfast.

I waved to the night clerk who was getting off duty and then walked across the attractive lobby to Joan, who was sitting in one of several seating areas that overlooked the Atlantic.

She smiled when she saw me; her shoes looked fine. Joan may have thought that I was grinning at her, but I was thinking that this would be the first time a prospective renter went shoe shopping to meet the owner of a bed-and-breakfast on Folly Beach. They must do things differently in Gatlinburg.

She had a cup of coffee and seemed more together than she'd been when we helped her to her room last night. She stood—her shoes appeared to hold her up quite well—and gave me a peck on the cheek. "I know I'm being a pain," she said, wrapping her arm around my waist. "I'm really nervous." She squeezed my waist. "And scared."

Shoe shopping was a strange way to express fear, but I could see fear in her eyes. It also entered my mind that if someone did want her dead, he could have followed her here. I didn't want to reinforce her fear by trying to hide her in the inn. If I was with her, I could help protect her from whatever danger may lurk.

Some of my irritation melted, and we headed to her Jaguar, which was still in front of the hotel. Jay winked at me as I passed him. I slapped him on the arm and frowned.

"Sure you don't want me to drive?" I said as she walked around to the driver's side.

"Got to learn my way around," she said and opened the door. "Might as well start now."

Joan cautiously pulled out of the Tides' parking lot and then gunned the Jag up Center Street, the main street and most direct way off the island. If it had been vacation season, we would have rear-ended at least three cars and flattened a couple of jaywalkers. Fortunately, Folly's only stop light was green, no cars dallied up the street, and all the prospective jaywalkers were in bed. We were going fifty when we crossed the bridge off the island.

The FASTEN SEAT BELT light on the dash flashed several times, and an audio reminder chimed and then finally gave up. Joan had told me decades ago that she didn't believe in wearing the "stupid" seat belt—something about not wanting to drown after getting trapped in the car if it fell off a bridge and in a river. I wondered if her husband had been wearing his seat belt when his car barreled off the road.

A Piggly Wiggly was on our left, and she asked if that was where she should do her grocery shopping. I said it was if she needed more than an item or two, and that Bert's, the small family-owned store a block from the ocean, was the convenience store of choice on-island.

She kept grunting in agreement, but I doubted she'd remember. Her hands trembled on the steering wheel. We were going sixty-something in a forty-five-mile-per-hour zone, so I also pointed to a condo complex across from the Pig, telling her it was where Folly's chief of police lived. That got her attention. She slowed, but only momentarily.

I directed her to King Street, Charleston's ritzy shopping area, where, like a laser-guided missile, Joan zeroed in on two designer shoe stores within a hundred yards of each other. Parking wasn't quite as easy, and we had to circle the block twice before a space opened on the one-way street. I groused while stuffing eight quarters in the parking meter. Meanwhile, Joan headed across the street to the stores.

An hour later, and Joan's credit card a few hundred dollars lighter, we sped along Folly Road and to our appointment at Water's Edge Inn.

"Oh, crap," she said as she looked in the rearview mirror. "Crap, crap." Her palm pounded the steering wheel.

We were on a two-lane stretch of road before the bridge to the island. *She was followed*, I thought. Then I was relieved to see the reflection of blue flashing LED lights in the mirror. She slammed on the brakes and pulled over on the berm, reaching for the glove box. This was obviously not a new experience for my ex. The patrol car pulled in behind her.

"May I see your license and proof of insurance please, ma'am?" said the polite and familiar voice of Officer Cindy LaMond. She dipped her head down and saw me next to Joan. "Oh, hi, Chris," she said with a confused expression on her face.

Joan turned toward me while at the same time handing her license and registration out the window. "Do you know everybody?" she murmured.

Cindy looked at the license. "Ma'am, Ms. McCandless, I clocked you at seventy-five in a forty-five zone. I also notice that you do not have your safety belt fastened. South Carolina law requires it."

"Why for heaven's sake would that flat, straight stretch be forty-five?" said Joan.

Cindy, who could stand toe-to-toe with the biggest bruiser while maintaining her calm, cheerful, and humorous demeanor, smiled at Joan. "Ma'am, I didn't write the law or stick that ole sign up there," she said. "They just ask me to enforce it."

"Oh, never mind," said Joan. She drummed her hand on the steering wheel. "Just give me the ticket."

"Ma'am," said Cindy, "I see you're not from these parts, so I should tell you that not only were you speeding, but I should cite you for reckless driving." Cindy bent farther down and looked at me. "Today we'll stick to speeding." She turned and walked back to her cruiser to write the ticket.

Joan had calmed down and almost appeared gracious by the time Cindy returned with the ticket and told her to have a nice day. Cindy told Joan that she was also from Tennessee. Joan grinned and said, "That's nice." I silently thanked Cindy for not hauling Joan off to jail. But I knew the sun would not set without my getting a call from Officer LaMond, asking me all about the irritating, rude, and all-around obnoxious Ms. McCandless. I ventured to guess that she would be the first in a long line of inquisitive residents.

The day turned brighter, literally and figuratively, when Paul, the owner of Water's Edge Inn, greeted us at the car. We were a few minutes early, so he must have been watching for us. He showed Joan the large three-bedroom, three-bath villa. The dark hardwood floors contrasted nicely with the off-white kitchen cabinets and the traditional white beds. The villa was larger than my house, cheerful and as attractive as the nicest homes on the island. Joan's enthusiasm increased with each room we toured. I think she was already sold, but when he told her that cocktails were served each day, the deal was sealed.

Joan registered as Jane Mitchell and said she would be paying cash. Paul glanced at the register and said, "I'm sorry—I thought your first name was Joan."

Joan looked at me, and I gave a slight nod. She then told him an abbreviated version about being concerned that someone might come looking for her—someone she wanted to avoid.

"No problem," said the astute innkeeper, who then asked how long she would need the room. He was interested in her answer. But he wasn't nearly as curious as I was.

"Let's start with two months," she said as she continued to look around. I saw the reflection of dollar signs in Paul's eyes. I felt burning acid rising in my esophagus.

CHAPTER 28

"**It was no accident** that the box fell," Charles said between bites of pizza.

It was Thursday night, and I hadn't seen Charles most of the week. The island was nearly deserted of vacationers, although a hardy group of season-pushers from Toronto had stopped in the gallery—more out of boredom rather than to buy anything. Charles had worked each night at Cal's and rested his ankle during the day. I'd locked the gallery door an hour earlier, and Charles arrived with the pizza. We were in the small multifunctional room behind the sales gallery. The refrigerator was well stocked with beer, a few soft drinks, and in the summer, a couple of bottles of white wine.

"What makes you say that?" I said, taking a sip of Cabernet to wash down the doughy delight.

"Cal's crew is finally talking to me," he said. "They're learning that while I'm slightly older than any of them, I'm not totally worthless."

"Slightly older?" I said.

He rolled his eyes. "They call me gramps behind my back—nary a molecule of respect for their elders, you know."

I held back a laugh and said, "They said you're becoming a good bartender?"

"Didn't say that. They just realize that I'm not worthless." He hesitated and shook his head. "They think I'm funny—'cept I'm not trying to be."

"So what are you doing that's not totally worthless?" I asked. This was fun.

"I'm not breaking as many glasses," he said. "I'm not really the bartending type."

"Why not?" I asked.

"It's like golf," he said, swinging one of his crutches like a five iron. "As president Woodrow Wilson said, 'Golf is a game in which one endeavors to control a ball with implements ill adapted for the purpose.'" He finished his quote and feebly attempted a golf swing before he set the crutch beside the table. "I don't have the tools for bartending. Detecting's more up my fairway."

I bit my lower lip to avoid laughing. Instead, I raised my eyebrow. "So ... they're talking to you ... and ...?" I hoped he would get back on track—or at least out of the rough.

"They're acting like I'm one of them. Anyway, Kenneth told me that he was certain he put the case on the bottom shelf the day before. Said he put it there so the 'more feeble' employees could move it. It fell from the top shelf."

"Who's Kenneth? Is he sure where he put it?"

"The bartender with the mullet. He's got huge arms; he's a weightlifter. Moved here in July from Baltimore. Doesn't talk much. Drives an old Dodge Dart and—"

Before Charles told me even more than I wanted to know, I interrupted and asked again, "Is he sure about where he put the box?"

"Says so." Charles got up to get another beer. "I didn't have a lie detector with me so I couldn't test him."

"So who moved it?" I asked.

"Don't know but it sure was fixed to fall when I opened the door. I was lucky it only broke my ankle."

"Who knew you were cleaning the next morning?" I asked.

"Good question," he said. "I might let you work in my detective agency—just might."

He had said that, or something similar, several times over the last three years. I had consistently ignored him. I saw no reason to break that streak.

Charles studied his Bud Light before finally answering my question. "Who knew? Let's see. It was busy. All the bartenders and wait folks would have known. The schedule was behind the bar, but anyone could see it. Customers who weren't enjoying listening to themselves talk could have heard it mentioned."

"Doesn't narrow it down much," I said.

"Nope," he said. "Enough about this detecting stuff. What's the deal with the former Mrs. Landrum?" He reached down for one of his crutches and tapped it on the table leg. "And before I forget, I'm royally pissed at you."

Should I ask? What the heck—he was going to tell me anyway. "Why?"

"Why? Are you serious? Who was your best friend who was stranded here while you took a young, hot, smart chick with a gun to Tennessee?"

"You weren't in any condition to travel," I said defensively.

"I know that," he said. "But you were supposed to ask me so I could tell you that I didn't feel like going."

I grinned. "What would you have said if I'd asked?"

"What time are you picking me up?" he replied, oblivious to what he had said about not being able to travel.

I shook my head. "I rest my case."

"Enough of you being right," he said. "How long will she be here? Are you getting back together?"

I tilted my head toward him.

"Okay," he said. "Then … how's your sex life? With Karen? Or with your ex? Is Karen going to shoot your ex?" He paused for a breath.

"You'll be the first to know," I said.

"Know what?"

"The answer," I said. Since he'd asked a half dozen or so questions, I thought that should confuse him for the rest of his beer. He was due at Cal's in twenty minutes, so he wouldn't have time to pester me further.

"I'm sure you were getting ready to answer each one, but I have to get to work. Tell me next time."

"You know it," I said.

"Sure you will," he said. He finished the beer, grabbed his crutches from the floor, and headed to the door.

"Gotta go catch a thief," he said as he exited the gallery.

If he was right about the case being a booby trap, someone thought he was getting close and wanted to scare him off.

I hoped scare was all.

CHAPTER 29

The next three days were a blur. We had unseasonably warm temperatures, and several condo owners who would normally be happy in their homes in Atlanta or Columbia ventured to the beach to walk on the cool sand, eat in local restaurants, and go home to rub in their neighbors' faces how they had spent a few days at the beach. Some even bought photos.

Joan called at least twice a day. Friday she had called to ask questions that anyone at the Water's Edge could have answered—where she could get her hair cut, where the post office was, where she could get a good manicure. By the second and third call that day, she talked about how much she missed Daniel and her home. It wasn't long before she was sobbing. There were long pauses when all I heard was sniffling. She was in pain, but I was clueless about what to do. the last two times she called, she hadn't finished a thought before hanging up. Should I have gone to check on her? Should I have called back? I did neither and then spent the next hour feeling guilty.

I decided to check on her Saturday morning. The sun hadn't begun its slow warm-up, so I drove. During the short drive, I wondered if I should disturb her. Her car was gone, so my indecision went for naught. I returned to the gallery, and as I was pouring water in the Mr. Coffee, the phone rang.

"Did you just call?" said Joan. She sounded jumpy.

"No, why?" I said.

"They're trying to find me," she whispered.

"Who?" I asked.

I heard sounds in the background; I could barely hear her. "The ones who killed Daniel. The ones who destroyed my house."

"Where are you?" I asked.

"The grocery store—Piggly Wiggly. I'm scared."

"Okay," I said. "Take a deep breath and walk to the office. It's at the front of the store. Stand where a lot of people can see you. I'll be there in ten minutes."

I made the short trip off-island to the Pig in less than five minutes. Joan was out the door before I put the SUV in park. She was dressed more like she was going on a job interview than doing early morning shopping at a beach grocery store. She looked around the parking lot and back at the store while tightly squeezing her phone. She ran to the passenger door.

"Let's go somewhere … anywhere," she said. "I'll get my car later."

I hadn't had breakfast, but I knew if I asked if she was hungry, she would say no, so I headed to a spot where I was comfortable, the Lost Dog Café. Weekends were busy at the Dog, and today was no exception. We were given the last booth, and Amber was at the table before Joan removed her coat. This was only the second time that I was aware of that she had been in the Dog, and the first time that Amber had been working. I introduced the women but left out a few minor details, like my life with Joan and my history with Amber. I figured Joan wouldn't have known about Amber; but I would bet my left lung that Amber had already heard about Joan.

Amber smirked when I said that Joan was someone I had known years ago. "From Louisville," said Amber. "From high school, from college, from—"

"Coffee, two," I interrupted. I knew where Amber was going and didn't think Joan, in her current state, was ready to hear about her entire background with me from a server she had just met.

Amber knew that I knew she knew. "Sure," she said, heading behind the counter.

Joan's hands were shaking, and she craned her neck to see the front door.

"You're okay here," I said. "What happened?"

She closed her eyes for a moment. The smell of freshly brewed coffee filled the air, and the low background noise from several conversations provided a calming ambiance—at least to me. "I was in the store, and the phone rang. I always look to see who's calling before I answer. It said UNKNOWN. No one said anything. Then it went dead."

"Okay, and then what? Did you see them?"

"Well, no," she said. "I figured that it was a wrong number or that you had called from another phone, so I went about my business." She looked back toward the door again. "Then ... then it rang again ... *Unknown* ... I'm scared, Chris." She reached across the table, clasped my hand, and squeezed. "I'm so scared."

Had I missed something? She had received two hang-ups. There were no threats, no words spoken. She gripped my hand as if it were going to escape. "What makes you think it was someone trying to find you? How would just calling let someone know where you were?"

Her eyes narrowed; her grip tightened. "Because I know it's them. They killed Daniel. They ... they blew up my house to kill me, and now they're trying to get me. It was them."

I saw Amber heading to the table with two mugs of coffee. She appeared to notice the tension on Joan's brow and see how tightly she gripped my hand. Amber paused and then turned to another table.

I was torn. I wanted to joke about wrong numbers, but I could tell that whether Joan was wrong or not, she was terrified. How could I comfort her? Were her fears real? I couldn't say that everything would be okay. I thought it would, but ...

I stroked the top of her hand and said, "Do you remember anything else about the calls? Something scared you; help me understand." I hesitated as I almost said there was nothing terrifying about two hang-ups.

"There wasn't anything." She was nearly shouting. "I told you, Chris—there wasn't anything." She jerked her head around. "Where's that waitress?" She yanked her hand away from mine. "Why is she so slow?"

Amber had kept a respectful distance from the table, but she'd watched for a sign to return. I nodded, and she headed back.

Joan murmured, "About time."

Amber gave her customer-service smile and asked what Joan would like. Joan responded, "Bacon and eggs. Don't care how you fix them." She then waved her away.

I ordered oatmeal and mouthed, "I'm sorry."

Joan's emotions swung from fear to anger in a nanosecond. Neither was attractive.

She took a deep breath. "I don't know what you find so great about this damned island," she said. She sipped her coffee. "Shopping sucks ... Many of the houses—if you can call them that—are dilapidated, with weeds, grasses, and mangy-looking trees growing everywhere ... Service is pitiful ... Oh, never mind." She stared down at the table and shook her head. Tears formed in the corner of her eyes.

I reached for her hand, and she didn't pull back. I squeezed gently. "Let me tell you a couple of things about Folly," I said. "I've met more fantastic people here in the last five years than I knew in my first fifty-seven. Most of them would do anything for me. Also, you haven't been here long enough to know this, but it's the most unpretentious place I've ever visited. And—"

"Okay, okay," she interrupted. "I'm tired ... and scared." She wiped away a tear and tried to smile. "You've always had good judgment; truth be known, I should have paid more attention to you, but ... anyway. If it's good enough for you, I'll give it a chance." Her smile turned into a laugh. "Besides, I invited myself here. I'd better not make everyone mad." She nodded toward Amber. "What's her name again?"

Amber returned with our food, and Joan apologized for being rude and asked how long Amber had worked here and if she had any family.

Amber looked my way and then back to Joan. She said she'd been on the island almost fourteen years and had a fourteen-year-old son. Joan asked her what her husband did, and Amber glanced my way again. I thought Joan was doing much better, but when Amber told her that she didn't have a husband, Joan's smile disappeared.

"I don't have a husband either," said Joan.

"Oh," said Amber.

Considering the alternatives, I thought that was a good response.

Joan's eyes were downcast as she said, "Mine was murdered a couple of weeks ago."

Talk about a conversation stopper, I thought.

CHAPTER 30

A friend of William Hansel's had drowned near the Folly Pier four years ago. The police had ruled it suicide, but he stubbornly maintained that his friend was terrified of the ocean and would never have killed himself that way. William couldn't convince the police, but Charles and I knew him enough to know that if he said his friend was murdered, someone had better take another look. Charles and I did, and to make a long story short—or shorter—William was right, and my friend and I were nearly killed proving it.

William had suffered a nervous breakdown following the death, and he spent several days in a mental health facility. The good news was that he made a complete recovery. I held a college degree in psychology, but the last class I took was forty years ago. I had trouble remembering what I learned three days ago, so my formal education was decades past worthless. Maybe William could shed some light on Joan or recommend someone who might help.

His small, neat one-story house was three blocks from the center of town, so I decided to walk over and see if he was home. I wore a jacket, but I'd unzipped it. The sun made it feel several degrees warmer than it was. I also realized how ironic it was that I was walking. When I had dated Amber, she'd tried to get me to eat better and exercise more. Of course, I had earned a merit badge in male stubbornness by ignoring her suggestions—her wise, accurate, and helpful suggestions. Now here I was, no longer with Amber and walking to William's house—further proof that I hadn't remembered anything from my college psychology classes.

William was clearly surprised to see me on his stoop, but he invited me in and offered me a cup of hot tea. Tea was his drink of choice, seasonally adjusted in temperature so it would take a few minutes for him to boil water. I didn't know him when his wife died, but I suspected everything in his house had remained unchanged since her passing. There were feminine touches everywhere. Cream-colored doilies topped each table. Ceramic angel figurines were placed in groupings on the coffee table and the table in the entry hall. He had an ample collection of books on two bookcases in the living room, but it paled in comparison to Charles's book cave.

The professor delivered the tea on a silver platter that held two china cups with holly and red berries adorning the side. They were on matching saucers, and a white sugar bowl was in the middle of the platter. I thought of the contrast from my usual party accoutrements—Styrofoam cups, napkins for plates, beer cans, and screw-top wine bottles.

Steam ribboned from the tea as I tried to figure out how to get my finger in the cup's tiny handle. I wondered who the miniopenings were made for; they weren't for most guys.

"And what brings you out on such a lovely winter day?" asked my proper host.

"Couldn't I simply have wanted to visit a friend?" I asked.

"Of course," he said and rubbed his chin. "But I suspect that is not the primary reason."

"You caught me," I said with a smile. "Actually, I wanted to talk about Joan."

"Ah," he said. "And how is the lovely former Mrs. Landrum adjusting to our unique slice of heaven?"

I forced my finger in the petite handle, blew across the steaming liquid, took a sip, and shook my head. "Not well. That's what I wanted to talk about." I hesitated. "This is a delicate subject, and I apologize ahead of time if it's uncomfortable for you."

William set his cup on the table and gave me his full attention. "That certainly piques my curiosity," he said in his powerful voice. "Apology accepted prediscomfort."

I shared a little about Joan's erratic behavior and mood swings. I told him that I saw nothing unusual about the phone hang-ups and feared that her imagination was running wild. Then the delicate part. William was an extremely private person and had few friends. I was honored to be among them.

"William," I said reluctantly, "back when you, umm, suffered, umm—"

"When I was hospitalized with a debilitating bout of depression," he interrupted.

I sighed. "Exactly."

"Chris," he interrupted again, "You were there for me. It was a terrible time but one that I do not wish to conceal. I had a condition, a mental condition no different from a physical malady, and received professional treatment. You were my friend, you believed in me, and you found the evil perpetrators who took my friend's life. I'm forever indebted. Please do not be hesitant now."

The formal warm and fuzzy was so William, I thought.

"Thanks," I said. "You said the counseling saved your life. You told me that you were not a strong believer in that kind of help before you went through it." I took another sip and William sat silently. He knew not to interrupt. "I think Joan needs the same kind of help."

"I concur," he said. "I would highly recommend the counselors at Carolina Counseling. That's where I went after release from the hospital. They're near my campus, two blocks from my classroom." He walked to his bedroom and returned with the counseling center's business card. "How do you plan to broach the subject with Mrs. McCandless?" He handed me the card.

"Good question," I said. "Good question."

"Perhaps here's an even better one," he said. "How do you know that there's not someone out to harm her?"

"I don't. But there's also no reason to think there is."

"Allow me to share my thoughts," he said. I nodded and he continued. "In the last three weeks, Mrs. McCandless's husband has perished in a horrible automobile crash. Perhaps it was an accident; a longer shot, murder. And then her house was destroyed—probably an accident, possibly intentional. And now she's moved hundreds of miles from everything she was familiar with to a place that, on its best day, could be considered strange. She has contact here with only one person she has ever known, that being you, an ex-husband she hasn't seen or talked to in decades." He peered down into his empty teacup. "I would think that even the most mentally sound individual would be going, as Charles would say, bonkers under those circumstances."

William was right—in a professorial, class presentation sort of way. Still, he was right.

"True," I said.

"Then does not she deserve more sympathy and understanding?" he said.

I had to agree.

CHAPTER 31

After spending the day with Joan's irrational ramblings and mood swings, and then with the overly rational logic, combined with a minor scolding, from William, I needed to find my comfort zone. Cal's Country Bar and Burgers should meet that criterion, with an ample supply of comfort food and drink, a representative sample of the characters of Folly Beach, and good traditional country music provided by Cal and his country-infused Wurlitzer.

I knew I had made the right choice when the first person I saw was Charles behind the bar, wearing a black long-sleeved T-shirt with DETROIT BARTENDING SCHOOL in block letters across the front. He balanced one crutch under his left arm and tossed a can of Budweiser to Dawn, his younger and much more attractive fellow barkeep.

Cal was on the small stage, his back curved and his mouth almost touching the old-fashioned, softball-sized microphone on the stand in front of him. He was in stage garb and announced that he would be performing a set of "good ole-fashioned country classics" in an hour. "Until then, folks, I'll set this jukebox spinnin' some of the greatest hits from the ... the ... whatever number that last century was." He walked to the jukebox in the corner and pushed a few buttons until the sound of Lefty Frizzell and "I Never Go Around Mirrors" reverberated off the walls.

I inhaled and soaked in the aroma of stale beer and frying onions, letting the feel of Folly wash away my tension created by, as Cal would say, "a blast from the past."

The bar was two-thirds full, mostly with regulars. I recognized most of them, including Heather, who was at the table farthest from the stage. The chair to her right was tilted with its back rested on the table to announce that it was reserved. She had draped her yellow cloth jacket on the chair to her left. She waved me over, grabbed her jacket, and threw it on the chair on the far side of the table.

"Charles said you'd be here. He wanted me to save you a seat," she said.

That was interesting since fifteen minutes ago I hadn't known I'd be there. "You mean Chucky?" I said. I sat beside Heather and tossed my Tilley on the chair with her coat.

She gave me her best stage grin. "Aw-shucks, I know he favors Charles," she said. "I call him Chucky to annoy him. Getting under his skin is so much fun." She giggled.

I almost grabbed my hat so I could tip it to her. I matched her grin. "More power to you," I said.

"How're you and your ex getting along?" she asked.

I knew that I'd be hearing that question so often that I should walk to Cal's mike and share the answer with everyone. Instead, I said that we were getting along fine and hoped that would satisfy her.

A server I'd seen a time or two magically appeared with a pink drink of unknown content and set it in front of Heather, and she surprised me with a glass of red wine. "Charles said I didn't have to listen to you but to give you this glass," she said with a smile.

Heather watched her go. "That's Beatrice. She's a strange one," she said.

Coming from Heather, that was quite a comment. "How?" I asked.

Heather kept staring at the server and said, "Well, ding-dong. Who'd want to be called Beatrice? She was named after her grandmother, you know. Said some folks try to call her Bee but she hates it." Heather leaned closer. "She may be a witch ... A full moon tonight." Heather paused and took a not-so-dainty sip of beer.

"A witch?" I said. I had learned a couple of years ago that Heather had no problem talking, talking, and talking, but her conversation easily drifted like an unanchored fishing boat in a storm.

"Witch, yeah." She seemed to be trying to refocus. "She makes handmade jewelry—cutesy bracelets, necklaces, rings."

Heather's left wrist displayed three bracelets that I would call cutesy. "How does that make her a witch?"

She leaned close again and whispered as if she were sharing a state secret. "Some of them—especially the necklaces—have that star-looking thing on them."

"Pentagram?" I said.

"Yeah, that's it. That witchy symbol," said Heather. "Anyway, she's always trying to push her baubles, always short of money." She leaned even closer and kept her eye on the bar. "Charles thinks she might smoke the weed a bit too much."

I hadn't heard Heather say anything that would put Beatrice in the strange category. In fact, it sounded as if she would fit in well on my quirky island.

From the jukebox, Ricky Van Shelton yanked tears out of every note of "Life Turned Her That Way." The room was packed, and Charles arrived at the table.

"Break time," he said. He pulled a beer can of out of his pocket and set it close to Heather, put a half-full bottle of Cabernet in front of me, leaned his crutches against the table, and sat in the chair Heather had saved for him.

I looked at his shirt. "Been to bartending school?" I said, certain that I knew the answer.

He peered down at his chest. "Like it?" he said. "Ordered it on the Internet. Thought if I wore it, customers wouldn't scream at me for screwing up their drinks—me being a highly educated mixologist."

"Is it working?"

"Not yet," he said, taking a sip of beer.

I looked toward the bar. "Don't they need you?"

Charles looked back over his shoulder. "Nah. Dawn's got it under control. She raised two kids; had the guts to leave her abusive husband; and treats all the kids working here like a mother hen. Things are under control. Besides, I'm taking her shift Monday—poor thing's got to go to court to get a restraining order against her ex." Charles's eyes lit up like a lightbulb had gone off in his brain. "Speaking of exes, how's yours?"

Time to nip that one. My need to not think about it outweighed

Charles's insatiable appetite for nosiness. "Later," I said. "Caught the thief?"

He sighed. "Thanks for bringing that up."

Heather put her hand on Charles thigh. "Now, Chucky," she said and winked at me, "You know who it is." She shook her head. "Looking at all those employee folks is barking up the wrong totem pole."

I leaned closer to the lovebirds. "Who?" I said.

"Frank Fontana," she said, leaning back in her chair.

Where had I heard that name before?

"Sweetie," said Charles, putting his arm around Heather. "You know that may not be right."

"Now, Chucky, cutie," she countered, "you said it was a good thought. You said Frank had to be considered."

Sweetie … cutie—I was about ready to start talking about Joan rather than fall deeper into the syrup. Instead, I said, "Frank Fontana?"

I wished I hadn't. Charles glanced at Heather and then looked me in the face. "A spirit, phantom, spook, soul … He's a ghost."

It came to me: on Halloween, when old man Carr told me the story about the twins dying in a pavilion fire in the fifties—and about Frank Fontana and how he had disappeared, the rumor that his ghost was mad because no one tried to save the young girls.

I blinked, took a sip of wine, and thought I would need many more before the night was over. I turned to Heather. "How do you know it's Fontana?" I asked this as if it were a completely normal question.

"I knew it was the apparition of someone but didn't know who until Chester told me," she said.

"Oh," I said, turning to Charles. "Would that be the same Chester Carr who told you the tables had been rearranged by ghosts playing cards?"

"That's the one," said Heather, speaking for Charles. My sarcasm is often missed. "Chester said he thought more about it after he figured out why the tables had been moved. He never saw Frank in here—alive or in his current spirit state—but Chester knew that the bar that was on this exact spot was called Jerk's or Perk's or something like that." She pointed at the floor. "It was Fontana's favorite drinking spot. Since he was here, he must have played cards with the gang that's coming to play now."

"She could have a point," said Charles.

Whoever said that love was blind, definitely had twenty-twenty vision, I thought.

I turned to Charles. "Make sure I have this right. The spirit of Frank Fontana is stealing cases of whiskey and money, and it lifted a case of bourbon to the top shelf so it would fall on you."

"Told you Chris was quick," said Heather.

"Well," said Charles, "that's one working theory—I'm not certain. I'm considering other suspects."

"Human?" I asked.

Beatrice appeared at the table. She leaned over to Charles and told him that Dawn needed help at the bar. Charles huffed and puffed and then grabbed his crutches and hobbled off.

My plan had worked. I hadn't thought of Joan or William since I'd walked in the door of Cal's. *Thank God for comfort zones*, I thought. Then I left the bar and went home, basking in the warmth of the evening's fun and hoping for a great night's sleep. Like many things in life, you don't always get what you hope for, and change—for better or worse—is always right around the corner.

CHAPTER 32

I did something Sunday that I hadn't done in maybe fifteen years. I went to church. I parked in the public library's small parking lot across from the Baptist Church and hesitantly walked to the front of the simple white house of the Lord. I took a deep breath, waited until the last possible minute before the eleven o'clock service, and then walked up the steps and entered the double doors. I had been reared in the Baptist Church and had many fond memories of Sunday school, Wednesday prayer services, and vacation Bible school. As a kid, I'd had no idea what the preacher was talking about, but I could tell from his tone that it was important, eternally important. During my adult years, I understood what he was saying but didn't understand what it meant.

My fondest memories centered on such inspirational, melodious, and haunting hymns as "Precious Memories," "Just As I Am," and "Amazing Grace." None of those soothing sounds greeted me as I entered. No one from Folly knew about my church attendance prior to my moving here, but if they were observant, they would have known that I had never graced their door. It felt as if everyone in the sanctuary was staring at me as I slipped into the next to last pew. However, no one stood, pointed at me, and shouted "Sinner!" I was relieved.

The call to worship ended, and no one had paid attention to me more than anyone else. The preacher didn't even call me out and ask who I was. I finally relaxed ... until I spotted Joan seated three pews in front of me.

Despite where I was, and my best intentions, I was angry with her.

What right did she have to drag me into her life—her confused, tragic, and paranoid life. We hadn't had any contact for decades. On the other hand, maybe the guy we were worshiping brought her back to me for a reason. Could this be my chance to make amends for chasing her off in the first place?

Joan turned, saw me, and gave me the same sweet, alluring smile that had drawn me to her in high school. I had been deeply in love with her for many years. I added my anger to the list of guilts I already had this morning. I remembered what William had said about her having earned the right to be depressed, confused, and fearful. She deserved more understanding. Maybe it was William's words or the preacher's message about forgiveness, but I knew what I would do at the end of the service. With that resolved, I made a joyous noise unto the Lord as I joined the congregation in "Just a Closer Walk with Thee."

I waited outside. Joan came around the building and looked around until she saw me. She gave a high-wattage smile and rushed over to give me a warm hug. She appeared rested and quite nice in a dark green pantsuit.

"I enjoyed your church," she said after she let go and stepped back.

I didn't correct her. "I'm glad," I said. "Want to get lunch?"

"That'd be nice," she said without hesitation.

"I'll drive," I said.

She laughed. "If you don't speed." She actually winked at me.

I drove to downtown Charleston and found a parking spot on Queen Street, between King and Meeting streets, near the side entrance to the Mills House Hotel. Most of the year I wouldn't have found a parking spot within blocks and would have been forced to park in one of the public parking garages. I was partial to small, quaint restaurants, so I escorted Joan across Queen Street to Poogan's Porch, a cheerfully painted yellow late-1880s Victorian home converted to one of the city's better-known eating establishments. Even though it was January, the restaurant was full and we had to wait for a table. Its Sunday brunch was reputed to be the best in the city.

Joan asked if Poogan was the owner, and I explained that Poogan was a scruffy neighborhood dog that had adopted the old house before it became a restaurant. After the renovation, Poogan hung out on the porch and begged for table scraps. He became a low-cost welcoming committee for patrons. Poogan retired from his greeter job and from his time on Earth in the late seventies, but he lived on as the name of the restaurant.

I noticed that Joan's hands were not trembling and that she was paying attention to what I was saying. I shortened our wait by telling her that it was rumored that the ghost of the former owner was often seen walking around the restaurant in a long black dress.

Her eyes lit up with mirth. "With Poogan?" she asked.

It was nice to see a sincere smile. I said that she should ask the server.

I was out of trivia about the restaurant when we were paged for our table. Charles could have drummed up another hour's worth of worthless information. The pleasant college-aged hostess led us to a table in an attractive room along the back of the restaurant. A mural of Charleston's famed White Point Gardens, better known as Battery Park, was on one wall, and our table was next to the Palladian windows that overlooked a patio—a prime seating area in warm weather. I ordered a mid-priced bottle of Joel Gott domestic Cabernet after pondering the extensive wine list. It was the first Cabernet that I could pronounce on the list.

Joan asked the server if Poogan accompanied the former owner on her haunting excursions. The server appeared confused but quickly recovered and said that she would check with the chef. Joan laughed after the befuddled woman left to get our wine.

The crowded room was noisy, and I slid my chair closer to Joan. "How are your parents?" I asked. I had realized on the drive over that I'd had several conversations with Joan in the last month, but all of them had been about recent events. I also didn't want today's conversation to sink to her paranoid fears and terrible memories of the last couple of weeks.

"Gone," she said.

"Oh, sorry," I said.

She gazed out the doors to the patio. "Long time ago ... Mom, cancer; Dad, car accident."

Way to go, Chris, I thought. *Great way to distract her from Daniel's death.*

The wine arrived, and we ordered from the brunch menu. I ordered the cinnamon french toast and wondered how Joan stayed so trim when she ordered a po'boy. I also wondered how a Cabernet would go with french toast. I didn't linger on that thought.

If someone had been eavesdropping, we would have sounded like two old friends catching up after decades of not seeing each other. We traded a few stories about college classmates—where they were now, what they were doing, who was married to or divorced from whom. I gave her a drastically abbreviated version of how I found Folly Beach and reiterated why I loved it so much. She said that she was shocked that I was friends with someone like Charles. I told her that I would have been shocked if I wasn't. She said she didn't understand; I said that neither did I. And she hadn't even met Dude, Mad Mel, and Heather!

As Joan shared a little about her career in the world of business, I held back a yawn of boredom. I was more interested in why Daniel had decided to move to Gatlinburg. Apparently, he never adequately explained why he had sold the businesses in California and why, with all the choices available, he selected the Tennessee resort community. She said she was more baffled about why he wanted to get involved with the Jaguar dealership, especially since he said he'd never liked the owners.

The conversation was drifting too close to the depressing reality of the last few weeks, and I suggested that we walk to Charleston's market. It was in the upper fifties, but in the bright afternoon sun, it felt warmer. The historic market was only a few blocks from Poogan's.

We approached the large Greek Revival entry, and Joan told me that she and Daniel had visited the popular tourist attraction several years ago. It wasn't new to her, but the more than one hundred vendors, who sold everything from handmade sweetgrass baskets to Harley-Davidson belt buckles to Low-Country traditional benne wafers, kept her distracted. We meandered through half of the several-block-long open-air market, and she put her arm around mine, squeezed, and said, "This is fun. Thanks."

Joan was talking to one of the women weaving a sweetgrass basket when my cell rang. "What are you doing tonight?" said Charles. I could hear voices in the background.

"Sleeping," I said.

"Overrated," he said. "See you at midnight."

"Whoa," I said, hoping to keep him from hanging up. "Where and, more importantly, why?"

"I've been thinking about what Heather said about ghosts," he said. "Think she's on to something ... oh yeah, be at Cal's."

"What're you talking about?" I said. Joan was about ten feet away and in deep conversation with the artist. Both were laughing.

"I've been hearing noises after closing," he said. "I never see anything. Dawn and Dustin told me that they've heard spooky sounds too."

"There are hundreds of mice and rats on the island," I said. "It's winter, and they want to get warm. You're hearing them moving to their winter condos. It's rats."

"Rats leave poop pellets," said Charles. "Haven't seen any—uh, not many. Besides, Heather said she has a feeling that unhappy poker-playing spirits are knocking the chairs over when they lose." There was a pause. "Talk more about it tonight—midnight ... Cal's. See ya." The phone went dead.

I was staring at the phone when Joan tapped me on the shoulder. She had two baskets in her left hand and a smile on her face. "Nice lady," she said. "I think I need to get home; I'm bushed."

I offered to get the car and pick her up, but she said she wasn't that tired and would walk back to the restaurant with me, even smiling when she said it. She dozed on the ride home and thanked me profusely when I let her out at her car. I followed her back to Water's Edge to make sure she was safe.

On the short drive to the house, I realized that this had been a pleasant day and that spending time with Joan wasn't half bad.

I suspected things would get geometrically worse at midnight. Rat patrol?

CHAPTER 33

The front entrance to Cal's was locked, so I went to the side door. It was a little before midnight. The overhead fluorescent lights that were off when the bar was open cast a stark shadow and accented how worn the dark brown carpet had become. Cal's, like me and most of my aging friends, looked better in dim light.

"About time you got here," said Charles.

If he hadn't been so tired after tending bar all night, I'm certain he would have said, "You're a real pal; thanks for coming. I owe you big time."

"Now that you've dragged me out of a night's sleep, why are we here?" I said, throwing my jacket on the table closest to the bar.

"Help me move these tables to the other side of the room, and then I'll give you the scoop." He pointed to two tables that had been scooted to the edge of the dance floor. He'd parked the crutches behind the bar and said he'd had enough of them.

We slowly moved the tables, arranged four chairs at each, and then Charles returned to the bar. He asked me to lift onto the bar a beer case–sized brown cardboard box that Heather had delivered to the bar. It had an inch-wide orange stripe around it that looked like it was hand drawn with a colored marker.

He leaned against the bar and rubbed his injured ankle. "It's been a couple of nights since the thieves visited," he said. "I figure they're due. Heather's ghosts make more sense than anything else."

Who am I to argue? I thought. Besides, it would be futile. And after all, the Low Country did have a storied history of ghosts.

"Heather thought we'd need this to catch the ghosts," he said. He started rooting through the box. He pulled out an aluminum device about twice the size of a cigarette pack. Two toggle switches, two dials, and a digital readout screen were on the face.

"Umm," I said, nodding toward the device that he set on the table.

"It's an ion counter, of course," he said.

Gee, I thought, *how could I have skipped that bit of knowledge during my long and not-so-illustrious life?*

"Of course," I said. "And other than counting ions—whatever they are—how is it going to help *you* catch a ghost?"

He shook his head. "Chris, Chris, Chris … ghosts stir up a gaggle of positive ions because they radiate high amounts of electromagnetic discharges."

"Ah," I said. "What number will that doohickey machine tell you is a high amount?"

"No clue," said Charles. "Heather didn't tell me everything. I think we'll know when it spots a spook."

"Speaking of Heather, where is she?" I asked. "Isn't ghost stalking one of her hobbies?"

"She said I was an idiot to stay out all night—and that she needed her beauty sleep."

My admiration for Charles's main squeeze increased.

Charles's hand was back in the box, and he pulled out a barometer, a compass, and another handheld contraption the size of his palm. It was similar to the ion counter, with a digital readout and a dial.

"And what's that?" I asked.

"A compass," he said with a grin.

"I know that," I sighed. "I meant that other thingie."

"Happens to be a three-axis gaussmeter—says so right here on the front." He held up his right hand. "Don't bother asking; I don't have any better idea what the numbers mean than I did with the ion counter."

"So when those digital meters start dinging, vibrating, or whatever they do when a ghost happens to stop by to visit two human idiots in a bar, you'll call Heather, wake her up, and ask what to do next?" I plopped down in the chair closest to the bar, leaned back, clasped my hands together behind my head, and then rolled my eyes. My shoulder and knee still felt as if I'd been hit by a beer truck.

"Didn't say the plan was perfect." He sat in the chair next to me. "This is what detectives do. Solving crimes is boring work."

"I think this is what ghost busters do," I said.

Charles studied the array of stuff he had removed from the box. "She said I couldn't be trusted with her infrared thermal scanner, hydrometer, and thermal imaging scopes." He shook his head and frowned.

Another feather in her yellow bonnet.

*   *   *

If the clock on the wall behind the bar chimed instead of just telling time and advertising beer, it would have chimed twice. Charles had lit candles on four tables and turned off the cold-hued fluorescent lights. Heather had told him that the candles were critical because ghosts can drain equipment energy and our flashlights may be useless. I found that information less than encouraging. Twice in the last hour, Charles said he believed he heard ghosts but soon decided that it was the normal cold weather creaking of the old building. Occasionally, the sound of a vehicle roaring past broke the middle-of-the-night silence.

"Charles," I said around three thirty, "let's pretend that the thief is a real person. If that's the case, and I know that it is *highly unlikely*, who are your suspects—excuse me, 'spects?"

He looked in the flickering candle on our table. "Between you and me—"

"And the ghosts," I interrupted, sarcasm getting the better of me.

"And the ghosts," Charles continued. "I'm not as certain as Heather about ghosts. Don't tell her, okay?"

I frowned as if I were giving it serious consideration and then nodded.

"It could be anyone on Folly," said Charles. "But it would make more sense that it's an inside job. The employees know where Cal keeps the money, when the liquor's delivered, and where it's stored. They also know the most expensive bottles and know their way around the bar."

"Yes, but so do any of the barflies who hang out here more than they do at home," I said.

"True," said Charles, "but aren't the odds greater that it's an inside job?"

I nodded again.

"I guess it could be any of them except Kristin. She went home to Nashville over the college break and wasn't within several hundred miles when the last theft occurred." He hesitated. "If I had to rank the 'spects, I'd put Nick at the top, then Kenneth, and then maybe Dawn."

"Why?"

"Nick doesn't like me—that rocketed him to the top of the list. He's been here three years and knows his way around the bar. He's always flashing a fistful of cash. And every time Cal mentions the thefts, Nick's quick to blame vacationers or some of the homeless folks who call Folly home. He's never said it could be someone who works here."

I'd witnessed their near confrontation on Christmas and knew they'd never be fishing buddies, but I didn't believe disliking Charles should put someone at the top of a suspect list. It was interesting, though, that Nick wouldn't think it was an insider. "Why Kenneth?"

"Nothing specific," said Charles as he walked behind the bar to the industrial strength coffeemaker and poured a cup for each of us. "He's almost as secretive about his past as you are. Greg hired him before he left. Hang on a second—let me show you something." He headed off to the storeroom.

I wondered where he thought I might be going.

Charles returned with a crinkled-up manila file folder in his left hand. "I was sort of going through the personnel files—"

"Sort of?"

"Okay, I was nosin' through them," said Charles. "Detective stuff, you know." He handed me the file. "Look at this."

The name Kenneth Landry was scribbled in blue ink on the top tab. I laid the file on the table and opened it. There was only one sheet of paper in it: an application for employment. The top two lines of the application were filled out with the applicant's name, Kenneth Landry, and his social security number. An address on James Island was listed under residence, but it was scratched out and replaced with an apartment on Folly.

I waved the application in Charles's face. "What am I supposed to be looking for?" I asked.

"Look at the oodles of information on it," said Charles.

The only other thing on the application was the name of two bars listed under references. In fine print at the bottom of the application was a notation written in a different color pen: *Hired. Only applicant!*

"Did Greg check references on his other hires?" I asked.

"Yeah. It looked like he called former employers. But not with Kenneth."

"You're right," I said. "It is strange. But I wouldn't use it as a reason to consider him the thief."

"True," he conceded. "But it's enough to get him on my list."

Our conversation was interrupted by the loud siren of one of Folly's fire engines as it left the station across the street. The high-pitched attention-grabbing noise bounced off the walls.

I waited for the truck to get around the corner and the noise to subside. "Why Dawn?"

"It's funny," said Charles who was trying to balance his cane vertically with the rubber-tipped end on his palm. "She's on the list for the opposite reason as Nick. Dawn's always broke. Her ex-husband hasn't done anything but cause trouble. He dumped her with a spittoon full of debt. Her two kids skipped the state once they were old enough. She doesn't know where they are. She's always getting calls here from people she owes money to." The cane flipped out of his hand and bounced off the table. "Whoops," he said.

After suggesting that he keep his bartending detective job and not join the circus as a juggler, I asked if poverty was the only reason he suspected Dawn. A scratching sound coming from the ceiling interrupted our conversation.

Charles jumped out of his chair and grabbed the ion counter and a candle. He pointed to the ceiling and stared at the digital screen on the counter, where nothing, absolutely nothing, happened.

The scratching appeared to scurry to the other side of the ceiling, and I laughed. Charles put his finger to his lips for silence.

"It's a mouse," I said. "I told you there's a bunch of them here. I'm not the expert on the unnatural like you and Heather, but I know a mouse when I hear one. Is that what you've heard after closing?"

"Could be. I never thought of it in rodent terms," he said, clearly disappointed. "How about the ghost of a mouse?"

I ignored his desperate stretch and suggested that we give up ghost watching for the night. I thought the mouse population would be here all the time, and no self-respecting burglar would be out at three in the morning.

"Another half hour?" he asked. His tone was close to begging, so I figured it wouldn't hurt to stay thirty more minutes. We settled back in our chairs, and I pinched my arm to to keep from falling asleep.

"Heather says Daniel's alive," he said without looking at me.

Considering the source, I would tend to dismiss Charles's comment if I hadn't been thinking the same thing after I let Joan out at Water's Edge. "Why does she think that?"

"Said she would know if he had crossed over to Deadsville."

"She never met the man," I said. "She's never been to Gatlinburg, and she hasn't even met Joan. How would she know that?"

"Good question," he said. "I asked the same thing. She said she knows my vibes, and I'd spent time with Joan and even visited the scene of the intentional accident. She seemed mighty confident." Charles paused and then carried his cup over to the coffeepot. He refilled it, picked up his cup, and then set it back down. "Do you know why he may have faked his death?"

I didn't tell Charles that I'd had this same conversation with myself within the past twenty-four hours. "He was mysterious with Joan about why he got out of the Jaguar partnership. Actually, he was evasive about why he'd decided to leave California."

"Sounds like reasons to me," said Charles. "Think he wanted to get away from her? It'd be mighty cruel to fake his death and leave her hanging, unless he wanted to vamoose."

"I don't know enough about their relationship to say. I think she has emotional problems, but in the last day, I've seen glimmers of the kind, wonderful lady I fell in love with years ago. But really, no clue."

"Hmm," said Charles as he walked around the bar and blew out candles. "Anyway, that's only Heather's psychic whatever speaking."

"Do you have a different idea?" I asked.

"Yeah," said Charles. He turned on the fluorescent lights, blew out the last candle, and said, "I think Joan killed him."

I didn't see that coming. "What makes you think that?" I asked.

"What do you really know about her?" he asked. "I know all the blah, blah, blah stuff from when you were married. That leaves out the last twenty-four years. A lot can happen in that amount of time."

"I can't argue with that. But why do you think it was her?"

He shrugged. "No good reason. Just think it should be considered."

I offered a silent prayer that neither Heather nor Charles was right.

CHAPTER 34

I hadn't heard from Joan the last couple of days, and then I literally ran into her at Bert's. She was carrying cleaning supplies and a quart of milk. I knocked a box of dish soap out of her arm.

"Sorry," I said. I leaned down and picked up the box, smiling at her. "I didn't think you liked the shopping on Folly."

She returned my smile and then looked around the iconic store that sold everything from beer to bait. "I possibly mistook character for grunge. I figured if it was good enough for you, I'd chance it."

That was the second time that she'd said something like that. I nodded as she paid Eric, whose dark hair and beard were almost as long as some of the tales I'd heard in the grocery store.

"Want to get some lunch?" she said as I followed her out to her car. She had parked on the side of the store that was covered by a painted mural featuring a larger-than-life likeness of Bert.

"Sure," I said, offering to pick her up at her place. My car was at the house, within sight of the store. She said it wasn't necessary and for me to hop in. Before she pulled out of the parking space, she stopped, studied the mural, and then turned to me. "Folly?"

"You got it."

She stopped at Water's Edge and took the bag to her villa while I waited in the car. I mentioned the Charleston Crab House, and she said, "Why not?" The restaurant was off Folly Road, about nine miles from the island.

I then said a silent prayer for a safe trip as she got behind the wheel and failed to fasten her seat belt, a habit that I had given up trying to break back when George H. W. Bush was president. We weaved through a residential area of Folly, past some of the quaint, rustic cottages that contributed to the island's unique charm, and slid onto Folly Road. I grabbed the door handle and Joan reached over and patted my knee. "Don't worry," she said, "I've had high-performance driver training."

I didn't loosen my grip on the handle but managed to ask, "Why?"

She laughed. "Daniel said that if I was going to be driving cars that cost more than starter homes, I needed to know how to not wreck them." She passed a driver who had the audacity to drive the speed limit and almost rear-ended a bumper sticker–adorned minivan. "Besides, I think he liked to brag to his friends about his 'cool race car–driving wife.'"

Her conviction that speed limits didn't apply to her ensured that we arrived ahead of the lunch crowd. We were escorted to the best indoor table, which overlooked Wappoo Creek. In the summer, diners would be entertained by dozens of small boats packed with laughing, happy groups enjoying the scenery and the occasional dolphin that chose the peacefulness of the creek over the rambunctious Atlantic. Today one small pleasure craft motored by on the creek that was as wide as many small rivers.

A typical fish restaurant menu matched the décor and featured some of the freshest seafood in the area. Joan ordered a bottle of Cabernet without asking what I wanted—perhaps she knew me better than I thought. I recommended the coconut fried shrimp plate and ordered the fried flounder plate for myself. She sat back in her chair and took a deep breath. A faint smell of frying fish reached our table.

She smiled. "This is nice."

I returned the smile and asked how she was adjusting to Folly Beach and her villa.

"I'm trying to make the best of a bad—scratch that, a terrible situation." She tilted her head to the left and then to the right. "I don't want to be here, but … I can't turn back the clock. Daniel's gone; my home's gone. And I think I'm getting used to your island."

The wine arrived, and we each took a sip and looked out on

the waterway. Joan was much more relaxed than the last time we'd talked.

"Remember," she said, continuing to stare outside, "the time we drove up to New York City and the car broke down on the Pennsylvania Turnpike?"

"And you said, 'Who wants to see that old Empire State Building, anyway?'"

"Yeah," she laughed. "I was thinking about that on the way over here from home, er, Gatlinburg. If Daniel and I had car trouble, he would have cussed, fumed, and been mad for days. All you did was say not to worry. Said we'd get the car fixed and still see all there was to see in the Big Apple." She paused; a sparkle appeared in the corner of her eye. "I also remember that night in the roadside motel with the squeaky bed and all."

I thought I might be blushing. "I remember too," I said.

"Maybe you're not so dull after all. I could've used a lot more of that calm in my life." She finally turned toward me and smiled.

"'Not so dull.' Gee, thanks."

Our lunch arrived, and we ate in silence until she said, "Tell me about Amber."

I nearly choked on a hush puppy. "What about her?"

"I've been in the Dog a couple more times, and she waited on me once. Said she knew you pretty well. She didn't say it, but I had the feeling there was history between you two."

I hesitated and then realized that there wasn't any reason not to tell her about Amber—but also no reason to tell her. I gave her an abridged version of how I had met Amber, how we had been friends for a year or so before going out, and what had occurred that ended our dating.

Joan surprised me when she said, "Her loss." My next sip of wine was larger.

"So now you're dating Karen, the 'government worker' who happens to be a detective with the sheriff's office," she said with a wink.

My face reddened; it was no big deal what Karen did, but we had hidden it from Joan. "We've gone out some. I don't know how serious it is."

"I hear her dad's Folly's police chief," she said.

How can I keep Joan away from the Lost Dog gossip pit? I wondered.

"Yes, Brian's the chief and a friend," I said. I wanted to change the subject. I knew if we stayed on this topic, Joan would start thinking about the alleged killer. The lunch was too pleasant to sink to that. I told her about Charles and how we had met, mentioning our shared interest in photography and a little about the history of the struggling gallery.

"Remember when we went to the Four Tops concert in Cincinnati?" I said.

"Yeah, I remember that you complained the whole way." She held her wineglass up to me as if she were toasting something. "You kept saying, 'Motown, Motown, and a two-hundred-mile drive. Yuck!'" She laughed. "I also remember your saying on the ride back how much you liked the concert."

"The point is—"

"The point is," she interrupted, "that you finally surrendered and started liking the Supremes, the Temptations, and the other groups that I liked—groups you wouldn't listen to before."

"True," I conceded, "that's one point, but I brought it up because it's similar to you and Folly. You said you didn't like the feel and look of the place, but the more you give it a chance, I guarantee it'll grow on you."

"So," she said, rubbing her chin in an exaggerated motion, "because you like the Supremes, you think I could start liking weird president-quoting scruffy ole Charles?"

I laughed. "I wouldn't go that far. Take it one step at a time."

The longer we sat, the more we drifted to the kinds of conversations we'd had in college. We talked about the things we agreed on and some of the same things that we had debated some forty years ago. She still couldn't understand how I could like both the Beach Boys and George Jones. I said it was an *admirable eclectic musical taste*; she said it was just weird. Her laughter came more naturally. She shared how she had acquired an interest in opera and ballet. I said I would be glad to give her any tickets I was given to either of those events.

I glanced at my watch and was surprised that we'd been there three hours—a pleasant trip down memory lane, reconnecting with someone who had only been a bad memory at best for many years, and a good meal to boot. She said we should be going. I don't think either of us actually had anywhere to go, but I agreed.

She put her arm around my waist as we walked to the car. It felt strange yet almost familiar. She still insisted on driving.

We had just passed the road that veers off Folly Road and leads to Charleston when the car suddenly jerked to the left. The high-pitched sound of steel on steel ripped through my skull. My head banged off the headrest. Joan uttered a profanity, yanked the wheel to the right, and looked in the rearview mirror.

I turned my head and saw a high silver grille on a large black pickup truck fill the rear window. It fell back a few feet and then accelerated. I tightened my grip on the door handle.

"Hang on!" yelled Joan.

I turned back toward the windshield and saw temporary concrete barriers guarding a road construction project. It was directly in front of us. *I wonder if air bags really work*, rushed through my mind as quickly as we were headed at the massive gray concrete wall.

Joan's options were limited. The road narrowed because of the construction. Traffic rushed toward us in the left lane, and the barrier loomed in front of us on the right.

We were less than a hundred feet from the concrete wall. The pickup rammed us again. I lost my grip on the door handle and twisted sideways. Instead of trying to stop, Joan stomped on the accelerator and turned the wheel. We were in a controlled skid. Horns from the oncoming traffic blared. Joan muttered, "Calm, calm, calm," and then the truck rammed us again.

My life did not flash before my eyes. All I saw in front of me was the huge unforgiving concrete barrier.

CHAPTER 35

We were close enough for me to reach out and touch the barrier. There couldn't have been more than ten feet between the deadly concrete wall and the line of traffic passing us on the other side of the car.

The truck nudged us one more time before catching an opening in the traffic to our left and roaring past us. It's surprising what one notices in time of crisis. The truck didn't have a license plate. The other thing I noticed was the Jaguar hitting a glancing blow to the concrete barrier. We scraped it for no more than a couple of seconds.

A heavy dose of luck and Joan's deceased husband having sprung for high-performance driver training had saved us. Joan had masterfully maneuvered between the oncoming traffic and the concrete barrier and skidded to a stop in a small shopping center on the other side of the construction. The truck that had come precariously close to ramming us into oblivion was nowhere in sight.

A couple of shoppers from a small grocery store in the shopping center rushed out to ask if we were okay. Joan and I were standing by the car and looking at the seven-foot-long gash along my side of the car. Apparently, someone had already called the police. The high-pitched sounds of police sirens rapidly approached.

A middle-aged machine shop owner who was following the pickup had pulled in to see if we were okay. He had been behind the truck for the last quarter mile and thought the driver was drunk because of the way he had weaved across the lanes. The Good Samaritan thought we'd be goners when he saw the pickup hit us before we reached the bridge. He had called 911 and waited to tell the police what he had seen.

Two other Charleston patrol cars arrived almost simultaneously. It was in the lower sixties and sunny, but Joan was shivering. I convinced her to get back in the car with the heater running. Two of the officers came over to the Jaguar and one of them checked out the damage. Chips of concrete from the barrier were imbedded in the side of the car. The third officer talked to the witness and then leaned down to Joan's window to share what the other witness had said.

"Officer," said Joan. Her voice crackled, and her hands shook. "It *was not* a drunk driver. He tried to kill us."

"Ma'am," replied the patient officer, "you said you recently moved from Tennessee. Who here would want to kill you?"

She didn't respond. I pictured wheels turning in her head—how much should she tell the cop? She sighed and then said, "I saw the truck parked beside the restaurant when we came out. It followed us."

"Ma'am, do you know how many big black pickups there are around here? How do you know it was the same one?"

Joan glared at the cop. "It wasn't just a large black pickup," she said, her voice growing stronger. "It was a Ford F-250 Super Duty Crew Cab, probably an oh-eight."

Being married to a car dealer had its benefits.

The officer remained polite and wrote down the information. He said he would issue a BOLO but stuck to his view that it was a drunk driver. He said that was how the man who had called the police described it.

Joan gave an exasperated sigh, her shoulders slumped, and she mumbled, "Whatever."

I asked if she wanted me to drive; she said no. For the first time since I had known her, Joan slipped on her lap belt and then pulled back on Folly Road and headed toward the beach.

Her hands clasped the steering wheel; her knuckles were white. "You believe me, don't you?"

Much more than I did an hour ago, I thought. "I don't think it was a drunk. He knew what he was doing and waited until we were near the narrowest section of road."

That was not a yes to her question, but it appeared to satisfy her. "How did he find me?" She accelerated. "How, Chris ... how?"

"I don't know," I said. I wondered if he had attached some sort of tracking device to her luggage or her car. Could he have simply followed us from Tennessee? If he did, why hadn't he made an attempt on her life earlier? If he was from Gatlinburg, he had to follow us from Water's Edge to the restaurant. Had he come in when we were eating? Did I notice anything unusual about the lunch crowd? Clearly, Joan hadn't seen a familiar face. "I don't know," I repeated.

She offered to drop me at the house, but I told her to go home and I'd walk from there. I wanted to make sure everything was okay at her place but didn't say it. After a quick look, she said that everything was the same as when she had left. She had added some personal touches, and it had a homey feel. She walked around the living area and lit three candles neatly arranged on two tables in the main room. She had added some fresh-cut flowers in a crystal vase on the glass-topped casual dining table. The bag from the grocery store was on the island in the kitchen.

I awkwardly stood in the entry hall, and she leaned against the entry table. She looked in the kitchen and then at the stairs that led to the bedrooms. "Please help find who's doing this," she said. "They do want to kill me, you know."

I nodded. "I'll do my best, but—"

She put her arms around me and then stepped back. She then hugged me again and kissed my cheek. "Thank you," she said. A tear rolled down her face.

I left her at the door and looked around for a black truck. I then inspected as much of her Jaguar as I could see without crawling around under it. How had he found her?

CHAPTER 36

I walked to the gallery instead of home. I fired up the Mr. Coffee, turned on the lights, and took the OPEN WHEN I'M HERE—CLOSED WHEN I'M NOT sign out of the window and hoped customers would wander in. I hadn't opened on Wednesdays since the summer but thought it might distract me from the day's events. I was wrong.

I rearranged two large photos displayed on the wall. I even swept the foot-worn floor, something I usually saved for Charles. Then my undistracted mind took over. Could someone really have followed Joan? How could he, or she, have known where she was? Did anyone other than Charlene and her husband know that Joan was here? Could they be involved?

If someone wanted to kill her, why? Who could she be a threat to? Was she keeping something from me?

I paced, gazed out the front window, and then paced some more. Could Heather's far-fetched theory that Daniel was still alive be true? If he was alive, would he want to kill his wife? Wouldn't today's ramming eliminate Joan as a suspect in Daniel's death? All I concluded was that the floor was cleaner.

I didn't believe in coincidences. The recent events—the death of Joan's husband, the destruction of her house, and now the incident on Folly Road—were beyond any reasonable chance of being random.

If that weren't bad enough, I started thinking about Amber and Karen. Both were in their early forties and nearly twenty years younger than I was. I knew that Amber's favorite musicians included Tracy

Chapman, George Michael, and two groups I'd never heard of—all whose music was alien to my ears. Talking to Joan about our favorites from the 1960s reminded me that I was from a different world, at least chronologically, than Amber and Karen. Was that chasm too wide to bridge in a relationship? I didn't want to think so, but …

I shook the thought from my mind and then smiled. The thought of Charles, the budding detective, trying to catch either a mouse or a ghost who had been stealing from Cal's lightened my mood. I was laughing when the front door opened.

"What be hilarious?" said Dude, bounding in and skipping over to me. His oversized corduroy coat flapped open and his signature tie-dye shirt glowed under it.

"Just thinking about something," I said, and offered to take his coat. "Who's manning the surf shop?" I carried his coat to the back room and pointed to the coffeepot. His preference was tea, but he'd stoop to sipping coffee in a pinch.

"Don't need manning," he said. "Surfers in short supply the long *J* month. Stick smiley face on door and scoot."

Dude made enough the rest of the year, during the busy season, that he didn't have to unlock the surf shop from Christmas to April if he didn't want to. He spent most of his downtime sitting in the Dog, reading astronomy magazines and questioning regulars about why business was slow. The regulars used to tell him that it was because no one was here. Now they simply said, "Don't know." That satisfied him.

He set his coffee mug on the table, parked his trim body on an old wooden chair, and put his feet on the corner of the table. "Hear your ex-surfer chick be making goo-goo eyes at you." He had a sly grin on his sunken sun- and seawater-wrinkled face. "Wantin' to respark, they say."

Wow, that was the beginning of a conversation that I hadn't expected. "Where'd you hear that?"

"Here, there," he said. "Hear she's a Benny."

Charles usually served as my translator for Dude-speak. I was on my own. "Benny?" I asked.

"Benny, duh," said Dude. "Be someone from big city and dissed beach."

"Oh," I said. "No, I think she's having a hard time adjusting to Folly and some of the strange folks around here. She's okay."

"Who be strange?" said Dude.

Pots calling kettles black. Still, I understood his warped perspective and ignored the question. "Who said she wanted to respark?" I tried again.

"Peeps at Pup," he said.

I assumed that he meant the Lost Dog Café, and I knew that was all I'd learn. I got the coffeepot and poured more for my sentence-challenged friend.

"Where's Chuckster?" he said, his eyes darting around the small office area as if he thought Charles had been standing in the corner the entire time.

I told him Charles had been working nights at Cal's and was spending less time in the gallery; and besides, there weren't enough customers for me to need help.

"He be detectin'?" asked Dude.

I nodded.

"Hope he's better at detectin' than barkeepin'," said Dude. "Hear he narrowed thief to peeps, ghosts, and rodents."

Dude should start a newspaper to compete with the *Folly Current*. It would have fewer words, but it would be accurate and definitely entertaining.

I laughed. "I think those are his top suspects."

"Martians added to list?" said Dude with a straight face. "Hear they stopped by last full moon."

I'd bet he didn't hear that at the Dog. "I'll tell Charles," I deadpanned.

"Me not a detective," he said. "But if thief not a ghost, or Mickey M., or little green men, could be human." He nodded, and I responded with a nod. "If human, how be gettin' in? Figure that out and be catchin' bad guy."

Dude suddenly hopped out of the chair, grabbed his coat, and was gone as quickly as he had arrived. I took two seconds to not count my sales, turn out the lights, turn off the coffeemaker, lock the door, and head home.

Dude be right, I thought.

CHAPTER 37

Thursday began as a glorious sunny winter day; it was to reach the midsixties by noon. I had overslept, something I rarely did, and I didn't start my day until nine. I rationalized that since I'd had fish for lunch yesterday—even if it was fried—I could have something significantly less healthy for breakfast, so I walked next door to Bert's for a package of powdered sugar doughnuts and coffee. I then walked to the lobby of the Tides and sat at one of the soft, comfortable beige chairs that overlooked the hotel's pool, the Folly Pier, and the magnificent Atlantic Ocean. A large section of clear etched glass separated my seat from the hotel's restaurant, so I didn't think eating doughnuts would bother the management. They didn't serve sugarcoated doughnuts anyway. Two rationalizations and it wasn't even noon.

As I was reaching for my phone to call Charles, it rang.

"I saw him. I saw him!" screamed Joan. Her voice trembled, and I couldn't understand what she said next.

"Where are you?" I said.

"In the car ... in front of ... oh, what is it ... that big real-estate building near the gas station—"

"Avocet Realty?" I said.

"Yeah."

"Can you park on Center Street?"

"I think so," she said.

"Pull over. I'll be there in two minutes."

She inhaled, and then said, "Hurry."

I made the trek in record time—record time for me, that is. Her Jaguar was on the sloped drive that led to a Kangaroo gas station from the side street next to Avocet. It took her three tries to hit the button to unlock the door.

"Thank God," she said. "Thank you."

"Are you okay?"

Her hands had a death grip on the leather-trimmed steering wheel, but she nodded.

"Who did you see? Where?"

She took a deep breath and then rubbed her left hand across her face. "I was on the way back from Bert's. I needed coffee filters and ... never mind. I was ..." She pointed down Center Street toward the ocean. Her finger shook. "I saw him go around the corner by Avocet. I wasn't paying attention at first, and then it struck me. I'd seen him before. I thought it was from here, but then I realized it wasn't."

"Did he see you?"

"I don't think so."

"Where did you remember him from?" I asked, reaching out and touching her trembling hand. She grabbed my wrist.

"California, maybe," she said. "It could be Tennessee." She took another deep breath. "I'm not certain ... not certain. I know I've seen him. It had to be the guy in the truck."

"Did you see where he went?"

"I didn't see him after he turned that corner." She again pointed back over her shoulder.

"Okay," I said. "I'll drive."

She didn't argue but only hurried around to the passenger's door. I avoided the block where Joan saw him go, instead circling around to the house and parking in front. This was Joan's first visit. We walked to the front door, and I wondered what condition I had left it in. Company was the last thing I had expected when I left.

It wasn't too messy, and I picked up the newspaper from the floor by my favorite chair while she looked around. "Nice," she was kind enough to say. I offered to fix coffee. My old coffee machine had seen better days, and its performance was subpar compared to Bert's, but it was better than nothing. I didn't think she'd complain.

Joan seemed calmer, but she still paced the small living room and the most unused room in the house, the kitchen. I called Officer Cindy LaMond's cell phone. She answered on the first ring.

"Hi, Chris," she said. I detest caller ID and cringe when someone knows who I am without my telling them.

"Working?" I asked.

"Yep, but go ahead. I'm just sitting at the bridge harassing speeders to have something to do." She gave a faux yawn to punctuate her excitement.

"Then this is your lucky day," I said. "If you come by the house, I have something you'll be interested in."

She laughed. "You hired a male stripper?"

"Come over and find out."

"On my way," she said.

Cindy was as good as her word. In fewer than five minutes, a white City of Folly Beach Department of Public Safety patrol car pulled up behind Joan's Jaguar.

Cindy looked at me and turned to Joan. "Let me guess: you were going ninety-seven miles an hour down Center Street and want to turn yourself in." A twinkle of humor appeared in the corner of her eyes.

Joan, to her credit, laughed. Cindy then smiled. And I took a deep breath. Cindy had done more to ease Joan's fears than I had with comforting words and crappy coffee.

I escorted both women to the kitchen, and the three of us sat around my small table. Cindy accepted a cup of coffee, and I refilled Joan's mug. I gave Cindy a synopsis of Joan's recent tragedies and yesterday's encounter with the truck. She had already heard much of it from Charles and Amber. I then told her about what happened this morning with the mysterious person.

Cindy went into police mode and took notes. She lifted her head from her pad and turned to Joan. "And you're certain you don't know where you've seen the guy before?"

"Sorry, no," said Joan, "As I told Chris, it could have been from California or Tennessee." She paused and looked at the coffeemaker. "It wasn't from here."

"Describe him again," said Cindy, her pen poised over the small notepad.

"Brown hair," began Joan. "I guess he was average height, maybe five ten or so. His weight, also average."

"Around one sixty?" asked Cindy.

Joan shrugged her shoulders. "I guess."

"Clothes?"

"Dark slacks, long-sleeved shirt, maybe brown. No coat. Sorry, that's the best I can do—I only saw him for a second."

"No, that's great. Age?" asked Cindy.

"Not too old; not too young," said Joan.

That will help a lot, I thought.

Cindy tilted her head in my direction. "Older than old man Chris here?"

Joan grinned. "Much younger than that," she said, tapping me on the arm.

"Okay," said Cindy as she pretended to jot down a note. "Pregeezer."

That got a bigger laugh from Joan than it deserved. But I was pleased that the two were getting along and that Joan was relaxing. Cindy took the description of the pickup from yesterday. Joan was pleased that Cindy took her more seriously than the Charleston cop had.

Joan told us that she couldn't remember anything else, and then Cindy turned to me. "I can't put this through the system, but Allen Spencer's on patrol. I'll get with him and give him this description. If that truck's on Folly, we'll find it."

On her way out the door, Cindy touched Joan's arm and said, "I'm sorry for your troubles. If you need anything while you're here, please let me know."

"Nice lady," said Joan as she watched Cindy drive away.

CHAPTER 38

Charles, William, and I were at the gallery the day after Joan saw the "killer." I had told them about the truck ramming, Joan spotting the "familiar" person, and our meeting with Cindy.

Then Charles said, "Cindy called you a geezer?"

He needed more detective lessons. I ignored him.

William took the high road and said, "From what you have so eloquently shared, it would appear that your initial concerns about Joan being paranoid with an overextended imagination could be highly inaccurate."

I figured that meant that William thought Joan was telling the truth. "I can't be certain about the death of her husband or the explosion, but yesterday's love tap by a monster truck was bone-jarringly real. Her defensive driving was all that saved us from a trip to the hospital or worse."

"I surmise that Officers LaMond and Spencer did not find the gentleman," said William.

"No," I said. "Cindy called last night and said they 'covered the island like a bad blizzard' and saw 'neither hide nor follicle' of man or machine."

"Too many places to hide a truck," said Charles. "Besides, there's no reason to think he's staying on-island, is there?"

I shook my head.

"Chris," said William, "I don't wish to complicate this matter more than it already is, but—and tell me if I could be wrong—the gentleman somehow following Joan to Folly doesn't preclude the possibility that her husband faked his own death and ignited the explosion to the family home or hired the gentleman Joan saw to set it."

"That's possible." I thought for a second. "She could have recognized him as someone she'd seen with Daniel."

"If that's true," said Charles, "why kill her?"

"Why does anyone want her dead?" I said. "Apparently someone, someone who could be Daniel, believes she knows something that's a threat."

"And," added William, "she may or may not know what it is."

We weren't getting anywhere—at least, anywhere productive—so I changed the subject. "Charles, what's the latest on your hunt for the bourbon bandit?"

Charles huffed. "Thanks for bringing that up—again," he said. "This morning the tables were rearranged and a deck of cards was placed on the center of one of the rearranged tables. Five chairs were knocked over and scattered around on the floor. Dawn locked up last night. She said that everything was fine when she left."

"What was purloined?" asked William.

"That's what's strange," said Charles as he shook his head. "Nothing—absolutely nothing was missing."

"The ghosts played a few hands of poker?" I asked.

"That's what Heather said. What's worse, I think word's out about me. Some of the 'spects are asking who I think's doing it."

"Our island does have a storied history involving ghosts," said William.

That got my attention, although I'd heard bits and pieces about ghosts in the Charleston area as well as on Folly.

"The Fifty-Fourth Massachusetts Volunteer Infantry Regiment was one of the first African American units in the Civil War. They were called colored units—and much worse." He slowly shook his head. "Anyway, the regiment fought gallantly for the Union. Accounts reveal that the unit left Massachusetts to head here in excellent spirits despite the Confederate proclamation to put all African American soldiers under what amounted to a death sentence."

"*Glory*—Morgan Freeman," said Charles.

"Correct," said William.

"Huh?" said I.

"The movie *Glory*, from the late nineteen eighties, depicted the exploits of the Fifty-Fourth," said William. "Now, Charles, if I may continue." He looked at Charles as if he were one of his students throwing spitballs at the cute redhead two seats over.

Charles leaned back. "Please do, Professor."

"In eighteen sixty-three, the regiment fought a courageous battle at Fort Wagner, which was on Morris Island, off Folly Island, past the decommissioned coast guard station. They suffered more than two hundred and fifty casualties, including fifty-three men who died in the battle or later from wounds suffered."

"Your point, Professor?" said the inpatient private investigator.

"Ah, patience, my friend," said William. "Fifty-two of the men from the Fifty-Fourth—and, a little later, the Fifty-Fifth Massachusetts Volunteers—were never accounted for, and many of the dead were buried on Folly. I have been told by people who have heard it on good authority that the ghosts of some of these young men, cut down in their youth defending their country, still haunt the island."

"Any bourbon drinkers?" asked Charles.

Scary as it seemed, I think he was serious.

William took a sip of tea I'd managed to brew and then smiled. "Most likely," he said. "Whiskey was the alcoholic drink of choice of many in those days, but I never heard it specifically mentioned. Most recent reports talk of strangers walking up to someone and even speaking before disappearing in direct view of the startled observer. Others reported smelling burning flesh and seeing shadows near the graffiti-clad concrete foundation from one of the demolished coast guard buildings. One person even shared that the ghost saved a life by telling the person about deadly rip currents and saying that others were in danger." William hesitated and looked toward the door. "I'm not certain that I believe these stories, you understand; I'm simply repeating what I have been told."

Charles pointed his cane toward Cal's. "You may not be certain," he said, "but Heather is convinced beyond a shadow of a ghost that Cal's is haunted and the haunters are stealing whiskey, money, and having a jolly good time playing cards."

William listened patiently as Charles presented Heather's theory and waved his cane around dangerously close to my head. "Let's for a moment go out on a limb and say that Miss Heather is incorrect," said William. "If a mortal creature is responsible, how is he or she entering Cal's?"

I liked the limb he was on and waited for Charles. Both Dude and William had asked the same question.

"I've not the foggiest idea," he said.

And I waited for that, I thought.

"I am not a detective like you," said William with a straight face, "but I would think that if you determined the method of entry, you would have traveled a long way toward solving the crimes for which you are being compensated to decipher."

Go, William, go.

Charles pointed his cane at William. "I don't have my official private detective license and decoder ring," said Charles. "But your question has been right up here." He put the tip of his index finger to his head. "It's got me befuddled."

"Could he or she possess a key?" asked William.

"The first couple of times, sure," said Charles. "There were several keys to the building and to where the cash was stashed. Cal had Larry change the locks. There are two keys now. Cal has one, and I have the other. If others open or close, they get the key from Cal." Charles reached in his pocket and pulled out a key ring that held three keys and a mangy-looking rabbit's foot, holding it up as if we had never seen a key ring before. He took each key and pointed it at us. "This is for my apartment; this one's the key to Cal's; and I don't know what this one's to."

"And what would be the significance of the Leporidae?" asked William.

I speculated that he meant the rabbit rather than the Latin name for a silver key ring.

"Dang, William," said Charles. "Am I going to have to start hauling a dictionary with me in case I cross your path?"

William chortled. "Sorry, my friend," he said. "I had assumed that you were smarter than the average Ursidae. Leporidae is a rabbit."

Ah, William does have a sense of humor to go with his extraordinary vocabulary, I thought.

Charles sighed and dropped his arms to his side. He refrained from asking about Ursidae and said, "Why didn't you say so?" He then waved the rabbit's foot in William's face. "Heather said it would ward off evil spirits." He looked at the appendage in his hand. "I think she may have made that up so that I wouldn't worry."

"Shocking," I said. I had had enough Latin lessons and was curious to hear how well Charles had checked out possible ways a nonghost could have entered Cal's.

Charles apparently had expanded his vocabulary as much as he could take. "Back to my point," he said. "The unsub—that's what we detectives call the unknown perpetrator, you know—didn't use a key to get in. There was no evidence that the doors were jimmied. They look good as new, or as new as an old door can look."

"It's an old building," I said. "Are there other openings like a crawl space or loose wall boards, or openings where pipes enter the building, or ... anything?"

"I've walked around it I don't know how many times," said Charles. "I can't see anything. It sits smack-dab on the ground; there's no crawl space. Three of the sides don't touch anything, and the other side shares a wall with Ada's Arts and Crafts."

Ada Yurt, an eighty-something-year-old native of Folly Beach who painted landscapes of scenes from along the coast, was the owner of Ada's Arts and Crafts. She painted as well as Heather sang and as well as sea turtles flew, but she was likable and sold dozens of paintings each year. Most of her sales were of foot-long pieces of driftwood with a grinning—according to the artist—seagull painted on them. The quality of the unique pieces of art was dreadful, but Ada was so sweet that guilt usually convinced vacationers to purchase one.

"Could someone get in Cal's through Ms. Yurt's store?" asked William.

"Already checked," said Charles with his chin held high. "Ada let me inspect the connecting wall. Checked it twice. All that's against the wall is a shelf with tubes of oil paint on it. There's no way anyone could get in Cal's from there. And if you know anyone who would like to buy a lovely painting of a seagull on driftwood, let me know." He shook his head. "I'm now the proud owner of two."

Neither William nor I jumped at that opportunity.

Perhaps it really is a ghost, I thought.

I may have had doubts about whom or what was stealing Cal's bourbon, but it wasn't a ghost that wanted to cause serious harm to Joan. And that was frightening.

CHAPTER 39

I blocked out thoughts of Joan's problems and Charles's ghosts for the next two days. The beach had an unusual influx of off-season vacationers, and I was surprisingly busy in the gallery. Charles had stopped in and hinted that he was exhausted from tending bar—until I said that I could handle the steady stream of customers by myself. He yawned, thanked me, and headed home to get his "beauty sleep." He would normally have knocked me out of the way to assume his sales manager role. He really was tired. And although he wouldn't admit it, he was worried about catching whomever or whatever.

Charles and Heather stopped by the gallery late Saturday afternoon. He wore a crimson sweatshirt with NEW MEXICO STATE AGGIES and what looked like a gunslinger on the front. Heather was more muted in a dark green blouse under a fuzzy light green jacket. She said that "Chucky" was taking her on a date and they were going to supper at Woody's, Folly's pizza restaurant of choice.

I thought about telling them to be careful, not do anything that I wouldn't do, and to be home early, but went with, "You kids have fun."

Heather wrapped her arm around Charles and giggled. "We plan to," she said.

Charles rolled his eyes toward the brim of his Tilley.

Heather stuck her tongue out at him and then turned toward me. "Hey," she said, "why don't you and Joanie double-date with us?"

Charles pulled her close to his side.

"I've had good sales today," I said. "I'm going to hang around a couple more hours. Besides, Joan and I aren't dating."

"That's not her fault," said Heather. "I heard—"

"Time to go," interrupted Charles.

Heather wasn't to be deterred. "Oh, Chucky, Woody's isn't that busy." She elbowed Charles. "Chris, Amber tells me that Joanie the ex has been in the Dog a few times asking about your social life. Heck, I saw her there myself. She was asking more questions than a lawyer on an hourly rate." Heather gave her head a big stage nod. "Yep, she's out to rehook you—no doubt."

Heather had finally said her piece and then allowed Charles—Chucky—to guide her toward the door and on their way for a hot date at Woody's.

Charles and Heather hadn't been gone five minutes when Karen called. She asked if I wanted to get something to eat. It was rare for her to call, and this was the first time she had asked me out. I said sure, adding that I was closing in thirty minutes; curiosity trumped last-minute sales.

We met at Applebee's off Folly Road, halfway between the island and her house. I preferred locally owned restaurants—McDonald's being the exception—but Applebee's was convenient, with a predictable and reasonably priced menu. Besides, I wasn't about to go against Karen's suggestion. Curiosity also trumped restaurant choices.

Karen was in a booth when I arrived. She stood and kissed me on the cheek. It felt comfortable. She wore tight black jeans, a maroon turtleneck, and her lightweight bomber jacket.

We each ordered an entree and a glass of red wine before she got to the reason for the unexpected invitation.

"I thought about the incident on Folly Road, especially in relation to the other two events that Joan went through," she said. I had called Karen the day after the truck ran us off the road and told her what had happened. "I called Officer Norton in Gatlinburg. I got his cell number when we were there."

I said I was pleased with her initiative.

"I caught him playing in the snow with his kids, but he was cordial. He asked how Joan was; he said he wondered where she had gone. Said everyone at church was praying for her." She looked at the floor as if trying to remember anything else he had said. "Anyway, I told him about the incident with the truck, and he was stunned. I didn't want to come across as telling him how to do his job, but I shared my view that the three incidents were related."

"What did he say?" I asked.

"Said he agreed—in fact, he said he wasn't happy with what happened there but couldn't convince the higher-ups to do anything. Norton said that his guys just gave a cursory look at the scene. There are several gas leaks this time of year, and occasionally one causes an explosion. He then started talking really low and said something about the medical examiner's office screwing up the tests."

"DNA?" I said.

"Yeah," she said. "They finally determined that it was Daniel in the car."

"Wow. That sure eliminates him as a suspect," I said.

"Yeah, but not much else."

"What can Norton do?"

Karen laughed and shook her head. "He asked for a description of the truck and the man Joan saw. When I finished, he said, 'Okay, all I have to do is find an average-looking guy driving a black pickup truck in the pickup capital of these here United States?'"

She reached across the table and patted my hand. "He said that he could find fifty people who fit that description in fifteen minutes and asked if I wanted to hold while he rounded them up." She laughed again. "He said he knew three people in the police station who qualified."

I smiled. Her warm hand felt good on my fingers. "I suppose finding the right one will be the problem."

"That's what he said." She squeezed my hand and then let go. "He also said that a couple of people in the church who knew some about Daniel's car business said that the last few months he seemed distant and worried about something. One of the men told Norton that when he asked Daniel what was wrong, he waved him off and said that he was having some paperwork problems with the California sale. 'Stupid tax stuff,' was how he put it."

"Did they think it was serious enough to be connected to his death?"

"They didn't know, but they were surprised that he would have missed that curve. All of them said he was a good driver."

Karen and I talked more about Daniel's situation, and she said that Officer Norton seemed interested in digging further and said he'd keep her apprised. "He told me to say hi to Joan."

We talked about a couple of her more difficult cases, how her father was doing now that he was back as chief after suffering two heart attacks; about her cat, Joe; and how beautiful the Smoky Mountains had looked during our brief visit. Something was bothering her, and she covered it with small talk.

"What's on your mind?" I asked.

She took a bite and after a moment said to me, "You do know that Joan has her heart set on getting you back, don't you?"

My mind flashed back to my first few months on Folly, when some of my new acquaintances had said almost the same thing about Amber. I had only talked to her at the Dog, and I knew that Amber had flirted, but I had seen her doing that with other customers, and she even hinted that there could be more with me. I couldn't imagine that it was true. My friends were right; now some of them were saying this about Joan. Was I wrong again?

"Come on Karen," I said. "She's lost her husband. Her house exploded. She's in an alien environment. I'm the only person she knows here."

She gave me her skeptical detective stare and nodded.

I shook my head. "We have a history, but it ended decades ago. I haven't heard from her in all these years. She needs a familiar face to give her some semblance of order, that's all. There's ... nothing there."

"Then why do I hear that she's asking about your love life? Who you've been dating? If you are in a serious relationship? Where she can find a good beautician? If anyone knows of a good Realtor she can talk to about buying a house?"

Good questions, Ms. Detective, I thought. *Good questions.*

Chapter 40

I was half daydreaming as Dude rambled on in small bursts of Dude-speak about three galaxies that I had never heard of nor cared about. We were in the Dog minutes after it opened. While Dude expounded on astronomy, I was thinking about Karen's comment after I'd walked her to her car last night. "Chris, for someone who's fairly bright, you're an idiot when it comes to women." She then firmly planted her lips on mine so I couldn't ask her to explain. Actually, at that point, I didn't care.

"Yo—wipeout!" said Dude.

Dude jolted me out of my daydream. I turned toward the door to see who he was looking at. Charles hobbled toward us. He had a two-inch square flesh-colored bandage stuck to his forehead below the brim of his hat.

"Log smack you?" said Dude.

Charles set his cane on the floor and dropped his hat on top of it. "Nope. I wasn't hit by a surfboard." He turned his back on Dude, and I was sure it was to find someone to bring coffee.

"Then what happened?" I asked, needlessly of course. He would tell us even if we had begged him not to.

"Detecting," he said, waving for Amber.

"Detectin' a tree trunk?" said Dude.

"Coffee first, story second," said Charles. His mood reflected a blow to the head.

Amber brought a cup of steaming coffee to the table, noticed Charles's bandage, and leaned over and gently kissed it.

"See," said Charles. "That's the way to treat the handicapped. Thank you, Amber. It feels better now."

"Me not be smoochin' Chuckster," said Dude as he leaned away from Charles and the table.

"Charles," I said, sounding slightly more frustrated than I was. "What happened?"

He blew across his coffee and took a sip. "Okay, if you insist."

Dude and I nodded—the nods were closer to curious rather than to insisting.

"I thought I'd figured out how the thief was getting the bourbon out of Cal's," he said. "I can't see how it's done when the bar's closed, so it must be when it's open. I figured that he had to be sneaking the whiskey cases in trash boxes and then taking them to the Dumpster. There's nothing strange about someone taking trash to the Dumpster."

Dude and I nodded again.

"After I closed last night, I got my trusty detective flashlight. Actually, it's Heather's ghost-catching flashlight. I hadn't given it back to her—"

"Story?" interrupted Dude.

"Anyway," continued Charles—finally. "I stood on one of those old wooden crates that Cal saves for some reason. I leaned over the Dumpster to find the stolen bourbon. Then I sort of leaned too far. Next thing I knew, I was in the middle of the Dumpster, stepping on boxes, moldy hamburger buns, and something that smelled like a dead duck-billed platypus."

There was no way I was going to ask how he knew that. Fortunately, neither did Dude, so Charles continued.

"I looked around using the trusty detective flashlight and noticed spots of red on a box in front of me. My eyes, and then a pain on my noggin, told me it was blood—my blood."

"Go to docville?" asked Dude.

"If that means hospital," said Charles, "no." He pointed to his forehead as if we would have forgotten where he was injured. "Not too bad; went home and dabbed some of that stingy stuff on it to kill germs and tiny varmints. Had this bandage in the bathroom since Y2K—don't remember why."

"Find firewater?" asked Dude.

Charles shook his head. "Nope."

"Bummer," said Dude.

I held back a laugh and echoed Dude. "Bummer."

Charles took another sip. "If you think that's a bummer, catch this. I went by Cal's to get a daylight view of what was dead in the Dumpster and then went inside to see how much cleanup I'd have to do later." He hesitated and then shook his head.

"Another card game?" I asked.

"Yep. Another card game. Dirty glasses on four tables, three chairs tipped over, three tables rearranged, and—you guessed it—another case of our finest bourbon gone."

"That be boss ghost party," said Dude.

I couldn't argue with that. But I wasn't ready to buy into the ghost theory. "I assume all the doors were locked?"

"As always," he said.

"Is it possible for someone to exit the building and the doors lock by themselves without a key?"

"They're deadbolted; need the key to get out. Larry made sure of that."

"So that eliminates the doors," I said.

"Guess so."

"So we're back to how they get in and out," I said.

Dude listened attentively, switching his gaze from Charles to me and then back to Charles.

"Inside job," said Dude.

"Why?" I asked.

"Know firewater there … know best hooch to steal … know where cash stashed … had time to figure how in and out. Be inside job."

"You still think so, Charles?" I asked.

"Yeah," he said. "Last night Nick told me he knew I was there to catch a thief. He said again that it had to be an outside job. It could be him. He's working too hard to direct me outside instead of looking at the employees. I don't trust him."

"Why not?" I asked.

"I think he's shorting the cash drawer," said Charles. "I can't prove it, but he's mighty secretive around the register—just a feeling. Besides, it seems like we should be doing better than we are, and he keeps flashing around money." Charles shook his head. "Cal said that if this continued, he'd be broke and the bar history."

"Is Dawn still on your list?" I asked as Amber poured more coffee and gave Dude a fresh cup of tea.

"She borrowed a twenty from me last night," he said as a nonanswer. "She needed it to pay her electric bill. I don't know if she could be doing it, but she needs money."

"What about Kenneth?" I asked. "Didn't you say Greg hadn't checked him out?"

Dude waved his right hand in the air. "Mullet man?" he asked.

Charles looked at Dude. "Kenneth has a mullet. Why?" said Charles.

"Mullet man moved here last sizzling season," said Dude. "Asked Dudester for job. Mullet filled out application. Dudester did due diligence, called references. All fake. The employers never heard of mullet man—faux."

I didn't know if I was more surprised that Dude checked references or that he knew what due diligence meant.

Charles was more interested in Kenneth's fake credentials. "He never worked at bars in Baltimore?"

"Not a ticktock," said Dude. "If I was a great detective like Chuckster, be flipping mullet man to top of bad guy list."

"Not a bad idea," said Charles. "Not a bad idea."

Dude flipped his hand in the air again. "That's enough detectin' today." He grabbed his *Astronomy* magazine and headed for the exit.

Charles watched Dude leave and then turned back to me. "Between this knot on my head and the thefts, all I have is a headache." He closed his eyes and gently touched the bandage. "I thought I could really do this. Thought I could be a detective. I'm as big a fake as Kenneth." He shook his head. "Let's talk about something else."

I felt for Charles. I felt his frustration but didn't know how to help. I also had no idea about Kenneth, but having worked in a human resources department for years, I knew the importance of checking references and the backgrounds of potential employees. I also realized that I knew very little about Joan's husband. Could something in his background have started the ball rolling downhill and the string of disasters and near disasters? One thing was sure: he had never set foot on Folly Beach, so there wasn't anything I could learn here.

"Charles," I said, "ready to take another trip to the mountains?"

"No," he said, grabbing my phone off the table. He punched in a number and after a few seconds said, "Cal, got a family emergency, gotta be away for ..." He held three fingers up to me. I nodded. "Three days ... okay, thanks." He pushed the END CALL button, set the phone back on the table, and said, "I'm ready now."

CHAPTER 41

Charles had been unusually silent for the first half of the drive. We were now on the Tennessee side of Asheville, on a curvy stretch of I-40. The temperatures were in the upper thirties, and the the snow-covered peaks of the mountain chain were directly in front of us. It was cloudy, and the sky was gray on gray. I couldn't tell the mountaintop from the gray sky. It was as if winter had sucked the color out of the hills. The look matched my mood and, apparently, Charles's as well.

"What're we going to learn?" asked Charles.

"It would be nice to learn who killed Daniel," I said—a response that seemed more than obvious. "But I'll take whatever we find."

We were on the stretch of road that occasionally suffered rock slides and had been closed for months in recent years. Mesh screening that looked like steel shrimp nets was draped on the side of the more unpredictable slopes to catch boulders instead of swimming crustaceans.

I focused on the treacherous stretch of highway but glanced at my passenger. "Joan's telling the truth about someone trying to kill her. She's in danger. A very real person rammed us off the road."

"That's good enough for me," he said. "But again, what do you expect to learn? Who's going to tell us anything?"

I didn't give him the satisfaction of hearing that I didn't know. "First, we need to visit Jaguar of Knoxville and snoop around some. And then—"

"Whoa," he said. "You mean we get to ride seven hours so we can be swarmed on by a lounge of lot lizards?"

"Lounge?" I said.

"Sure," said Charles. "That's what they call a bunch of lizards."

"Whatever," I said. "There's a higher level of reptile at Jaguar dealers. Yes, we'll check it out. You'll be in the market for a new car."

"No prob," he said. "Remember, I am a detective."

"How could I forget?" I said.

Charles was getting excited about faux-buying a new car as we passed a handful of white-water rafting billboards and then took our exit. I thought we should also visit Joan's cop friend and talk to Charlene.

The Gatlinburg Police Department was on our way to town, so I took a chance and pulled in the lot. I saw what Karen meant about black trucks. There were five trucks in the small police lot—three were black. Officer Norton was on duty but on patrol, so I told the person at the desk that I was a friend of Joan's and wanted to talk to Norton. He radioed him, and Norton agreed to meet us. He was at Ober Gatlinburg, taking statements from a couple whose car had been vandalized, and he said we could meet him there.

Charles was shocked as we drove by the ruins of the huge home that he had visited not that many days ago. I cringed when I thought of how close Karen came to falling through the floor to the concrete basement floor twelve feet below. The contractors had begun demolition and had taped large sheets of plastic on the remaining windows and stretched blue heavy-duty tarps on the portion of the roof still standing. Charles whistled. "Joan was lucky—very lucky," he said, looking back at the ruined structure.

We rounded the curve and pulled into Ober Gatlinburg's large parking lot. A City of Gatlinburg patrol car was parked in a yellow striped NO PARKING space near the entrance to the lodge. Exhaust poured from the tailpipe. I pulled in behind the car, and a trim middle-aged police officer about my height got out and waved for me to park behind him in the restricted area. His face was still tan from his Florida vacation. He greeted me with a strong handshake and a cautious grin; he was handsome in a rough-hewn way. If it weren't for ears that would put Dumbo's to shame, he would have been a striking authority figure.

I introduced Charles, and Norton suggested that we go in the lodge and get warm.

The interior of the large building looked like an oversized ski lodge. The large dining area had a massive cathedral ceiling with a view of a large wood-burning fireplace and floor-to-ceiling windows that overlooked ski runs snaking down the hill toward the lodge. A steady stream of skiers in brightly colored jackets and hats followed each other down the slope. A few weren't as successful and were sprawled in the snow—skis strewn in one direction, bodies and arms in another.

The tables near the windows were full, so we commandeered one by the railing beside the indoor skating rink. "What interest do you have in Joan?" asked the officer as we sat down. His hands were pressed against the table. His smile faded.

I would have been more comfortable with a few more courtesy comments before rushing to the meat of the visit. I started to explain that Joan and I had been married many years ago and that we had not had any contact for years, until the week before Christmas.

Norton raised his right hand and aimed it at me as he would at a car that he wanted to stop. "I got that," he said. He gave me a penetrating stare. "Detective Lawson told me your history with Mrs. McCandless." His hand returned to pressing the tabletop. "I'm talking about now. Why are you involved?"

"Her friend Charlene called after Daniel was killed," I said, skirting around the question. "Joan says she trusts me and believes that she's in danger."

He remained in a defensive pose, but his shoulders slackened slightly. He took his eyes off me and looked up at the colorful banners located around the edge of the ski rink. "She's a nice lady. She really is," he said.

It struck me as I watched him daydream that there was really no reason to trust the cop. I didn't know what was going on, and he was someone she knew fairly well. Did he like her as more than a friend? How much should I tell him about the person Joan saw on Folly?

Norton leaned closer. "Joan trusts you, so I'll try to trust you." He gazed around the dining area. "I met Joan and Daniel through church shortly after they moved here. She was all friendly like, volunteered to teach Sunday school, helped in the kitchen, and did whatever was needed. Know what I mean? Now ..." He paused and studied his hands. "I don't like to speak unkindly about the dead, but Daniel was different."

"How?" asked Charles.

Norton looked at Charles and then back to me. "Don't get me wrong. Daniel was nice and friendly, but there was something about him. He tried too hard. Know what I mean?"

I nodded but wasn't sure.

"And then he was closemouthed about his business," continued Norton. "Joan told me that he had some car lots in California. I'm a car buff, but every time I asked him about cars or auto dealers, he clammed up ... like he was hiding something." He looked back at the banners. "He would put on that car salesman smile and say some nice words—nice words without saying anything. Know what I mean?"

Charles and I both nodded this time.

Norton also nodded. "I didn't trust him—just didn't." He hesitated. "Not like I trust Joan."

"Did he give you reason not to trust him? Learn anything about him?" I asked.

The side of his mouth worked its way into a smile. "This is bad," he said. "I'm almost embarrassed to tell you." He paused, fortunately not too long or Charles would have jumped in. "I have a cousin who lives in California and works security at the Monterey airport. Daniel told me they'd lived near Carmel, and I knew Monterey was near there. I called him to see if he'd heard of Mr. McCandless. My cousin hadn't, but he said he would have a friend of his, a cop with the Carmel police, call me." He paused again.

Charles evidently decided the pause was too long for his liking. "Did he?"

Norton turned to Charles. "Yeah," he said. "The next day, I got a call from—get this—the Carmel-by-the-Sea Police Department. That's really the name of the city."

Charles reached for his pocket. I'd bet money that he was looking for a pen to write *Carmel-by-the-Sea*—another piece of useless trivia. He evidently couldn't find a pen, and he resumed listening instead.

"A sergeant called and told me that he was a good friend of my cousin's or he wouldn't have called. He didn't know Daniel, but a few of his guys had talked about him over the years." Norton looked at his watch and smiled. "Apparently, Daniel's right foot weighed more than his left. He averaged a half dozen speeding tickets a year. The sergeant said the reason Daniel still had his license was because he was a big donor to police charities and other big causes out there. Daniel was known for throwing money around. Any group with a need and a sad story hit on him. Know what I mean?"

"Sounds like a nice guy," I said.

Norton frowned. "I was beginning to think so until the sergeant started whispering. He said everyone who knew Daniel was shocked when he sold the businesses. It happened almost overnight. Rumors were that the buyer had mob ties and Daniel was somehow caught up in something, but no one knew what. Understand now—these were only rumors."

"Did Joan say why they left California?" I asked.

"Only that Daniel wanted to retire and move," said Norton.

He asked what we planned to do while we were in town. I told him that we wanted to visit Charlene. He said that we'd better hurry since she and her husband were leaving in the morning on a Caribbean cruise and wouldn't be back for a week. Charles looked at me as if to say, *Good planning*. I then told Norton that we were going to visit Jaguar of Knoxville and asked for directions. Charles added that he might buy a Jag while we were there.

"Must be nice," said Norton who then gave us directions and checked his watch again. "I've got to go guys. Sorry I couldn't help."

"We'll walk you out," volunteered Charles.

Norton stopped before he opened the door of the Chevy patrol car. "One other thing never made sense to me," he said. "Joan said they moved here so Daniel could retire, and what does he go and do but become a partner in the Jag dealership." He shook his head. "That didn't compute. But he almost single-handedly made it a success. The clowns he went into business with had no idea how to run a luxury lot. They were good at selling volume cars like Kias and Nissans. Selling high-ticket rides is another ball game, know what I mean?" He shook his head. "It bothered her so much that she never even visited the Jag lot. She thought retired should mean retired."

He was clearly in a hurry, and it was cold. I didn't ask anything else.

"I really like Joan," said Norton before closing the door. "Call if you need anything. Oh yeah," he said as he winked, "be sure to say hi to Detective Lawson for me. Know what I mean?"

I believed I did.

CHAPTER 42

We were exhausted after the drive and meeting with Officer Norton so we vegged out at the becoming-all-too-familiar Hampton Inn and headed to the car dealership just after it opened the next morning. I called Charlene on the way to the dealership and put the phone on speakerphone. She said she was glad to hear from me. I told her about the wreck on Folly, and she wanted to know all the details. She seemed sincerely shocked.

"Regardless what may have happened over the years, I don't think Joan's being paranoid," I said. Charles leaned close to the phone. "Is there anything you can add to help me find out what's going on?"

She hesitated, and then I heard her tell her husband that she'd be right there. "Umm," she said, "I hate saying this, but I never trusted Daniel."

"Why?" I asked.

"Can't put my finger on it," she said, and then she paused again. "He was too slick, too smooth. To be honest, I wouldn't have been surprised if he was involved in something illegal."

"Any idea what?" I asked.

"Not really," she said, "but it must have something to do with the car lot." I heard someone say something in the background. "Sorry, Chris. I really have to go. Please let me know if there's anything I can do."

I agreed that I would and then wished her a wonderful cruise.

We stopped at a red light about a half block from Jaguar of Knoxville.

A larger-than-life silver likeness of a jaguar—the animal, not the car—sat atop what appeared to be a marble pedestal, and a lot full of shiny new luxury cars greeted us as we pulled into a CUSTOMERS ONLY space in front of the space-age contemporary structure. To the right of the Jaguar of Knoxville building was its multiacre used vehicle lot.

"No lizards yet," said Charles as he looked around.

My cell rang before I opened the door. It was Heather. "Charles's answering service," I answered.

"Hee-hee," she said. "Is you-know-who with you?"

Instead of telling her, I simply held the phone out for him. "Are you ever going to get one of these?" I asked.

He shrugged and took the phone.

"At your service," he said to the receiver. "Uh-huh … not yet." He paused to listen, tapping the fingers on his left hand on the center console. "Really … No, I'm sure you saw the ghost … Of course … Tell Cal I'll catch it when we get back … You bet … You too."

I looked at the door to the dealership and then at Charles.

"Heather saw the ghost of Frank Fontana in Cal's last night."

"Oh," I said. "Anyone else see it?"

"Don't think so," he said. "She sort of sees things that no one else does."

This was the last conversation I wanted to be having now. "Guess you'll be catching the ghost when we get back?"

He shook his head, but said, "You know it."

I reminded him why we were here. He was to act interested in buying a luxury car, and I was to nose around. He asked me again what we expected to find; I once again told him that I had no idea. He murmured something like, "Well thought out," and we entered the double doors at the front of the curved entry.

There may not have been a lounge of lizards waiting for us outside, but the front door had barely opened before we were approached by a tall gentleman with a muscular build. He couldn't have been out of his twenties, but he carried himself like a fifty-year-old. He held his head high, had his shoulders raked back, and wore a smile that could have melted a snowball.

"May I help you?" he said as he rubbed his left hand across his temple. His hair was shiny black with a small patch of gray over each ear. I would wager that the gray was added for credibility. "I'm Bradford."

I would also wager that if he worked at the Kia lot, he would be Brad. I introduced myself, and Charles stepped to the foreground, gave his name, and told the hungry salesman that he was interested in a new Jaguar.

"My friend, you've come to the right place," said Bradford. His full attention was now focused on Charles and the burgundy Southwestern College sweatshirt with a black jaguar on the front. I was off his radar, and that was good. Bradford grabbed two brochures from a rack near the front door and asked if Charles would be so kind as to join him in his office. Charles was that kind and followed Bradford to a small office in the back of the showroom. I did not follow.

The front half of the large room was shaped in a semicircle, and five sparkling new Jaguars were symmetrically arranged on the polished granite floor like spokes on a wheel. In the center of the circle was a red version of Joan's convertible. Its top was retracted, and the sleek car was ready to drive off in the snow. Two of the other vehicles had huge red bows on the hoods—or were they the bonnets in Jaguar-speak? Elevator music filled the showroom.

I saw Charles and Bradford through the glass windows that divided the sales floor from the office. The young salesman was slowly turning the pages of a brochure, which Charles studied intently. I dreaded the ride home since I would have to listen to hundreds of bits of trivia about Jaguars.

Bradford was the only salesperson on duty, so I was able to wander around unbothered. Every wall in the salesroom except one was a huge window that either opened to the lot or the sales offices in the rear. The lone nonglass wall was dark blue and held a dozen attractively framed items. There were nine letters from "happy," "thrilled," or "elated" customers gushing over their "marvelous" new Jaguar—or the salesperson or service department. A Jaguar of Knoxville mission statement held a prominent place on the brag wall and reassured customers that the dealership looked out for their best interests and was dedicated to providing quality, ethical service, and attention. The other two frames featured professionally matted studio photos of men who appeared to be in their forties. An engraved one-by-three-inch silver plaque under the photo on the left read TAG HUMBOLDT. Alil Munson's name appeared under the other frame. To the right of Munson's frame, in the size and shape of a third frame, the paint was much brighter. I assumed that a photo of Daniel McCandless had been displayed there until he severed his relationship.

"Handsome fellows," came a voice from behind me.

I jumped as if I'd been caught checking out the *Playboy* centerfold.

"Sorry to startle you," said a smiling Alil Munson, an older version of the Photoshop-improved photo on the wall. He shook my hand and gripped my forearm with his left hand. I introduced myself.

He motioned toward my SUV. "Nice Infiniti," he said. "I'm guessing you're not here to buy yourself a new car. Perhaps a New Year's present for the missus?"

"No, actually I'm here with a friend. He's with Bradford," I said.

"Then he's in good hands," said Alil. "Anyway, it was nice meeting you. Remember, nothing says love more than a new Jaguar."

Alil walked away as quickly as he had appeared. I wiped my hands on my slacks and willed myself to forget his comment about love. Other than learning that a wall needed repainting and an owner was too vain to display an accurate, recent photo of himself, I wondered what I had thought we could determine about the death of Daniel and the explosion at Joan's house by visiting Jaguar of Knoxville.

Charles miraculously resisted Bradford's polished sales presentation, and we left with two glossy brochures proudly proclaiming "Sporty Luxury at its Finest."

"Learn anything?" I asked the budding detective as we pulled on the road to Gatlinburg.

Charles looked back toward the building. "Think I'll buy a golf cart to tool around Folly. Those cars are too powerful for our little island."

I had hoped for information that was more relevant. "Anything else?"

"Yes," said Charles. "Bradford goes by Brad, except when he's at work. His mother's originally from North Dakota; dad's from Alcoa— that's somewhere around here. He lives at home and drives a ninety-four Mustang with rust in the wheel wells. And—"

I waved my hand in front of his face. "Charles! Did you learn anything about Daniel?"

"Uh … no," said Charles. "Bradford said that he was a nice guy, but he didn't deal with him much. He did say that things changed after Daniel left. Sales dropped, and they let three salesmen go. They even eliminated two jobs in the service department—almost started a revolt with the remaining service techs because of the extra work they had to do. The vast majority of the dealer's sales are from the used-car lot, and those cars always need work."

"Charles."

"Oh yeah, he said he sure wished I was going to buy a car. He needed the money. I told him that I would have to wait a couple of months until some CDs matured. He started to jabber about easy finance terms. I stopped him and said that I only pay cash for my new cars." He turned to me. "That's the truth, you know. I've never bought a new car, but if I do, I'll pay cash."

On the way back to Gatlinburg, we decided that there was no reason to hang around the mountain resort, so we stopped at the hotel and checked out. Charles insisted that we stop for a pound of fudge before leaving town. I thought it was his best ideas in months.

The ride home would be more productive than anything we had learned in Gatlinburg.

CHAPTER 43

Charles unplugged my phone from the charger and called Cal to tell him he would be able to work tonight. He put it on speakerphone, so I was able to listen. I learned that Cal would be thrilled if Charles could make it in and close. His other employees were getting tired, cranky, and irritated by low tips. Cal also shared that no bourbon had been missing since Charles had left town.

Charles set the phone on the console and stared at it. "President Rutherford Hayes was wrong when he said, 'An amazing invention— but who would ever want to use one?' This phone thing is handy-dandy. I should get one."

He had stubbornly refused to get a cell phone, although he was using mine more often. Charles believed that stubbornness was next to timeliness, which bordered on godliness.

I shook my head and then took a turn with the phone. I called Sean Aker, a friend and attorney on Folly. Charles and I had helped prove his innocence last year when he was accused of killing his law partner. A relieved Sean had said that he owed us several favors and to call if we ever needed anything. I briefly told him about Daniel and how he had sold his businesses in California and then his share of Jaguar of Knoxville. I told him my suspicions about Daniel and asked if he could access public records and find anything about the sales, especially anything unusual. He said he'd do better. He had a fraternity brother who was a big-shot lawyer in Knoxville who should be able to find more than what was in the public records. He also knew someone in Carmel and would see if he could get anything from her.

The phone beeped three different times while I was talking to Sean. When I hung up, I saw that I'd missed a call from Joan. I returned her call, but she didn't answer. I left a message.

Charles was quiet for nearly fifty miles—a minor miracle—before he said, "I have a hunch who's stealing the stuff."

"Who?" I said.

He stared straight ahead at the interstate. "I'm fairly sure it's Nick," he said.

"Why?"

"Nothing concrete," said Charles, who glanced at me out of the corner of his eye. "The cash he keeps throwing around—and how he's always trying to blame it on outsiders."

"That's not much," I said.

"I know … I know. It's a feeling." He turned back to the road and didn't say anything for several miles.

"So," I said, "how are you going to prove it?"

"Good question," he said. "Think there's an online course in confession wrangling?"

"I doubt it," I said with a straight face. "I wouldn't count on getting him to confess."

"Then I'll catch him," he said with a nod.

Here we go again. I was glad he'd said *I'll* instead of *we'll* catch him. I wasn't ready to spend another candlelit night in Cal's, chasing rats, ghosts, or Nick.

We were thirty miles shy of Columbia. Charles was getting ready to share his master plan on how he was going to catch Nick, and I was soon to learn that President Hayes was right about the phone being an amazing invention.

The phone rang. It was Joan. "Thank God I got you this time," she said. She sounded out of breath, as if she had been running. "I saw him again. He's still here."

"Where are you, and where was he?" I asked. We were more than two hours from Folly.

"I'm home … God, I'm scared … He was … he was at the light by Snapper Jack's … He was in a silver Camry this time."

"Did he see you?"

"Don't think so … He was going toward the beach. I was walking." She hesitated. "Where are you?"

I told her and said I'd try to get Cindy to stay with her until I got back.

"Hurry," she said, ending the call.

Cindy was off duty and at the Pig when she answered. She was checking out and said she'd drop the groceries at home and then go to Water's Edge until I got there. After I told her about the mystery man being in a different vehicle, she asked if Joan could have imagined seeing him. I said that anything was possible.

I took Charles to his apartment and drove two blocks to Water's Edge. Cindy's car was in front, and she answered Joan's door. She held her service revolver behind her back until she saw that it was me. Joan had been at the top of the stairs, and she rushed to hug me before Cindy closed the door.

Her arms were tight around my waist, and I heard sobbing. Cindy stood in the entry. She shifted her weight from one foot to the other and back.

Joan finally moved back a step. "Thank you," she whispered.

Cindy grabbed her heavy jacket from the entry table and slipped the Glock in its holster. "I'll ride around a while and see if I can find the Camry. I'll call if I learn anything."

Joan hugged Cindy and thanked her for coming.

The next hour was discomforting at best. Joan offered me a drink and then something to eat. I declined. She then told me exactly two times what she had shared on the phone about seeing the Camry. She paced the living area and then flopped down on the couch. She kept asking, "Why?" I never had a satisfactory answer, and most of the times I didn't respond. There was nothing I could say that hadn't been said countless times.

I shared what Charles and I had done in Gatlinburg. Joan was irritated that we hadn't taken her with us, but then she seemed relieved that we had left her behind. She asked what her home looked like and then held her hand in front of my face to stop me before I could answer. She said she didn't want to know.

The tension slowly subsided. She occasionally yawned, her hands stopped shaking, and she stopped staring at the front door as if terrified that someone would come bursting in. I would have preferred to think my calming demeanor had helped, but it was most likely the three glasses of Maker's Mark she'd consumed.

It was nearly midnight, and her eyes fluttered. She leaned back on the couch with her bare feet on the coffee table. For the last half hour, she had drifted back to the years we had spent together, asking me if remembered various trips we had gone on—a week in Phoenix, a two-week trip through Canada, the long weekend in Cancun. I didn't remember much about the vacations. They were ancient history to me, but Joan knew the names of the places where we had stayed, what side trips we had made, and even the decor from a couple of the rooms.

Cindy didn't call, so I assumed that she didn't find the Camry, and I wondered what she would have done even if she had. There was no proof that the driver had done anything wrong. It was after midnight, and I wondered how I was going to say I had to go.

I thought she was almost asleep, but her eyes popped open, and she leaned forward on the couch.

"Stay with me."

CHAPTER 44

I was standing in the gallery and looking out on Center Street when Charles came in. He almost appeared to be back to normal, or as normal as Charles could look.

"Sleep well?" asked Charles. It was in the lower forties outside, but he only had on a bright red University of Louisville sweatshirt, faded jeans, and a Tilley. He tapped his cane on the wooden floor.

"Yep," I said. I was curious about why he asked since he wasn't usually interested in my sleep pattern.

"Hmm," he said, heading to the back room. I followed.

He slid his cane on the table and carefully placed his hat on the cane. "How's Joan?" he said as he sat.

"She was scared last night," I said, as abbreviated an answer as I could muster.

His eyes twinkled. "How about this morning?"

"Don't know," I said. "Haven't seen her."

"Oh," he said. "Well, there was an SUV that looked exactly like yours at Water's Edge when I took my morning walk."

Ah, there it was. Charles taking a "morning walk" would have been as rare as a surfing squirrel. Water's Edge was on a dead-end street that was not on his customary route from his home to anywhere, especially considering his limited mobility.

"Interesting," I said, sipping my coffee.

I interrupted Charles's not-so-subtle probing and asked if he wanted anything. He said coffee; he had to get to Cal's to clean up. I pointed to the Mr. Coffee machine. He murmured something and then said that it would be great if he could find someone to help him. He said he had asked everybody working last night, and no one was interested. Imagine that. I felt guilty and volunteered. After all, he had nearly bought a Jaguar for me.

I drove to Cal's, and he turned on the harsh fluorescent lights. I immediately knew why none of the employees wanted to help. The place was a wreck. I was afraid that ghosts from a hundred miles around had gathered for a card game and barroom brawl, but Charles assured me that last night's crowd was celebrating who-knows-what, and the mess was made by living, breathing drunks. It was there when he'd left at midnight. I started collecting beer bottles and plates from the tables, and Charles went to the kitchen to sweep the floor.

I was placing two bottles in an industrial-strength trash bag when Charles screamed. I dropped the bag and ran around the bar. Charles yelled, "Help!" He was in the small storage room, wedged between a tall Ice-O-Matic machine and the wall. He was on his knees with his left hand at the side of the ice machine. His eyes were wide, his pupils the size of quarters. His body shook uncontrollably.

"E-electric!" he yelled. His feet kicked behind him and his arm appeared stuck to something beside the machine.

He was being electrocuted. His feet were trying to push his body away from the machine, but he slipped in a puddle of water oozing out from under the machine. It was as if he were superglued to the electric cord.

Electricity would knife through me if I tried to pull him away. Neither of us would survive.

I desperately searched for the electric panel. Where was it? Had I seen it before? Stay calm … stay calm. It was nowhere in sight.

I grabbed the wooden broom handle that he had been sweeping with. I wedged the handle against the icemaker and pulled sideways on it. It moved most of his body away from the cord, but his hand held on as if it were still glued to the wire.

I moved the broom so the end was under his arm and yanked up. The handle slipped out. I moved as close as I dared and pushed the handle under his arm again. I yanked up on the handle, and his hand flew off the cord.

Charles moaned and then crashed to the floor. Sweat poured from my forehead. My hands shook.

He lay motionless. Was he dead? Should I run to the fire station for help? Should I leave Charles? Was he alive?

A weak voice coming from my prone friend answered my last question. "That was ... a shocker," said my not-always-funny friend.

At that second, those were some of the funniest words he'd ever spoken.

"You okay?"

He exhaled. "Sort of, I think."

He was still on the floor but had scooted a couple of feet from the stainless steel ice maker. He held his cane vertically with his right hand and pulled himself up on it. His face was chalk white.

"Should you be standing?" I went to his side to help. "Let me call 911 or go across the street to the fire station."

He shook his head. "Give me a minute," he said. "I'm fine ... I'm okay." He then lowered himself back to the quarry-tile floor, took a deep breath, pulled up his knees and, rested his head on them. "A minute and I'll be fine."

I was tempted to call for help but knew that would only make him mad. I squeezed his shoulder. I then carefully peeked around the side of the ice machine to see what had happened. The large machine blocked the light from the two-tube fluorescent fixture in the center of the ceiling. I had to wait for my eyes to adjust to the dim light before I could see the black electric cord that was plugged into the duplex outlet beside the machine. Three inches from the plug, the insulation on the cord was cut or frayed.

Charles's breathing was almost steady, and he raised his head from his knee and turned it toward me. "What the hell happened?" he asked.

"You sure you're okay?" I asked.

"Uh-huh. What happened?"

"Is there a flashlight here?"

He hesitated and then said, "Behind the bar, right side, big ole silver one."

I returned with the light and found that Charles had managed to stand. He wasn't shaking but was using his cane for its intended purpose.

"Let's get you to a chair," I said, nodding toward the tables in the bar.

"In a minute," he said, leaning toward the corner plug.

I pushed him back and squeezed between Charles and the ice machine. I pointed the beam at the plug and saw that I was right about the cord. The insulation was separated, and the bare wires were clearly visible. Charles was leaning over my back and saw it. "I'm lucky to be standing," he said, barely above a whisper.

I helped him to the nearest table and steadied him as he lowered himself in the chair. He argued the entire way that he was fine. I turned the breaker off and unplugged the machine; I turned the breaker back on and moved to the chair closest to Charles.

"What happened?" I asked.

"Not much," he said. His voice had regained its strength, but he wasn't back to being Charles yet. "I went back there to clean and noticed that the ice machine wasn't making any noise. Usually goes *grrrr*."

"Got it," I said with a smile.

"Cal had been having trouble with it. The building's so old that it didn't trip the breaker when the machine kicked off. He was afraid it'd start a fire. He told each of us who opened to check it first thing to be sure it was okay." He paused again, caught his breath, and then continued. "I didn't hear it working and opened the electric panel to see if the breaker had been tripped. It was fine, and then I checked to see if it was plugged in. It was unplugged, so I put the plug in the thingamajig on the wall and ..." He shuddered. "And ... well, you know what happened."

"Did Cal tell you last night to check the machine?"

"Yeah," said Charles. "He pestered us about it every night. I think he was finally ready to call a repair man."

"Who was here at closing?" I asked.

"Let's see—there was Cal, of course; Beatrice and Kristin had been waitressing and were here; then—let me think—Dawn and Nick were bartending and closed last night." He hesitated. "That's it, I think."

"Did they know you were going to be cleaning today?"

"Sure," he said. "None of them wanted to do it, so I made a big deal about coming in."

"Charles, you saw the wire," I said. "It's been stripped to the bare wire as sure as we're sitting here. Someone tried to electrocute you. And it had to be someone here last night at closing."

He stared at me and then glanced toward the ice machine and shook his head. "Nick again," he said. "He and Cal were the only two here when I left." He shook his head again.

CHAPTER 45

Charles and I had griped at each other over the years, occasionally sniped, had minor arguments, hurt each other's feelings, and shared a couple of brief shouting matches, but we had never had a major battle. Until now.

I insisted that we had to call the police. He said no. I said that someone had tried to kill him, and we couldn't let it go. He said not only could we, but we were going to. I threatened to call anyway. He said if I did, he would deny that anything had happened. I said he was being foolish and had a death wish. He said it was his death wish and none of my damn business—period!

My business or not, I was just about to cross the street to the police station when Cal came in the side door.

He had on his sweat-stained Stetson and a plain gray sweatshirt instead of his stage garb. He looked at the mess left from last night. "Hells bells, Illinois, this place won't clean itself while you're sitting there jabbering," he said. He tried to hold a frown, but it quickly turned to a big stage grin. He walked to our table. "Hey, Kentucky," he said.

I nodded but didn't say anything. Cal saw my expression and turned to Charles to see that he wasn't smiling.

"Whoops. Did I interrupt something?" said Cal. "You two look like someone burnt the wrong brand on your heifer."

That must have some important meaning in Texas, Cal's native state, so I looked at Charles to see what he would say. He didn't say anything. He was angry and, I suspected, scared. I gestured for Cal to grab a chair and then proceeded to tell him about what had happened. I didn't mention Charles's suspicions about Nick. There was no proof, and it might get in the way of Charles's "investigation."

Cal said we had to call the police. Charles emphatically said no.

Cal looked at Charles, then at me, and then back at Charles. He stood and looked toward the storage room, returned to his chair, took a deep breath, and then said, "Charles, you're fired."

"Huh?" said Charles.

Cal shook his head. "A few cases of whiskey and a few bucks—"

"A few bucks, hell," interrupted Charles. "You said the cash had been short for weeks. It could be big bucks. You said you might have to close."

"Regardless," continued Cal. "It ain't worth you getting yourself dead over." He shook his head more quickly. "I'm not going to have anything to do with you getting kilt. Your friendship is worth more than that. Yep, you're fired."

Charles tapped his fingers on the table. He looked up at the water-stained ceiling tiles and then turned his attention to Cal; then he abruptly looked back at the ceiling. "Two more days," he said. "You keep me on the payroll two more days, and if I haven't caught you a thief, I'll fire myself—won't demand severance, won't sue because of sort of discrimination, won't go postal on you, won't—"

Cal held his arms out. "Okay, okay, I surrender; forty-eight hours."

Charles looked down at the table. "Thank you," he whispered.

I thought Charles had made a terrible and dangerous mistake by not bringing in the cops. I didn't know what he had in mind with the forty-eight-hour reprieve, but I could tell he had a plan. Cal helped us clean. Charles avoided the ice machine but appeared none the worse from the shock. Cal didn't whistle while he worked, but he did hum and sing snippets of at least a hundred classic country tunes as he cleaned and moved the furniture back to its opening locations.

Sean Aker called around eleven and said that he was in Columbia for the day but had some information he thought I'd be interested in. We set a time to meet in the morning.

Joan called as we took the last two full bags of trash to the Dumpster and asked if I wanted to visit Boone Hall Plantation, one of the area's historic and beautiful plantations, located about seven miles on the other side of Charleston. I had been there a couple of times and didn't want to go, but I said yes anyway. I cared about her and knew her mental state was precarious at best. And she didn't need to be out alone. She said she'd pick me up in a couple of hours.

What a morning, I thought as Charles and I left Cal's. I had possibly saved my best friend's life; learned that Sean had actually found out something about Daniel's business dealings—something, I hoped, that would shed light on what was going on; and made a date with my ex-wife. And it wasn't yet noon.

What could possibly happen next?

CHAPTER 46

Joan's car pulled in front of my cottage and looked, with the exception of the unsightly gash on the passenger's side, as if it had just come off the showroom floor. I walked outside before the Jag came to a stop. I opened the door to a bright smile and slipped in the passenger's seat. She kissed me on cheek. She was classily dressed in black wool slacks and a bright green turtleneck sweater.

"Thanks for staying with me last night," she said. We roared up Center Street and across the small bridge off Folly Beach. "How was your room?"

"Great," I said. "I didn't want to wake you this morning, so I tiptoed out."

I didn't bring up her seeing the mystery man, and she didn't mention it. It would have been futile to tell her that I thought she shouldn't be out by herself. I knew she'd say that she couldn't stay cooped up in the villa.

As we approached downtown Charleston, she talked about how nice the weather was, how little traffic there was, and how pretty the boats looked on the Ashley River. She laughed and then became irritated at the stop-and-go traffic as we crossed the city. College of Charleston students had returned from the winter break and were lining each side of the street, lost in their own worlds. I prayed that one of them didn't step off the sidewalk in our path. The way Joan gunned it between each stoplight, I knew she wouldn't be able to stop. We got green lights at most of the intersections—a near miracle.

"You know …" she began. She had both hands on the wheel and her eyes focused straight ahead. She paused, and her lips parted a sliver and then closed. The traffic had lightened, and we approached the bridge between Charleston and Mt. Pleasant. As was our good luck this morning, she caught the last light before the bridge green. "Don't hate me for saying this," she slowly continued, "but I was disappointed when you said you'd take the guest bedroom." She continued to avoid eye contact with me.

I was speechless. She was extremely vulnerable—for good reason. Did she really mean what it sounded like? Was it simply her traumas speaking? How should I respond? Fortunately, I didn't have to.

"Do you think," she said, turning her head in my direction, "that we could ever get back together?"

Joan pulled onto the entrance ramp to the imposing cable-stayed Arthur Ravenel Jr. Bridge and accelerated. The two-and-a-half-mile-long eight-lane bridge arched up in the middle for a fantastic view of the Cooper River and the World War II aircraft carrier USS *Yorktown*, which was the centerpiece of Patriots Point Naval and Maritime Museum.

The sun glistened off the river far below the majestic span—soft, billowy clouds made it a picture-perfect day—but that was the last thing on my mind. Now what did I say?

"Joan, I … I know—"

"Oh, shit!" she said.

I looked at her and then down at the speedometer. It was pushing eighty.

Joan pumped the brake. Nothing happening. Traffic on the bridge was heavy, and there were cars on each side of us.

"Shit," she uttered again, yanking on the emergency brake lever on the console. Nothing happened. The Mt. Pleasant end of the bridge where the lanes split at the exit ramp was less than a half mile away.

I instinctively shoved my feet into the firewall.

We were in the next to right lane but had to move a lane to the left. If we didn't, we would be on the exit ramp and be going too fast to safely make the sharp curve at the bottom of it.

A green Ford Taurus was in front of us. Its driver was clueless that we were seconds from rear-ending him. Joan swerved left. Our bumper caught the rear of the Taurus but neither car lost control. The Taurus pulled to the right, and I caught a glimpse of the angry driver's face. Joan continued to ram down on the unresponsive brake. We rocketed toward the end of the bridge.

I had a death grip on the door pull. We slowed some but still topped seventy.

The yellow safety barrier that separated the exit ramp and the main road was directly in front of us. We were fewer than a hundred yards from the ramp and had to veer left into another lane to miss the deadly barrier.

Horns were blowing. The startled look of nearby drivers burned into my brain.

Joan twisted the wheel to the left fifty yards from the steel and concrete barrier. There was a tiny window of opportunity. We were almost there.

A Dodge minivan from the far left lane pulled in the opening Joan was aiming for. She yanked the wheel to the right to miss the Dodge. The seat belt and my grip on the door pull kept me from slamming into her shoulder.

The ear-shattering sound of screeching metal on metal knifed through my head. The front of the Jaguar rode up the safety railing. The yellow-and-black cushioning barrier accordioned as easily as an elephant stomping on a Styrofoam cup. A huge steel light pole shattered the windshield.

My world turned upside down. We spun sideways. The pavement raced below me. The air bag smashed my face. I heard screams. I didn't know if they were Joan's or mine.

My world faded to black.

CHAPTER 47

Stark white light ... Shut *my eyes ... Sledgehammer pounding my head ... Voices ... Who? ... Why? ... Don't understand ... God-awful ringing in my ears ... fade back to black.*

Blink ... bright lights ... pain's gone ... What's that irritating methodical beep behind me? Tube in my left arm ... Why? Where am I? ... Drifting away.

I can turn my head—ouch! Is it good that my head hurts? Does it mean I'm alive?

I try to speak—nothing. My lips sting; feel like I've swallowed sun-baked sand. There's a door to my left. A white marker board's beside it. Words and numbers are on it, but I can't read them. Everything starts to spin ...

"Mr. Landrum ... Mr. Landrum ... can you hear me?"

"Uh ... water ... dry ..." I cautiously opened my eyes. The spinning had stopped. Someone was standing to my right. "Where? Who?"

"Welcome back, Mr. Landrum. You're in the hospital. I'm Dr. Schaeffer. Do you know what month it is?"

"January," I said tentatively."

"Where do you live?"

"Folly Beach," I said.

"Do you know what happened? Why you're here?"

"I ... n-no," I stammered. *Isn't that something I should know?*

"You were in an accident," said the doctor. "You need to get some rest. I think you'll be fine."

The back of his head was all I saw as he turned to leave. I raised my head from the thin pillow to ask him what had happened. What accident? A sharp pain radiated up my neck. I let my head fall back down, and darkness returned.

*   *   *

"So how long do you plan to goof off?" Charles's familiar voice had come somewhere to my right.

My eyes fluttered open. I remembered what had happened the last time that I raised my head, so I kept it still. An IV tube was taped to my left arm; I still heard the mechanical pinging from behind the bed. There were two vases of flowers on the small table under a window on the left.

"Water?" My lips felt like sandpaper.

"Sure you don't want wine?" said Charles. He didn't wait for an answer but filled the blue plastic cup with ice and poured water over it. He topped the exotic drink off with a flexible straw.

I smiled. My lips stung. "Good job, bartender." The water tasted better than any wine. "What happened? How long have I been here?"

"Don't you remember anything?" he said.

I took another sip and shook my head.

"You've been here three days," he said. "The doc said you're extremely lucky. Your seat belt and air bag saved you. A concussion's all they're worried about. I told them not to worry. Nothing could hurt your hard head. Other than that, you have a sprained wrist and a bunch of bruises. You've been in and out most of the time—mostly out."

A couple of memories drifted through the fog—a bridge, a yellow barrier ... and ... and nothing. "What happened?"

Charles had pulled a heavy-duty green hospital recliner close to the side of the bed. "You really don't remember, do you?" he said.

I was afraid to turn my head, so I couldn't see his face. "No."

"Oh, damn," he whispered. He turned his head toward the door and then back. "I'm so sorry."

"What?" I interrupted.

Upside down ... in passenger seat ... air bag in my face ...

"I shouldn't say anything," said Charles. "Let me get the doctor."

"Charles, what?" I was almost screaming.

He reached over and put his hand on mine, something he had never done in all the years I'd known him. "You were in Joan's car," he said. He hesitated. "I don't know where you were going, but she lost control at the end of the bridge. The car slammed into a concrete divider."

Screeching, ear-shattering sounds of steel hitting steel and concrete, upside down, sparks flying, car skidding to a halt, convertible top shredded, head inches from pavement …

I slowly turned toward my friend. Tears were streaming down his cheeks.

"Joan's gone," he whispered. He squeezed my hand.

I heard his words, but nothing registered. I was chilled, and my head began to throb. I stared at a tear that slowly rolled down his face and fell to his University of Maryland sweatshirt.

He slowly shook his head. "She's dead, Chris. She was thrown out when the car flipped. She never had a chance."

I closed my eyes and let darkness suck me in.

CHAPTER 48

The soft touch of warm lips felt good on my forehead. I opened my eyes. Karen then leaned back over the side of the bed and delicately kissed my lips.

"Good morning, sleepyhead," she said.

"Thank God," I said. "I was afraid it was Charles."

She stood up straight and smiled. I blinked twice and then returned her smile. My lips stung, but it was worth it. Karen asked how I felt. I told her I felt terrible. She said she was sorry and then stepped back from the bed. A tall, burly gentleman in his thirties, wearing a navy blazer, a red-and-tan striped tie, and a close-cropped law enforcement haircut stepped to the spot that Karen had vacated.

"I hope you're feeling better," he said. His low, deep voice sounded much older than he looked. I'm Detective Adair, Charleston County sheriff's office. Do you feel like answering a few questions?"

I glanced at Karen, but she remained silent. I whispered yes.

Detective Adair turned to Karen and nodded toward the door.

"I'll be outside," she said, backing out of the room.

Adair leaned over the bed. "I know you're weak and hurting," he said, "so I'll keep this brief. I'm investigating the wreck." He waved a small notebook in his left hand. "I've talked to three motorists who witnessed what happened, and I want to get your take. Is that okay?"

"Sure," I said, "but I don't remember much."

"Yeah," he said, "the doc said that's not unusual. It may be weeks before you remember everything. Tell me what you can."

My memory was fairly clear on what led to the wreck. I remembered how happy Joan seemed to be despite seeing the mystery man the day before. I shared everything I could about both times she saw him. Adair asked if I believed that she was in danger or only imagined it. I said that I was skeptical at first, but she had convinced me there was someone.

I also remembered what she had asked about us getting back together, but I didn't tell him. I did say how desperate she had seemed when she discovered that the brakes had failed. I repeated everything twice at his request—or maybe to prod my memory of what had happened.

He said that if I remembered anything else, I should call. He put his card on the bedside table.

"I have a question," I said. He had already turned to leave but stopped and looked back at me. "It wasn't an accident, was it?"

He shook his head. "No, Mr. Landrum, it wasn't. The brakes had small cuts in them—both the front and rear lines and even the emergency brake cable. Someone wanted that car to wreck … but not until you had some time on the road. Unfortunately, they gave out at the worst possible time. I'm sorry." He turned and was gone.

Karen was back at my side before Detective Adair had time to leave the building. She pulled up the same chair that Charles had sat in the day before—or I assumed it was the day before. I was fuzzy as far as time. She was off duty and wearing the black jeans she'd had on in Gatlinburg, topped with a cream-colored sweatshirt.

"Detective Adair is good," she said. "If anyone can figure out what's going on, he can." She looked over at the flowers and then back. "I'm so sorry about Joan," she said. "She seemed like a nice lady."

I fought back tears and nodded.

"I saw Charles out there," she said, motioning toward the corridor. "Did you know he's been in this chair for hours at a time? He spent the first two nights here." She tapped the side of the chair, looked toward the door again, and then smiled. "I had to threaten to shoot him if he didn't go home last night. He said he would leave only if I stayed."

I dried my cheeks with the back of my right hand. I was touched. "What did you say?"

"I didn't say anything," she said. "He knew I'd stay here. He grumbled and grumbled and then finally left." She grinned. "For what it's worth, this is not a comfortable chair."

I halfheartedly said that nobody had to stay. She firmly said that yes they did, end of discussion.

"Oh yeah," she said, "Charles said they're releasing you tomorrow. Said you'd need to take it easy, but they can't do any more here."

"The doctor told Charles that? When were they going to tell the patient?"

"They thought Charles would tell you. He pestered them so much that they finally told him to shut him up."

That I believed. I knew it violated some laws, but I also knew Charles.

"Are you working with Detective Adair on this?" I asked.

"No," she said softly. "It's a murder investigation, and I'm too close to one of the people involved. It's in good hands."

Karen stayed another hour and helped me take a short walk a few doors down the corridor. I hurt, but it felt good to move on my own.

Dosage of my meds must have been reduced. I couldn't sleep. It wouldn't do any good to wallow in self-pity about what had happened during our marriage. I couldn't beat myself up about not saving her. I had a few flashbacks of the crash but even more flashes of anger. Joan was murdered, plain and simple. I had to do something about it—I had to.

CHAPTER 49

"Whee! This is fun," said Charles.

The nurse had experienced a serious lapse in judgment and had given Charles the reins of the wheelchair with orders to push me "slowly and carefully" to the car parked in front of the hospital. He was in his sixties, and she probably thought that his ever-present cane would hold him to a reasonable pace. Wrong! He was weaving the chair—with me gripping the armrests—around the brightly colored floor tiles and trying not to hit any of the patients walking down the corridor, slowed by the rolling IV stands they were pulling. He would never admit it, but I knew his antics were to distract me from the harsh reality of the last few days.

As much as Charles's childish driving jarred my already aching head and sprained wrist, I was glad to be riding to the exit. I declined his offer to help me in the car. I could see nothing good coming from his balancing the wheelchair, the car door, and me. He pouted but finally stood aside and let me maneuver inside unaided. The backseat was full of vases and flowers from my friends. Giving me fresh-cut flowers was like giving Ray Charles a portrait of Big Bird—they were useless to me—but it was the thought that counted. And I was blessed to have friends who cared. My stomach soured when I realized that Joan would not get to know them as well as I did.

I was in a haze for the next five days. Karen came by each day after work. She brought food from various restaurants. Her dad, Chief Newman, called each morning. I had a hunch his daughter made him call to see if I was alive. Dude called four times for a total of under three minutes although three minutes of Dude-speak was equivalent to about two hours of normal conversation. William Hansel stopped twice on his way home from school. Amber hadn't called or visited, but Charles assured me that she had asked about me regularly.

Cindy LaMond rode by several extra times when she was working and had her colleague, Officer Spencer, make extra runs when she wasn't on duty. Finally, Cal got the biggest laugh from me when he called and sang three verses of "Drop-Kick Me, Jesus (Through the Goalposts of Life)."

Regardless how many friends called or stopped by to cheer me, feed me, or just to see that I was still kicking, my mind kept going back to one of the last things Joan had said: "Do you think we could ever get back together?" Did she mean it? We had reconnected some during the last few weeks, but she didn't know who I was or, more accurately, who I had become. True, I was developing feelings for her; we did have many years of shared experiences—mostly good times and, of course, a few bad. I had loved her deeply those so-many years ago, but … it didn't matter now. She was gone.

Charles was on my doorstep each morning at ten o'clock sharp. He had convinced Cal to let him work a couple of more weeks as long as he didn't do anything stupid like grabbing a hot electric wire or spending the night alone in the bar trying to catch either a thief or a ghost. He blamed me for needing the extra weeks. The second day I was home, Charles and I walked around the block. It took longer than it should have, but I made it. Charles had never had a real need for the handmade cane he'd carried as long as I'd known him—until now. We were quite a pair: me with my bandaged wrist and walking at the speed of a tired turtle, and Charles still walking with a slight limp.

The next three days, we walked two blocks to the beach and another couple of blocks in the sand. The winter fog rolled in from the ocean and was so thick two of the days that we couldn't tell the sea from the sand and the sky. It felt good to be moving, and at the end of the fifth day, I declared myself well. I figured I could only hurt myself. Besides, all the phone calls and visits were driving me crazy. It seemed that I alternated between being depressed over Joan's death and happy that I was alive.

My friends were a great help and went out of their way not to mention the wreck. But I knew I had to do something—I owed it to Joan.

"Chris," said Charles after we had returned to the house from our walk the fifth day, "I know how the thief gets in."

"Really?" I said. I had asked him about it each day, but he had avoided answering. This was the first time he had brought up the topic since the wreck.

"Ceiling," he said.

"And?" I prodded.

"You know how the tables are messed up, cards everywhere, and a chair or two on the floor?"

"Yeah, ghosts," I said with a dash of sarcasm.

We had grabbed our usual chairs around the table in the kitchen. I got each of us a Diet Pepsi, anxious to hear the rest of his theory.

"Wants us to think it's ghosts," said Charles. "Here's what happens." He nodded his head like he was trying to convince both of us. "The water-stained ceiling tiles got me thinking, so I borrowed a ladder from Larry and pushed up a couple of them—those over by the wall are shared with Ada's Arts and Crafts. I knew the thief wasn't coming thorough a door. We checked the walls and found nothing, and the building sits on dirt and sand—no way short of digging a cave to get in from under it." He pointed his cane at the ceiling. "So it had to be the ceiling. Did you know that Cal's building is about a half story taller than Ada's?'

I could honestly shake my head no.

"It is," he continued. "There are plumbing pipes in the space betwixt the drop ceiling and the roof. And here's the key. There's an entry hatch between the roof of Ada's and Cal's for plumbers to get to pipes and stuff. Can't see it from the ground."

"Hmm," I said.

"Yep," said Charles, who by now was feeling pretty full of himself— perhaps for good reason. "There are crossbeams in the ceiling and a four-by-eight-foot sheet of plywood plopped down on two of them. And get this: there's one of those screwed-to-the-wall ladders to the roof of Ada's on the other side of her store. It's behind the trash Dumpster, well hidden. The thief bops up the ladder to Ada's roof, hops over and opens the hatch, works his way on the support beams, stands on the plywood, lifts a ceiling tile out, and drops down to the table."

"Isn't the ceiling in Cal's about nine feet high?" I asked. "He—I mean, your perp—wouldn't be able to reach a tabletop, would he?"

"Good thinking. Eight and a half feet to be exact. Measured it myself," said Charles. "Getting in's the easy part—just drop down a couple of feet to a table. Since the dead bolt needs a key, getting out's a bear. That's where the ghosts come in." Charles folded his arms as if to say, *So there.*

Maybe it was the effects of my concussion, or possibly I wasn't as good a detective as Charles, but I needed more.

"Okay, my brain-addled friend, I'll slow this down for you. To get out with the loot—liquid and monetary—the thief has to carry it to the table he dropped down on and then put one of the chairs on the table and then use the table and the chair as a ladder so he's high enough to set the loot on the plywood in the ceiling and then climb back out. Follow so far?" He held out his hands, palms up.

I went to the gurgling coffeepot and poured two cups. "It's Nick."

"Why'd you say that?"

"You keep saying *he.* I figured that eliminated Dawn, and you said he was there the night before you were almost electrocuted."

"Yep, it's him—no doubt, I think," he said. "Let me continue."

"Go ahead," I said, putting my feet on the stool and leaning back in the chair.

"So now he has the loot and could easily leave the same way he got in, but the problem is that there's a chair on the table in the bar. With that big clue, one wouldn't need to be as brilliant a detective as yours truly to figure out how the thief got in and out."

"True," I said. "So he moves some of the tables around, puts cards and glasses on them to make it look like someone was playing, and knocks a couple of chairs over so when he leaves he can kick the chair off the table and it will look like the ghosts did it."

"I think your noggin's back to normal," he said. "You got it."

"Can you prove it?" I asked.

"Nope," he said. "And before you give me a lecture about thinking something and proving it being two different things, I know that. I've got to catch him."

"And how do you plan to do that?" I asked.

He frowned. "I'm going to catch him tomorrow night."

Uh-oh. I shook my head. "How?"

"He's going to break into Cal's," he said. He pointed his cane toward the ceiling again.

"What makes you so certain?" I said, looking to where he pointed the cane.

"I may not be exactly certain," he said, "but I'm almost sure." He paused, and I stared at him. "Last night I worked until midnight. We were busy. There were tourists from Quebec at the Tides, and they came over for libations—"

"Okay, I got it. Now back to Nick."

"Hmm," said Charles. "He and I were tending bar. You know how cranky he is. Well, he kept humming. It was the happiest I've seen him. He said he's ready to 'skip this burg' and is heading out day after tomorrow."

I hoped that wasn't all he had. "Tomorrow night?" I said.

"Oh yeah," he said. "He got a call from some guy about eleven. He was in back, so I asked if I could take a message. The guy on the phone told me to tell Nick that he expected his stuff in two days, or else."

"Who was it? What stuff and 'or else' what?" I asked.

"He didn't say. Said Nick'd know. When he got back, I gave him the message. I asked if everything was okay. He laughed and said fine. His face was laughing. His eyes said it was a big fat lie."

"So you think he's stealing for this guy?" I said.

"What else could it be?" he said, nodding as if it were as clear as a confession.

"Let's say I buy the story," I said. "What's to say he won't break in tonight? Why tomorrow?"

""Your mind's working fine," he said. "Remember I told you that everyone who's working at Cal's seems to know why I'm there?"

"Yeah, you said a couple of them asked if you had learned who was stealing the stuff."

"Last night Nick asked me if I figured out how the ghosts were getting the whiskey out of the locked building." He paused and peered at the bottom of his coffee cup. "He must think I'm really dumb to think it's ghosts. I told him that I was going to spend tonight—all night tonight—in the bar and try to catch the ghosts, or in the unlikely event it is a human, catch him."

"What'd he say?"

"That it sounds like a good plan." He wiggled his forefinger back and forth. "He didn't mean it."

"So you figure he'll wait until tomorrow night, get the case to whoever called, and then head out of town."

"Yep," said Charles. He held his chin high and grinned. "And Detective Charles will be there to thwart the perfect crime."

"So what time do I meet you there?" I said.

Charles smiled. "I hoped you'd say that," he said. "Besides, there's something I want to show you."

If I'd known how important what he had to show me was, I wouldn't have waited.

CHAPTER 50

The funeral home director wasn't able to find any relatives of Joan's. He had left messages for me at the hospital. When I returned the call, he had visited my hospital room the first day that I could speak coherently. I'd told him that I didn't think she had any living relatives but to check with her friend Charlene. I also said that she wanted to be cremated like her husband.

The director called early in the afternoon to say that Charlene didn't know of any relatives either, and that he had verified with the funeral home in Tennessee that Daniel had been cremated. Only then did he honor Joan's wishes. I was irritated that he had to verify that Daniel had been cremated; I didn't see what it had to do with her wishes. He was speaking in his best "I am so sorry" funereal voice, so I just thanked him. I told him I would pick up the urn in a couple of days. I wasn't ready to face reality.

I was still weak and stretched out on the couch, trying to nap. I should have known not to be so optimistic. Karen called as I drifted off.

"Wanted to see how you felt," she said.

"Much better," I said, and hoped she couldn't tell that I was nearly asleep.

"Feel up to a ride?" she asked.

A change of scenery would do me good. I said yes, and she agreed to pick me up and deliver me back to the house. I said I couldn't ask for a better deal. She laughed and said she'd see me later.

*   *   *

"Detective Adair thinks you're in danger," said Karen.

We were driving through the historic areas of Charleston, south of Broad Street.

I looked at her and then at the stately mansions. "Really?"

"If Joan was killed by the person who killed her husband, he must have thought that she knew something incriminating against him. I'd guess something that either she learned on her own or that Daniel told her." She hesitated. "It would be logical that the killer thinks Joan told you what it is."

"I know," I said, and paused. *I want him to come after me*, I thought, but I didn't tell her that. Karen didn't speak, so I continued. "How's the investigation going?"

"Nothing new," she said. "Whoever cut the brake lines knew what he was doing. The lines were cut only enough so they'd drain slowly. She'd have time to drive several miles. That would increase the chances of her building up speed and having a more devastating result. I suspect that the person knew about Joan's history of speeding." She paused and slowly shook her head. "But that doesn't narrow it down much since any mechanic or someone good with tools could have done it. Instructions are all over the Internet."

"That's comforting," I said.

"The lines were tampered with the night before," said Karen. "There aren't surveillance cameras near where she parked, and apparently no one saw anything." She shook her head. "Both our guys and the Folly police have been looking for anything suspicious involving the kind of truck Joan reported, but we don't have any reason to stop every Ford F-250. Even if we did, we don't know what he looks like."

"What about the Gatlinburg police?" I asked.

We had parked along the elevated walkway overlooking the bay.

Karen gazed at the water and then back to me. "Good question," she said. "I called Kevin Norton and told him what had happened here and what we knew—more accurately, what we didn't know. He was devastated and said that he'd push to have the explosion checked, this time by the pros. Maybe that'll turn up something, although I doubt it since he said the contractor has almost finished the demolition."

I told her that I was going to the funeral home in the morning to get

Joan's ashes. She asked if I wanted her to go with me. I thanked her but said it wasn't necessary. I wanted to do it by myself. I also didn't see any reason to tell her about what Charles and I would be doing tomorrow night. I didn't want her to try to talk me out of going, and I knew she wouldn't stand a chance of derailing Charles.

On the drive home, she asked me if I wanted her to spend the night. I reached over and squeezed her arm and said that I would love for her to, but that I was exhausted and wouldn't be very good company.

She smirked and said that she wasn't looking for good company. "Next time," she said.

I smiled.

CHAPTER 51

The day Charles and I were going to catch a thief was supposed to be sunny and unseasonably warm—much like my last day with Joan. I slowly climbed out of bed before sunrise. I had been awake an hour before that. I wanted to sleep, but my mind wanted to relive the wreck, what Joan had said about getting back together, and the poignant moment that Charles, William, Joan, and I had spent in the bucolic cemetery in Cades Cove.

Listening to Mr. Coffee slurp out the last drops, I wondered what Charles wanted to show me and what Sean had learned about Daniel's businesses.

I spiraled deeper in the dark hole of reality as I wondered if I really was too old for Karen, or Amber, or any relationship. And then I wondered if I really was in danger. Did I know something and not realize it?

A steaming hot shower did more good than a few years of therapy might have done. I was refreshed, most of the negative thoughts washed down the drain, my aching wrist and legs loosened, and I was able to face the task of picking up Joan's remains.

"Why did you bring your camera?" I asked Charles. The trip to the funeral home had been physically and emotionally exhausting, and as strange as it sounded, I was almost looking forward to whatever the night would bring. We were sitting in the dark bar at Cal's. The only illumination came from the Bud Light neon sign behind the bar. Charles had left work before Cal, Dawn, Nick, and Beatrice, and he said that he made a big deal about going home. He told them he was tired and would be glad to have a few days off from work. I thought he might have overdone it, but he was the detective.

He picked the Nikon up off the table. "If it isn't Nick, I thought I'd photograph a few ghosts," he said. "Just kidding. Look at this." He switched the camera on, turned the three-inch playback LCD monitor toward me, and pushed the view button. A photo of a man in his thirties coming out of the Piggly Wiggly was on the screen.

I didn't recognize him. "Who's this?" I asked.

"I was thinking," he said.

"Dangerous," I said, rolling my eyes.

"Pay attention," he continued. "When you were lounging around in the hospital," he pointed his cane in the direction of Charleston, "I was looking for a murderer. You told me you hadn't seen the person who Joan saw—the person from her past."

"I didn't," I said.

"Think about it," he said. "Maybe you saw him when you were with Joan—a time when she didn't see him but you did. Could have been someone who was looking at you two and you subconsciously noticed. Or …" He stopped and perused the room as if he thought a ghost had appeared and was eavesdropping. "Or someone you noticed doing something strange and you didn't think about it at the time."

I looked down at the camera and shook my head. "Charles, that's a mighty leap," I said.

"I know," said Charles. "Humor me. I cased a few popular visitor places over the last week and took pictures of fifty-nine people. They're all there," he said, nodding toward the camera. "Flip through the shots and see if anyone strikes your fancy. What else do you have to do?"

"Why not?" I said. I figured there was a zero chance of seeing anything significant but was touched by Charles's work while I was lounging around the hospital.

I recognized Piggly Wiggle in the background of some. There was also Bert's, the Tides, Planet Follywood, the Folly Pier, the Morris Island lighthouse, the Dog, and even city hall. But I didn't recognize any of the men in the monitor. I had seen several of them around town but not recently. A few were out of focus, and there were five who seemed more familiar than the others, but that was it.

I felt bad that Charles had spent hours taking the photos. I thanked him and said that it had been worth a try. I handed him his camera, and he nearly dropped it when we heard a screeching sound from the direction of the wall between Cal's and Ada's Arts and Crafts. It wasn't a mouse this time. It sounded remarkably like the sound effect that old movies used when someone was opening a rusty-hinged door in a haunted house. My first thought wasn't about a ghost but a real person—a real person who might drop in on us any minute … a real person who could have a gun, a knife, or a variety of other lethal weapons, when all Charles and I had were his cane and the Nikon.

Bad ankle, sprained wrist, concussion or not, we quickly slipped behind the bar before the intruder began to lift the ceiling tile. I had barely caught my breath before a stained tile disappeared above the ceiling and a beam of a light came from the opening and illuminated the top of the table directly under it. A pair of legs in tight black jeans then dangled down.

The body connected to the legs gracelessly dropped from the ceiling to the table. The landing pad rocked and nearly tipped over when the feet hit. Cal's mysterious thief was standing twenty feet in front of us. It wasn't the ghost of Frank Fontana or any of his poker-playing, whiskey-drinking, bar-wrecking ghost buddies. Detective Charles was half-right—a real live human being hopped off the table.

But it wasn't Nick.

CHAPTER 52

"Oh, damn! Crap," she said as Charles aimed his flashlight at the intruder. "Who's there? Put down that damn light."

Charles lowered the light and walked to the front of the bar. He stood between the intruder and me. He raised the light so it reflected off his cane. "Hi, Dawn," he said.

The beam from Dawn's small penlight tried to find us. "Is that you, Charles?" came the crackling voice from beside the table. "Damn, it is you."

"You know my friend, Chris, don't you?" The ever-polite private detective shone the flashlight at my face. I raised my hand to block the blinding beam.

"Yes," was all she said. Charles pivoted and aimed the light back at her face. She looked toward the exit door and then back at Charles. Her shoulders sagged. "Don't guess you'd believe I stopped by to clean?"

Charles chuckled but kept the light aimed at her as he walked to the switches behind the bar and flipped on the fluorescent tubes. Both hands were in front of her. One held the light, the other moved around as if it didn't know what to do with it. I was no longer worried about her having a weapon. She blinked when the lights came on. I saw tears in her eyes.

"Didn't think so," she said. "Oh, damn. You set me up, didn't you? You were supposed to be here last night." She shook her lowered head. She reminded me of a basset hound that had been yelled at for peeing on a new rug. "All I wanted was enough money to leave town." She held her thumb and forefinger about an inch apart. "Two more weeks and I would've been gone. Gone from my ex." She kicked the table leg. "Crap."

Charles tilted his head, looked at Dawn, and then turned to me. "Chris … umm."

He then turned back to Dawn, rolled his eyes, and sighed. "Chris," he said. His body faced Dawn, but he turned his head my direction. "Would you have a seat over there?" He pointed his cane at the table closest to the front door. "I'd like to talk to Dawn a minute."

I didn't see that I had a choice, so I walked to the table, grabbed one of the chairs, and sat. Charles motioned for Dawn to follow him, and he walked to the small storage area—the site of his near electrocution.

It was after three o'clock, and I was tempted to put my head on the table and fall asleep. My wrist ached from the wreck, and my shoulder still hurt from the fall in Gatlinburg. Regardless of what I had been through, I had no business being awake, much less in a bar, at this ungodly hour. I heard the muted voices of Charles and Dawn but couldn't tell what they were saying.

A half hour later—a half hour that seemed like three hours—Charles followed Dawn to the side door that led outside. He unlocked the door and handed her a small folded piece of paper. She hugged him and mumbled something before she left. Charles watched her for a minute and then closed and locked the door.

He put the flashlight back in its resting spot behind the bar and opened the beer cooler and took out a Miller High Life. He then walked to the cabinet in the back bar and took out an opened bottle of Cabernet. With a wineglass in hand, Charles hooked his cane on his forearm and headed to my table with the beer, bottle of wine, and wineglass.

He poured a half glass of wine and took a sip of beer. Three steps beyond confused, I didn't say anything.

He sat down, took a sip of beer, and said, "Heather was right. Frank Fontana's ghost and his gambling buddies have been stealing whiskey."

"Charles, you—"

He put his hand in front of my face. "I saw Frank and his friends." He looked around the bar and then directly at me. "Didn't you?"

I slowly shook my head. "If you did, I did," I said.

"I did," he said. "I think they'll be visiting every once in a while and slipping some money back in the till to pay for all the whiskey and cash they borrowed." He nodded. "Yes, I think they will."

I smiled at Charles. "Hope they stop playing cards and messing up your bar," I said.

"They'll be moving their poker game far away," he said.

Charles had bought whatever explanation Dawn had given him. I was tempted to point out that it wasn't Nick who dropped in, but I didn't want to ruin his catching the thief. I've always said that he would give you the T-shirt off his back. He was generous to a fault. Tonight he may have crossed that fault line. But if it was good enough for him, it was good enough for me.

"Can we go home now?" I asked.

"Not until you climb on that table and put the ceiling tile back," he said, pointing his cane at the hole in the ceiling.

What are friends for? I thought.

CHAPTER 53

Charles was driving my SUV up the mountain on I-26, between Spartanburg and Asheville. The doctor had told me not to get behind the wheel unless I absolutely had to, so I handed the keys of the Infiniti to the person who hadn't driven a motor vehicle since his Saab became a lawn ornament a couple of years back. Tractor-trailers were banished to the right lane, and Charles zipped by them as if they were at a red light. A thick layer of snow was on top of the mountain, but we were at a low enough altitude to enjoy the beauty of the white stuff without driving in it. A powerful cold front accompanied by several inches of snow was predicted for east Tennessee in three days, so I decided this would be the best time to make the long drive to Cades Cove and give Joan the burial that she had requested.

"I need one of these. This is fun!"

Charles asked if we got on I-40 at Asheville, and I was telling him to pay attention to the mechanical voice of the navigational system when my phone rang. It was Sean Aker, who said he had interesting news about Daniel's sale of the car dealerships in California and about selling his share of Jaguar of Knoxville. Sean's friends had accessed records of both sales. He said that I owed him a big fat juicy steak for what he was going to tell me.

Charles successfully navigated the transition in interstates, and I listened to Sean without interrupting. For fifteen minutes, he walked me through the complex financial transactions. He finished, and I asked him to dumb it down. He said that he'd try but doubted that it could be made that dumb. I gave the appropriate laugh, and he continued.

My heart was thumping so loudly when he finished that I thought we had a flat tire. I told Sean that he'd not only earned a steak, but I would buy him a bottle of Dom Perignon to guzzle before cutting into his entrée. He said he would hold me to that. I didn't have all the details, but I had been right about Daniel and his partners.

"Charles, do you still have those photos?"

He nodded and jerked his right thumb toward the backseat.

I turned and grabbed his camera from under a lightweight jacket that he had reluctantly brought along.

My heart raced. I began scrolling through the images that he had shared with me in the middle of the night. My hand shook so badly that I kept hitting the scroll button twice and skipping photos. A handful of the people looked familiar, and I assumed that I had seen them on Folly. I stopped when I got to number thirty-seven. It was one of the slightly out-of-focus images. I tried to burn it in my mind. I closed my eyes and then opened them and examined it again.

I turned the camera off, returned it to the backseat, took a deep breath, and then looked at Charles.

"I know who killed Daniel and Joan," I said. "And I know why."

Charles was overly enjoying being behind the wheel. He had cruise control set on seventy-seven and said whee each time he passed a car. After I made my proclamation, he pulled into the right lane and slowed to the speed limit. "Do I have to have to guess, or are you going to tell me?"

I agreed to tell him if he stopped saying whee. He said that I drove a hard bargain, but he would try. For the next twenty miles, I shared the dumbed-down version of what Sean had shared, and how I had recognized the killer from the photographs Charles had taken. He reminded me how *detectively great* his idea was to photograph the strangers on Folly. I agreed that it was a *good* idea.

"Can you prove any of this?" he asked as we pulled off the interstate for the final leg of the trip.

"Don't think so," I said. "All we know is that the killer was on Folly Beach when you took his picture."

He tapped his right hand on the steering wheel. "As a good friend of mine pointed out the other day, it's one thing to know something, another to prove it." He turned to me and raised his eyebrows. "So how are *we* going to prove it?"

"Let's figure that out tonight," I said. "This afternoon we're taking Joan to join her husband."

I made two calls before we got to Gatlinburg. Charlene was back from her cruise, and I was pleased when she answered. I apologized for the late notice and told her where we were going, asking if she wanted to be there when I spread her friend's cremains. She said yes before I had time to tell her when. I asked if she wanted me to pick her up, but she said she knew the spot and would meet us there in three hours.

The second call was to Kevin Norton. Karen had given me his cell number, and I caught him during a lull. I again apologized for the late notice and told him the plan. He said a band of bank robbers couldn't keep him away.

As we pulled on Parkway, the main road through Gatlinburg, Charles told me that he wouldn't be able to ponder how to catch a killer on an empty stomach. We had a couple of hours before gathering at the cemetery, so I directed him to a public parking lot, and we walked a couple of blocks to the Pancake Pantry for a late breakfast.

The Pantry was nearly full, so we didn't get one of the prime tables near the windows. We were seated, and for the first time I noticed that Charles had on a solid black sweatshirt—not adorned with a single college logo or name. If this wasn't a first, it was close, and I said that to him. He looked down at his chest and said it was out of respect for Joan; he was in mourning. His sensitivity was touching.

Charles's mouth was full of orange walnut pancakes, but he managed to murmur, "The way I see it, there are two ways we can get proof—an easy way and one that might get you killed."

"The easy way is?" I asked, taking a bite of chocolate chip waffle.

"Duh," he replied. "We call the cops. Let them figure it out." He waved his fork at me. "That's what you'd tell me to do."

"True," I said. "But I don't see what they would find. At best, there's circumstantial evidence."

"Then we either need to get a confession or let him kill you." Charles hesitated and waved his fork in my face again. "I suppose it would be better if he didn't actually kill you—just tried to."

"Thanks," I said.

We spent the rest of breakfast talking about possible ways to get the killer to confess or get caught *unsuccessfully* trying to kill me. We bandied about many ideas, but nothing approaching a foolproof plan emerged.

*   *   *

A thick layer of puffy white snow had fallen since our last visit to the peaceful, isolated cemetery. The small parking area was covered, and there was no evidence of recent visitors. The temperature was in the low twenties, so Charles and I waited in the comfort of the car for the other two.

A silver metallic BMW 650 pulled in beside us. Charlene was behind the wheel. She smiled but remained in the car. It was ten minutes before the time I'd told everyone to be there, so I figured we would wait in heated comfort until Kevin Norton arrived. We didn't have to wait long. A boxy older model black Ford Explorer turned in the lot and pulled up on the passenger side of my SUV. The side window of the Explorer was covered with dirt and dried slush, but as dirty as it was, I recognized Norton's ears.

I grabbed my coat from the backseat, and Charles and I stepped in the foot of fresh snow. Charlene walked around her BMW and greeted us with a sisterly hug. She had on a long black coat. As a concession to the conditions, she wore dark green rubber boots that looked as if they would be more at home in a garden. Officer Norton was in a dress uniform like you see when police gather at a funeral of a fallen colleague. He explained that he had taken a few hours of leave. He said he would do anything for Joan. He was near tears as we exited our vehicles.

The funeral home hadn't known what I had planned for the cremains, so they had selected a simple shoebox-shaped brass container to hold the ashes. I took it from the backseat, and the four of us created a path through the snow to the section of the cemetery where Joan had stopped on our previous visit. The top of the tombstones were covered with snow, the branches of nearby trees were topped in white, and a light, powdery snow had begun to fall. We huddled close together, and for an awkward minute, none of us knew what to say. I suggested a silent prayer, and everyone nodded. I wished William had been there to sing "Amazing Grace."

Charlene dabbed her eyes with a tissue that blended with the falling snow. Tears ran down Kevin Norton's cheeks as he stood at attention. Charles was uncharacteristically silent. My hands shook so much that I had trouble opening the latch that held the top on the container.

My fingers were numb, and the brisk wind out of the north swirled the falling snow around the graveyard. I opened the box and fumbled with the opener on the clear plastic bag inside. Charles took the brass container so I could handle the plastic bag.

I slowly sifted the contents in an arc in front of me. The only sounds I heard were the wind moving nearby tree branches and Charlene's sobs. Norton stared straight ahead. Charles held his Tilley over his heart and bowed in silence. I wiped tears from my cheeks with my forearm. It was all so sad.

Before she climbed into her luxury car, Charlene thanked me for inviting her and gave me a more sincere hug than she had during her initial greeting. Norton shook my hand as we reached his Explorer. His cheeks were still damp from tears. I was surprised when instead of shaking his hand, Charles asked Norton if he could meet us at the hotel. The police officer did a double take at my friend, looked at his watch, and said that he had some time before going back at work.

"Okay," I said. Charles and I pulled back on the loop road headed out of Cades Cove. "What's that about?"

His knuckles were red as he tightly gripped the wheel. He barely glanced my way and said, "Catching a killer."

I was confused. "I thought we agreed that we weren't going to tell the cops," I said.

"We're not," he said. "We're going to tell Joan's friend."

Who happened to be a cop. Charles shared his plan, telling me what he thought might work. I said that I hoped for something better than *might* work. I threw out some ideas. He gave his opinion and suggested other approaches. He said, "No way." I said, "I think it'll work." By the time we reached the hotel, we had agreed on the best plan that could have been created while driving in the snow along the stark, narrow roads, in the Great Smoky Mountains.

Now all we had to do was get some assistance—life-and-death

assistance—from Officer Kevin Norton. For a second, I wondered if I was wrong. What if the killer was Norton? He had the means and, I suspect, a thing for Joan.

Lord, let me be right.

CHAPTER 54

The highway department had done an admirable job of moving the five inches of newly fallen snow off the main roads. I was on mostly-clear Highway 441, between Gatlinburg and Sevierville, better known as the birthplace of Dolly Parton. This was the first time I'd driven since the wreck, and my hands were gripping the wheel so tightly that they were losing feeling. And I had only been on the road for ten miles of the thirty-five-mile drive to Jaguar of Knoxville.

Charles and I had met with Kevin Norton for an hour yesterday.

I shared with him who had killed Joan and why. Daniel had proof of the killer's illegal activities, and had used it against him. I said that it had gotten him killed.

Speaking of proof, Kevin had asked what proof we had.

"None," we admitted.

"So why are we here?" he'd asked.

That's when we shared our bare-bones plan. He told us we were idiots. I didn't totally disagree, but I reminded him of his comment that he would do anything for Joan. He thought we needed to go to the state police with our accusations, but after we walked through what we actually knew, he agreed that it probably wouldn't be enough to make a case. He knew that if he got involved, it would jeopardize his job. I reminded him of his commitment to his friend. He thought parts of our plan were too dangerous and made some excellent suggestions about how to minimize the risks. He finally agreed to go along but warned that unless I could get the killer to fall, completely fall, for my story, the plan was doomed. If that happened, Joan's and Daniel's killer would get away with murder and quite possibly add me to the list of victims.

*   *   *

I crossed the Tennessee River and looked to the left at a layer of snow on Neyland Stadium, the University of Tennessee's massive football shrine. I obediently followed the navigation system's directions and headed west on Kingston Pike. I saw the oversized silver jaguar in front of the dealership and pulled in a strip center adjacent to the car lot. I wanted to rehearse my story for about the hundredth time. I told myself that's what I was doing, but really, I had to get my rage under control. I felt tension in my shoulders. My hands gripped the wheel as if I wanted to strangle the life out of it. I was going to see a cold-blooded killer. He had murdered Daniel, and for no apparent reason, he had arranged the savage death of my ex-wife and come close to killing me.

Could I pull it off? How good would my performance be? I was out of time and was only a hundred yards from the killer. It had to work—it would work.

Remember, the devil I'll be talking to doesn't know me, I repeated to myself. *He doesn't know if I am a sleaze or saint, money grabber, or Gandhi in khakis. Breathe, Chris, breathe.*

I took a deep breath and told myself that my act wouldn't improve with age. I edged around a man on an orange-and-white Bobcat pushing snow off the lot and parked in the CUSTOMERS ONLY space. I had called before leaving Gatlinburg, and I knew that the person I wanted to see was there.

Bradford, the salesperson who had waited on Charles and me during our last visit, greeted me at the door. From the lack of salt on the black track-off entry mat, it was obvious that I was the first potential customer of the day, and Bradford did little to hide his disappointment when I asked to speak to Tag Humboldt rather than swooning over a new car and reaching for my checkbook.

"Let me see if he's available," he said. "May I say who's asking?"

I was tempted to say yes and nothing more, but I knew this wasn't time for levity. The poor boy was disappointed enough as it was. "You may tell him Chris Landrum. He knows who I am."

Bradford walked through the double doors at the back of the sales room. I turned my eyes to the wall and began reading the brag pieces that I had read during my first visit. I also stared at the eight-by-ten photograph of Mr. Humboldt beside the photo of Mr. Munson, as well as the blank space where the photo of Daniel McCandless had been removed. It only took a second to confirm that Mr. Humboldt was the man in the photo that Charles had taken on Folly Beach three days before Joan's murder.

Bradford returned from the bowels of the dealership and said that Mr. Humboldt would be with me shortly. He didn't stop to shoot the breeze but headed back to his waiting spot by the door in hopes that a real customer would venture out on this cold, snowy January morning.

"Shortly" stretched to fifteen minutes. It crossed my mind that Humboldt may have slipped out a back door and was miles away by now. Was this a colossal mistake?

I didn't have much time to ponder the error of my ways. Mr. Humboldt stepped through the door with a smile that would make Charles's faux grin appear extraordinarily genuine. Humboldt was about my height but thin. I would guess he was in his forties, but his dyed-black hair could have covered a multitude of gray, and he could have been older. He wore a long-sleeved polo shirt with the Jaguar logo on the left breast pocket. I understood how Joan had described the man she had seen as average.

"Mr. Landrum," he said. He continued to smile and extended his hand. "It's nice to meet you."

Good start. He was already lying.

"You too," I lied back, biting my lower lip. I wanted to slap the smile off his face.

He waved to the door to the back offices. "Shall we go to my office?" he said. "How may I be of assistance?"

I could tell from his pursed lips and curiosity in his eyes that while he might not know how he could be of assistance, he undoubtedly knew who I was. I didn't respond until we were in his office, where he offered me coffee or water. I said yes to coffee. That would buy time to calm down.

He slowly walked to a black Bunn coffeemaker on a glass and steel table in the corner. Photos of classic Jaguars in flattering settings were on the wall over the coffee machine.

He handed me coffee in the obligatory Jaguar mug. I took a sip and took slight comfort in the aroma. "Mr. Humboldt," I said, "I don't know if you know who I am, but I'm from Folly Beach and am the ex-husband of Joan McCandless."

He sat in an all-black mesh Aeron chair behind a contemporary glass and steel desk that matched the coffeemaker table. His elbows rested on the desk. Other than his elbows, all that was on the desk was a miniature version of the Jaguar symbol that was in front of the dealership, a black Montblanc pen, and a gray legal pad. Humboldt would be a good poker player. He showed no emotion or recognition.

"I see," he said. "Isn't this a long way to come to buy a car? There are excellent Jaguar dealers between your island and Knoxville." He grinned, artificial at best.

"Then let me explain," I said. *Here it goes; stay calm.* "For some reason—God knows why—Joan called me after her husband was killed. I hadn't heard from her in nearly twenty-five years. We had been married, and she walked out on me." Humboldt remained impassive. "She left me in ruins—I was broke, depressed, and suicidal."

"I see," he said for the second time. His hands were clasped together.

"She told me her husband had died and that she wanted to give me something," I continued with a chuckle. My eyes narrowed. "She wouldn't say what. I figured she owed me big time. But who knows." I shrugged and leaned forward. "Anyway, I have a small business on Folly, a business that's sucking wind. Maybe Joan wanted to give me money—guilt money for deserting me." I hesitated, but Humboldt remained still and silent. "What the hell, I thought, and drove over here to see if I'd hit the lottery."

Humboldt finally showed life. "I'm not sure what this has to do with me," he said.

I almost said, "I see," but instead I said, "I understand. Bear with me. I think the dots will be connected." I clasped my right hand in a fist and tapped it against the desk. "She gave me some damn cock-and-bull story about her dear husband being murdered. I was wondering what holy crap I had stepped in. I bolted as quickly as my car would carry me." I shook my head. "No money, no nothing—she screwed me again." I leaned toward Humboldt and then placed both palms on the glass desktop.

"I fail to see—"

I raised my right hand from the desk and held it in front of me, palm facing Humboldt. "Then her house burns, and the next thing I hear is that she's moving to Folly Beach. Can you believe that? What was I to do?" I shook my head again. "What was I to do?"

Humboldt's fingers began to tap impatiently on the desk.

"Neither here nor there," I said. "Then she keeps telling me this story about someone trying to kill her." I looked at Humboldt and laughed. "I was ready to add myself to that list." I rolled my eyes. "She even gave me this." I reached to my back pocket and pulled out a plain white envelope I'd borrowed from the Hampton Inn's office. It contained five sheets of blank copy paper from the hotel's printer and one sheet from a bank statement that Sean had faxed to the hotel. I had printed CHRIS on the envelope.

Humboldt glanced at the envelope as if it were a tarantula, but he remained silent.

"And then do you know what happened, Mr. Humboldt?"

His glance went from the envelope to me. He shook his head.

"You killed her."

CHAPTER 55

I had never understood why anyone would want a glass-top desk.
It would be a pain to keep hand and fingerprint free. Now one huge
advantage immediately sprang to mind. Humboldt couldn't reach under
the top and grab a gun without my seeing it. I slowly slipped the
envelope back in my rear pocket. Humboldt's eyes followed the envelope
until it was behind me.

He cocked his head. If he were a cartoon character, there would have
been a bubble over his head showing intertwined gear wheels spinning.
His face hardened, and then he laughed—not quite a knee-slapping
laugh, but close. "That's the funniest thing I ever heard," he said.

I doubted that but didn't say anything.

He looked toward the coffeepot and then in the direction of my back
pocket. "Okay, I'll play along," he said. His hands gripped the arms of
his ergonomic high-tech chair. "Why are you here?" He laughed. "To
arrest me?"

"Hardly." I leaned back. "You see, Mr. Humboldt, or may I call
you Tag?"

"Sure," he said through clenched teeth.

"I couldn't care less about Joan and what happened to her damned
husband," I said. "I never even heard of him until he was dead. She
threw my life in a tailspin decades ago. She shoved her way back in my
life a few weeks ago and almost got me killed." My eyes met his. "I don't
give a rat's ass what happened to her."

His hands continued to grip the chair. "Again, why are you here?"

"Simple," I said. "You could call it taking advantage of an opportunity. You see, I'm broke. I'm in my sixties, too old to get a job even if I wanted to, which I don't. And I don't have a penny."

He nodded in the direction of the parking lot. "That's not a bad SUV you're driving," he said, spoken like a car salesman.

"Leased," I said. "Three payments behind."

"Hmm," he said with a nod.

"Anyway, you want to know why I'm here. Joan gave me this envelope the day she got to Folly." I patted my rear pocket. "She told me to open it if something happened to her. I thought she was paranoid—she had a history of that. I'd forgotten about it. Threw it on a pile of magazines at the house." I hesitated and then smiled at Tag. "If I'd known what it was when she gave it to me, I'd have rented a safety deposit box for it."

"What's so important about it?" said Tag. He tried to appear nonchalant, but I saw the tension around his eyes.

I reached for the envelope, stopped short, and pulled my hand back. "I'm not certain what it all means—a computer printout, copies of checks, and handwritten notes." I pulled the envelope out of my pocket and opened its flap. I pulled out the fax, and then just as quickly slid it back in the envelope. Humboldt examined the envelope. "But it looks like evidence that you'd been falsifying mileage and history on cars going all the way back to when you bought a Kia and a Nissan dealership. This place too." I waved my hand toward the showroom. "Something about laundering cash as well. According to the printout, it's a multimillion-dollar scam. The notes—I guess Joan's husband wrote them—say that a bunch of federal and state laws have been broken. It also says her husband found out about the scam. He offered to let you buy him out for hundreds of thousands of dollars more than what his share was worth." *Thank you, Sean Aker, for calling with that information and the fax.* "Again, I don't know what it all means, but I suspect you do." I stared at him. "So would the cops."

"This is preposterous," he said. He didn't sound nearly as exasperated as I'm sure he intended to. "That's quite a fantasy. I still don't know what you want."

He may be a good poker player, but a slight twitch in his left hand told what I needed to know.

Now for the moment of truth—sort of. I took a deep breath and patted my rear pocket. "I'll make it simple. I'm not greedy. This envelope holds the only copy of the documents. I'm staying in Gatlinburg. Tomorrow morning at eleven, I'll be in my SUV in the parking lot of the Hampton Inn. At ten after eleven, I will be on my way home. Follow so far?"

He nodded.

"If you're there at eleven with seventy-five thousand dollars cash, I'll hand you the envelope and happily be on my way and out of your life. You'll never hear from me again. Never." I snapped my fingers. "Oh yeah, if you're not there with the money, I'll drive to the Gatlinburg Police Department on my way out of town and hand them the envelope. It's as simple as that."

"If I were stupid enough to play along with this imaginary scenario, how would I know that's the only copy? How would I know you wouldn't be back?"

Charles and I had debated for more than an hour about how much to ask for. I wanted it large enough that Humboldt would think I could be satisfied. It also needed to be small enough that he could get it from a bank without too much trouble. Charles said it had to be enough to seem like a real threat. Seventy-five thousand sounded like a nice compromise.

I grinned. "You wouldn't," I said. "But do you really have a choice?" I abruptly stood and walked toward the door. "Tomorrow, eleven o'clock, seventy-five thousand cash. Have a good day."

I practically jogged out of the building, my heart beating faster than my step.

CHAPTER 56

Charles flung open his door on the first knock and peppered me
with questions before I could unzip my coat. I took the "incriminating"
envelope out of my pocket and threw it on the bedside table. I said that
I'd answer his questions but wanted to wait until Kevin joined us.

It was Kevin's day off, and he joined us at the hotel. Charles had
managed to get three bags of chips and three soft drinks from the vending
machines. I gave them as close to a verbatim description of my meeting
with Tag Humboldt as I could. Charles, being Charles, wondered if
Bradford had asked about him. He was visibly disappointed when I
said that he hadn't asked and hadn't appeared to have remembered our
earlier visit.

Kevin was more interested in Tag's reaction and whether I thought
he had fallen for it. I wasn't sure, saying that time would tell, but I let
him know that I'd be surprised if he didn't show.

Kevin hid a microphone and transmitter in the sun visor of my
SUV. He told me that it was sound activated, and that I wouldn't have
to do anything but talk to start it. He also gave me a body mike and
transmitter as well as instructions on how to attach it after my shower in
the morning. He said duct tape wasn't very high-tech but was effective
in holding the miniature mike and transmitter. I said, "Ouch." He
smiled. Charles took the recording equipment and said he would have
fun sticking it on me, and more fun ripping it off. "Ouch," I repeated.

Kevin said that he would be across the street from the hotel by ten
thirty, adding that one of his cop buddies would be with him. We all

agreed that it was a good plan, and Charles said that he knew it would work.

I wished I was that confident.

Sunset wasn't officially until a little after five thirty, but the mountains that loomed over Gatlinburg combined with the heavy snow clouds that kissed the mountaintops, casting darkness on the resort community before five. By eight o'clock, I felt like a six-year-old on Christmas Eve—it would never end; the next day would never arrive.

Charles wanted to talk and I wanted to soak my aching body in a hot shower. Charles wanted to get more chips; I wanted to throw up the ones I had eaten. Charles wanted to castrate the slimy bastard who'd killed his new friend Joan, and I wanted to hand the killer over to the police and go home to the familiar confines of my quaint cottage on Folly Beach, South Carolina.

By nine o'clock, I had said all I could and told him that I was turning in. He said that was good, as he had a new mystery by Tennessee novelist Keith Donnelly. Just what Charles needed, another mystery. I took the kind route and said, "Happy reading," closing his door.

I tried to watch television. I wasn't in the market for a seven-piece knife set or a "perfect lab-created" diamond necklace with matching earrings or reruns of *Law and Order*, so I hit the remote's OFF button.

Then my mind woke up. Had I convinced Humboldt? Did he buy my "couldn't care less about Joan" performance? Could I have been wrong about him? What were the odds that he wasn't the killer? Would he show? Would I live to tell the story to the police?

I was too antsy to sleep, yet I didn't want to start another conversation with Charles. A walk might help. The temperature had dropped drastically, and light snow had begun to fall again. I would much rather have been walking on the beach, but the nearly deserted streets of Gatlinburg were a pleasant second choice. The soothing smell of wood-burning fireplaces surrounded me as I walked the deserted sidewalks past closed shops and then back to the warm confines of my room.

CHAPTER 57

I had just thrown my coat on the chair when I heard a knock. I knew I shouldn't have slipped out without taking Charles with me. I was caught.

"Yes, Charles," I said as I opened the door. "I know—"

"Hello, Mr. Landrum," said Tag Humboldt. "I couldn't wait." He was my size, but in my mind, he filled the doorframe. I could barely see his face as he stared out of a coal-black flannel hoodie. He wore black jeans and black boots. His hands were covered with black leather gloves. The only thing not black was a silver-plated nine-millimeter semiautomatic pistol in his right hand. It was aimed at my stomach. "May I come in?"

I stepped back, considered my other options, which numbered zero, and shrugged. He pushed me back with the muzzle, pushed the door closed with his foot, and then used his free hand to hook the security chain.

"How did—"

He rammed his elbow in my stomach. I gasped, and he shoved me in the chair on top of my jacket. "Where's the envelope?" he said. "Where?"

I couldn't catch my breath, much less speak. I shook my head.

"You didn't think you could get away with it?" he said. He looked at my suitcase on the table by the television.

"How'd you find me?" I squeaked.

"Dumb ass," he said. "You told me where you were. Didn't know what room." He pointed the gun toward the parking lot. "I've been waiting out there an hour. I saw you come out and walk up the street. Don't you know it's dangerous going out alone at night?" He chuckled at his joke. "Waited for you to get back and here I am."

"Why—"

"Shut up!" He aimed the revolver to my head. "Where's the damn envelope?"

I shrugged.

He walked to the suitcase and flipped open the unzipped top, looked in, and didn't see what he was looking for. He grabbed the handle and shoved the case against the wall. It barely missed the television, and everything in it flew out on the table and the floor.

He checked my socks, underwear, jeans, and a few other odds and ends that I didn't even know were in the suitcase. My stuff was everywhere. There was still no envelope. He was pissed.

The gun was still pointed at my head. He took two steps, took hold of the edge of the mattress, lifted it, and pushed it until it slid off the bed frame. He may have looked average, but his strength was anything but. Nothing was under the mattress, and he got madder. He pulled one of the pillows off the bed and hurled it at the wall. It hit the flat-screen television, and the screen bounced off the wall and then crashed to the floor.

"Stand," he said, moving around the mattress to the chair.

He had me turn around and saw that I didn't have the envelope on me. All I could do was stall and pray for a miracle.

He slammed the gun down on my wrapped wrist. It felt as if a train were running up my arm. I screamed.

"Shut up!" he repeated. He glanced around the room until he saw my car keys on the bedside table. "Out." He grabbed my shirt collar and shoved me toward the door.

I reached back for my jacket, and he hit my arm again. "You won't need it."

I unlatched the chain and stepped out in the frigid night. Other than a couple of lights under the overhang a couple of rooms away, the area was dark, and not another soul was around. We weren't near the office—no help there.

Humboldt held the gun by his side and with his free hand shoved me into the parking lot.

Then I heard a high-pitched bloodcurdling *"Ahhh!"*

"What the …?" muttered Humboldt.

I looked over my shoulder and saw Charles. He'd pounced on Humboldt's back and was trying to twist the hand holding the gun away from me.

Humboldt was still standing, and Charles imitated a backpack and wouldn't let go. Humboldt pivoted and tried to dislodge my friend, but Charles's left arm was wrapped around the gunman's neck. He had Humboldt in a death grip.

Humboldt managed to twist around until the gun was pointed at Charles's head.

I turned to the right, grabbed Humboldt's gun hand, and pulled it away from Charles's face.

The gun fired.

Large flakes of snow flew around my face, and I felt a sensation like a hot iron above the elbow on my right arm.

I let go of Humboldt's arm. He lost his balance. Charles was on his back, and both of them hit the sidewalk with a dull thud.

Humboldt's head bounced off the pavement. The gun flew out of his hand, slid a couple of feet, and fell off the sidewalk to the parking lot. The killer was momentarily stunned. I took advantage and twisted his right hand behind his back. I thought of what he had done to Joan and twisted harder. Charles rammed his knee in the prone killer's back and grabbed both hands.

I stood back, caught my breath, thought of Joan and the smile on her face as we started across the bridge, and kicked Humboldt in the ribs. He let out a roar, and I kicked him again.

Lights came on in two of the upstairs rooms, and a man ran out of the hotel's office and yelled, "What's going on?"

I shouted, "Call the cops!"

Humboldt tried to push himself up with his knees, but with both hands twisted behind his back, he slipped back to the pavement and hit his head again. Blood gushed from his forehead. Charles pushed harder on his back and had a viselike grip on his left hand.

The light snow began to accumulate on the sidewalk. It was a surreal scene.

It must have been a slow night for crime in Gatlinburg. Two city cruisers slid in the lot within minutes of my yelling. The officers saw two men holding a helpless man on the sidewalk. They politely but firmly "asked" Charles and me to slowly get up and step away from the gentleman on the walk.

I said, "This man killed two people." I gestured to Humboldt. I knew they wouldn't believe me, but I didn't want them to treat him lightly.

A third cruiser arrived. Two of the officers conferred and then asked Charles and me to follow them to the hotel office. One of them picked up the semiautomatic by the barrel and asked whom it belonged to. Charles quickly pointed to Humboldt. The officer nodded. The third officer had a firm grip on Humboldt, and he escorted him to the rear seat of the patrol car. The cop offered Humboldt a white shop towel to press against his bleeding forehead. The officer then slipped in the front.

My adrenaline had slowed some, and the pain shot through my arm when Charles and I stepped into the office. We moved close to the small fireplace in the corner. Charles pointed to my arm and asked if I was okay. It was a fair question since blood was running down my shirt and dripping on the floor. The cop helped me sit and asked the desk clerk to call an ambulance. The pain was back, and I felt light-headed.

Thinking I might faint, I quickly asked the officer to call Officer Norton, saying he could verify our story. That was all I remembered—until I looked up and an ER doc said that I was in the LaConte Medical Center in nearby Sevierville. He said the bullet had missed bone, and that I'd be okay with some rest, strong pain meds, and some TLC.

I really, really hated hospitals!

CHAPTER 58

Charles was in the waiting room when I walked out of the treatment area. He looked at my bandaged right arm resting in a sling, instantly decided that I was going to live, and lit into me about spending the last three hours sleeping while he was helping the police solve the "crime of the century."

Hadn't he accused me of the same thing days earlier? I saw concern on his face, ignored his slightly exaggerated analysis of the crime, and apologized for making him work so hard.

"How did you know?" I asked as we slowly walked to the car. My arm didn't feel pain, but it also didn't feel anything.

"The first hint was when I heard your suitcase slam the wall between our rooms. After all, I am a detective, and I detected that something was amiss. Then I put my ear to the wall and heard two voices," he said. "Knew you weren't a ventriloquist and detected that there was more than one person in there. One of you was extremely unhappy." He grinned and gazed at my patched-up arm. "Is that enough of an explanation, or do you want more?"

I offered a doped-up smile and said that would do.

"Good," he said. "Then I won't tell you that I detected that a television smashing against the wall wasn't a good sign."

Even in my drugged state, I'd heard enough foolishness. "You said you'd been helping the police. What's happened?"

"Glad you asked. Officer Norton arrived on a white steed, or perhaps it was his Explorer. He told his colleagues who the good guys were and who weren't—that's why there isn't a cop here to haul you away." He looked both ways and then eased the SUV on the road back to Gatlinburg and the hotel. "I told them about your half-assed plan to catch the bad guys."

"*Our* plan," I corrected for no worthwhile reason.

"Yeah," he said. "Here's the kicker. Kevin and I told the other cops that there was a good chance that Humboldt's partner in Jag-o-Knox, the guy with the stupid name, Alil Bunson or Munson, is as involved as Humboldt."

"It's Munson. And?" I said. I was exhausted. I would be beyond sore once the meds wore off, not to mention slightly confused about the entire chain of events. *Get to the point!* I screamed in my head.

"And, impatient one, the cops hooked up with the fuzz in Knoxville and made a late night visit to Mr. Munson. He got real vague about the mileage scam, falsifying documents, and money laundering, but he told the detectives that he knew his business partner had been on Folly Beach for a week or so." He tapped the horn. "Idiot," he mumbled toward a yellow Chevy Malibu that pulled out in front of us. He shook his head. "Where was I? Oh yeah. Munson even confessed that he overheard Tag talking to one of the service techs who had installed an imitation LoJack contraption on Joan's Jag when she bought it."

"Imitation LoJack contraption?" I asked.

"Uh-huh," said Charles. "It's something that lets a car's owner track it if it's stolen." He shrugged. "The cop said it uses GPS to tell where the car is. And don't ask me anything about it. I still don't know how a radio works. I'm just saying the cops said that's how he tracked Joan to Folly."

"That answers one big question," I said. "Okay, back to your story."

"About time," he said. "*Of course*, Munson didn't know who Tag was talking about. He also said he suspected good ole Tag of having something to do with the demise of Joan's hubby." Charles lifted both hands from the wheel and waved toward the windshield. "But *of course*, he knew nothing for sure, and that's why he didn't tell the police." Charles rolled his eyes and said, "Right!"

"So that's it?" I said.

"One more thing; you'll like this. I suggested to Kevin that he might ask his detectives to fib a bit to Munson. They told him that they had a witness who saw a car waiting in the pull-off area near where Joan's poor hubby went over the cliff about the time of the accident. And amazing as it might seem, the imaginary witness may be able to identify the person who was sitting in the car. Pretty smart on my part, don't you think?"

"Depends," I said. "What happened?"

Charles nodded with a huge smile. "The cops said that the sleazy car dealer lawyered up before they could finish the sentence. I think his mileage scam will be the least of his worries—I sure do."

"Great," I said to my full-of-himself friend. Maybe it was over. Finally over.

Charles wasn't done. "I also told my new best friend Kevin Norton what Sean told you about the overpayment to Daniel, and how Sean speculated that it was because Daniel knew too much about the scam and they tried to buy him off." Charles yawned. "Kevin was going to have a detective contact Sean." He punched me on the knee—one of my few good appendages—and smiled. "Of course, you could clear it all up."

"How?"

"Give them the envelope with all the proof."

If only I had one, I thought.

CHAPTER 59

The next day zapped most of the energy I had left. A pain in my left arm woke me about six in the morning. I took another pain pill but was too awake when it kicked in to go back to sleep. Charles had offered to stay in my room, but I declined. I told him that if I needed anything, I'd throw the television against the wall.

Karen would be at work, and I called to let her know what had happened. She feigned anger, calling me brain-dead for what I'd done. I told her it was all Charles's idea, and she said, "Uh-huh, sure." Then she asked when we would be home.

"Tonight," I replied.

"Please hurry," she said. "Call when you're near."

I took that as a good sign.

We were at the police station at nine o'clock and had to tell our story two more times—once to the Gatlinburg police and again to two detectives from Knoxville. They followed Karen's lead and called us brain-dead but in more polite terms. They also said that Officer Norton had violated a slew of procedures by helping, but since it resulted in catching the killer of one of the city's more prominent citizens, he would save his job and only have a reprimand put in his file. He told them it was worth it.

By noon, I was exhausted but famished. Unbeknown to me, Charles, my after-catching-a-murderer event coordinator, had arranged for Charlene to meet us at the Pancake Pantry for a congratulatory and going-away luncheon.

She approached me for a hug but couldn't figure out where to squeeze. I said it wasn't as bad as it looked. Of course, I could have been wrong since I was still medicated. She thanked us, and then thanked us again, for figuring out the tragic murders of her friends. Daniel's and Joan's killer would have lived happily ever after if it weren't for us, she said. She also told me how happy Joan was the night before she left for Folly Beach. Joan had told her that she might be able to right something that she had wronged eons ago.

Drugged or not, I couldn't hold back tears. Charles took the conversation from there and took it to a lighter conclusion—something I would thank him for later.

We said good-bye to both Charlene and Gatlinburg.

*   *   *

We were on I-26, on the Charleston side of Columbia. The snow was now behind us. The allure of Folly Beach, sand, the ocean, and good friends was ahead.

"Something's wrong with this picture," said Charles.

I looked over at him behind the wheel. He was seated erectly in the driver's seat and carefully keeping his eyes on the road. "Wrong?" I said. "What picture?"

He continued to gaze straight ahead but pointed his right forefinger at me. "There is Chris Landrum, owner of a tiny photo gallery at the beach. He solves two murders and an explosion." He then pointed his finger at his right ear. "And here's Charles Fowler, owner and sole employee of the Charles Detective Agency. All he sort of solves is the theft of some firewater by a passel of ghosts led by Frank Fontana, a poor guy who died trying to save two little girls in 1957. As President Bill Clinton once said, 'It was not my best hour. It was not even my best hour and a half.'"

"Could be that Frank Fontana finally saved someone," I said.

"Dawn?" he said.

I nodded. Charles then glanced away from the road and toward me. "Know what she told me before she left?"

"What?"

"Said that she stole the money and whiskey."

Not quite breaking news, I thought. "So?"

We passed a semi, and then Charles looked my way again. "Said she didn't prop that case on the shelf that fell on me. Didn't cut the electric cord either."

"You believe her?" I asked.

"Want to," he said.

Good nonanswer. "Then who did?" I asked.

He shrugged. "Ghosts."

He put both hands back on the wheel and rammed his foot on the accelerator. We raced past a classic white Ford Mustang. "Whee!" said Charles.

Whee, indeed.

Printed in the United States
By Bookmasters